AREA 53

The Casserole Ladies Go Where No Woman Has Gone Before

ALSO BY BILLY JOHNSON

ATTACK OF THE iFONES and Other Vertically Challenged Stories, ISBN: 978-1-7374282-1-3

LION IN MY BACKYARD, A Children's Picture Book, ISBN: 978-1-7374282-2-0

WITH LINDA JOHNSON
THE CASSEROLE LADIES, ISBN: 978-1-7374282-0-6.

All Billy's books are available on Amazon.

Visit Billy on Facebook at: www.facebook.com/Billy4GoodBooks

The characters and events portrayed in this book are fictitious. Any similarity to real persons, living or dead, is coincidental and not intended by the author. Elgin Air Force Base is a fictitious entity that is in no way meant to portray Eglin Air Force Base. Preble Hill Plantation is also a fictitious entity that is in no way meant to portray Pebble Hill Plantation.

Front and Back Cover design by Jillian McKenna Oliver

ISBN: 978-1-7374282-3-7

Dedication

We dedicate AREA 53 to all the literary agents who turned it down. May they soon regret their decision.

AREA 53

The Casserole Ladies Go Where No Woman Has Gone Before

Casserole Ladies: Older unmarried women in towns throughout the South who appear on doorsteps of recently widowed or divorced males. These women bring casseroles and other homemade dishes, such charity occurring when these men are most vulnerable to feminine sympathy. Potential companionship and/or matrimony often are motivating factors.

Chapter 1

Sunday, November 9th, 11:59 PM, CST

Babs and two other Casserole Ladies nervously sat in her Cadillac Escalade parked off a backroad in northwest Florida's Panhandle. The SUV's headlights shone on a six-foot-high chain link fence as well as the thick forest of pine trees and spiky saw palmetto bushes beyond it. The light did not reveal any of the deadly wildlife lurking out there, the worst being cottonmouth moccasins and alligators.

The owner of the land on the other side of the fence took the right of privacy seriously. Coils of razor-sharp concertina wire topped the fence, and ominous signs communicated messages which even scatterbrained Babs understood. The intent of 'RESTRICTED AREA' and 'WARNING' on one sign was obvious. What was not so obvious was the line below in smaller print. None of the three ladies remembered to bring their glasses. It read, 'US Government Property.' A more ominous sign next to this one threatened, 'TRESSPASSERS WILL BE PROSECUTED.' The most apocalyptic sign said, 'WARNING: ELECTRIC FENCE 7,000 VOLTS'. Electricity surging through braided wire atop the fence generated a staticky sound loud enough to be heard inside the Escalade.

"How we ever gonna get over a fence with that many volts in it?" Babs asked, interrupting a long period of silence on her part. The chatterbox of the group had said little since parking her SUV an hour ago. Instead, she fretted silently about her decision to undertake this mission. Fear, intensified by doubt, muted her vocal cords. Her doubt was fueled by the curse of the living—growing old. She thought, *sixty-three is way too old to be doing something like this.* Dread of growing older increasingly troubled her. Guilt also played a part in her apprehension as tonight's perilous misadventure was her doing. The two friends accompanying her did so as a result of an ill-considered assertion she recently made on a primetime TV reality show. In front of 1.81 million viewers, Babs had boldly asserted the existence of a top-secret facility called Area 53, supposedly somewhere in the forest beyond the fence now confronting her. She and her friends would prove it. For the umpteenth time, she rolled back the extra-long sleeves of the camouflage top she wore. Her sleeves were damp from the sweat of her palms.

"I knew this was a bad idea from the git-go," said Lilly, stating the obvious while fidgeting in the seat next to Babs. No one in their hometown of Thomasville, Georgia would have ever expected Lilly to agree to do what Babs had promised they would. True, most residents considered Lilly about as sharp as a marble and therefore an ideal patsy to be schemed. But she was too reserved, too genteel for this kind of stunt. They underestimated Lilly. True friends sometimes must do things they would not do otherwise in order to support each other. In this case, a sneaky rival of Babs had challenged her Area 53 assertion on the reality show. Against Lilly's better judgement, such as it was, she joined tonight's attempt to prove the mean-spirited woman was wrong.

"Not according to Madame Cassandra." Babs referred to a psychic in their hometown. Cassandra considered the old widow to be a rich sucker and, even better, a steady source of income. Babs usually visited the fortune teller once a month for advice but had gone twice in the last three weeks. Babs also dabbles in voodoo, astrology, and hypnotism among other oddball interests. "She gave me the green light on this… uh, what did we decide to call what we're gonna do tonight?"

"I think it starts with the word 'cluster' and ends with a dirty word," said Lizzie from the second row of the SUV. The four-time divorcee was not known for mincing words. "We're going to have to accept looking like fools and liars, tuck in our tails, and get this tank back on the road to Thomasville."

"Better that we look like fools and liars than go to jail," said Lilly. Light from the moon glimmered off her smooth alabaster complexion which starkly contrasted with her jet-black hair. Lilly's stylist normally colored her hair using an ash blonde shade. Tonight, all three women sported the same hair color, having spent three hours in a beauty salon Friday afternoon. All hated the color but considered it necessary camouflage for a successful break-in of a top-secret government facility. Lilly frowned. "Besides, orange ain't in my color palette." She had chosen a mix of colors in her camouflage outfit in harmony with her palette.

"It's not too late. If y'all want to bail on me, I'd understand. Orange ain't my favorite color either," said Babs. Anger began to overtake fear. "But after what that damn Thomasville City Council did to us Friday, ain't no way I'm not going over that damn fence."

As the wit of the group, Lizzie's first instinct was to retort with some sort of wisecrack. Composing a reply, she smiled. It was a smile enhanced by expensive lip implants a Kardashian would envy. A sudden mysterious noise somewhere in the dark outside the Escalade erased her smile. Instead of her usual snappy one-liner, she said, "We could do some serious jail this time, Ladies. How did I ever let myself get into this kind of a… this kind of a snafu?"

Chapter 2

Wednesday, October 15th, 11:40 AM, EDT

Twenty-six days before their midnight snafu, Babs sat with her two friends in Hong Yip. The Thomasville restaurant's extensive menu challenged anyone with a weight problem, especially Babs. Barbara Neauxgeaux (a name derived from her French ancestry and pronounced as 'No Go') is short and plump—5' 2" in stockings, weight not publicly available. Her deceased husband Avery occasionally teased her about both characteristics. When trying to be more tactful, he simply told her the only thing more distinctive than her small stature was her eccentricity. As a young wife, she would smile whenever he said this until she turned thirty-two and looked up the definition of 'eccentricity.' In her absence, Avery typically substituted the term oddball for eccentric when describing her personality to others. Despite his careless lapses, she always loved him and still missed him.

Babs recently decided that her age was a bigger problem than her weight, until she saw the size of the menu. Frustrated, she let it fall from her hands onto the table. "This menu's got too many choices. I mean they got one, two, three…" Babs picked the menu up again and counted. "Four, five… ten different chicken dishes to choose from under the 'POULTRY' section of this menu. And that don't include the chicken fried rice under the 'FRIED RICE' section. I cain't make up my mind. I see at least half a dozen things I want to order, but I know I should just get a salad."

"Just go with All-U-Can-Eat lunch buffet and eat all of them. Buffets solve the problem of what to choose… Maybe that's part of my problem," said Lizzie. The woman knew how to handle her problem. She gestured toward her stomach with a circular wave with open palms as if presenting the Showcase Showdown Prize on an episode of *The Price Is Right*. Lizzie flashed a wide smile enhanced by the four-time divorcee's chubby face. A listing of Elizabeth Sherbert's ex-husbands requires more words than an editor would permit. Besides, four husbands' first and last names are too many for a sixty-five-year-old gold digger to remember. She honestly acknowledged her quest for a sugar daddy and was quite successful at it. Ask any of her previous husbands, or better yet, look at the balances in her accounts at Sawgrass Bank.

"I vote on the buffet. It was always Wendell's favorite," said Lilly. Lillian White enjoyed true love with her husband, Wendell, for three decades until he died a year ago, shortly after her fifty-fourth birthday. Always a follower, Lilly tends toward naïveté and vanity, unlike her best friend Lizzie. In many respects, Lilly and Lizzie were opposites. Whereas Lilly is naïve, Lizzie is streetwise savvy. Lilly practices civility; Lizzie wisecracks. Lilly is thin; Lizzie is overweight. Lilly is fair skinned, blonde, and almost wrinkle free. Lizzie is ruddy, redheaded, and weathered. Yet, these two opposites gel very well. Lilly's eyes suddenly moved up from the menu to her companions. "Don't look now, but trouble's coming up behind y'all. It's Mitzi. What do you think, Babsie? Should I call the manager over and have her run off?"

Babs turned to see a woman competing with her to hook someone from among Thomasville's limited supply of older men. Mitzi Merchant was a manipulative widow as well as a long-term rival of Babs. Think Baby Jane and Blanche on steroids with Mitzi playing the spiteful Bette Davis part. Neither she nor Babs remembered who initiated the bad blood between them that began in kindergarten. Mitzi actually started it when she destroyed Mister Piggles, Babs' favorite stuffed animal. Babs retaliated by smearing cotton candy in Mitzi's hair. It took three miserable scrubbings to remove it.

Mitzi harassed Babs throughout their K-12 school years. Her torment of choice was highlighting Babs' weight problem, going so far as to nickname her Butterball Babs. The Mitzi-Babs rivalry often mimicked that of Nancy Allen tormenting Sissy Spacek in the movie *Carrie* with one big difference. Babs *always* responded in kind. For example, Mitzi started a malicious rumor their senior year that Babs was going to FSU because she could not get into UGA. Babs promptly got her revenge. She slipped Ex-Lax into a mix of chocolate brownies Mitzi was making in Home Economics class. It took Mitzi two days to recover and forced her to miss the senior prom. Their feud only intensified the older they got.

"It's nice to see Hong Yip has a table just for old folks like y'all. Where's the rest of y'all's coven?" asked Mitzi, ignorant of the irony of her quip. She referred not to a coven of real witches but to Daffy and Gidget who with Babs, Lilly, and Lizzie made up Thomasville's most famous quintet of Casserole Ladies.

"Ho, ho. Excuse me if I forget to laugh, but feeble attempts at humor usually screw up my memory. For your information Mzz Nosy Busibody, they happen to be on a cruise. In fact, I just got a text from Daffy this morning that their boat is off the coast of Miami right now," Babs said.

Mitzi smirked while twisting her knife in a recent wound to the Casserole Ladies' reputation. "I bet Daffy and Gidget would rather be anywhere right now than here in Thomasville after that stunt y'all pulled last Saturday."

"Right now, I'd rather be anywhere I didn't have to listen to you," Lizzie said.

Babs said, "Yeah. I believe the All-U-Can-Eat buffet is calling you, Mitzi. If that's not enough, you can always go to Waffle House and eat a dozen or so waffles."

The two women had been enemies since kindergarten so juvenile trash-talk between them came second nature. Mitzi sneered at Babs. "I heard one of your clients wrote your name and phone number on the wall of the men's bathroom in the Waffle House."

"I heard it was you that wrote it when you weren't wearing makeup."

Mitzi smiled an evil Maleficent smile and said, "At your age without your makeup, you wouldn't be able to show your face in public ever. They'd arrest you for scaring little children."

The age thing stung, causing Babs to raise her voice. "At least when I put makeup on, it's on my face and not on my butt!" Diners nearby looked over.

"At least I don't have to buy my makeup at PetSmart." Having sensed a touchy issue for Babs, Mitzi decided to double down on growing older. "Isn't that where you get your Botox treatments? Looks like you're long overdue for one, but it's easy to forget the essentials at your age."

Too angry to speak, Babs fumed as Mitzi abruptly turned and headed back to her table. She glanced over her shoulder as she walked away and hurled a question mocking one of Babs' widely known oddball interests. "Seen any little green men lately, Babsie?"

After Mitzi was gone, Lizzie looked at Babs and said, "Don't let that old bitch get to you. Just ignore her. By the way, what was that little green men thing all about? I thought you were off of your UFO thing… for a while at least."

“Yeah. I thought you were into fairies now,” said Lilly.

Babs’ face displayed one of her ‘Will they never learn?’ looks. She said, “It’s *pixies*, not fairies, thank you.”

“What’s the difference?”

“They’s a world of difference between a pixie and a fairy.”

Lizzie rolled her eyes and asked, “Such as?”

“Two inches of height for one thing. Pixies are four inches tall, while fairies are six inches. And pixies live in gardens, while fairies live in the hills. And pixies have butterfly wings, while fairies have larger wings……”

Wikipedia defines a shaggy dog story as “an extremely long-winded anecdote characterized by extensive narration of typically irrelevant incidents and terminated by an anticlimax.” Babs was infamous for hers. Recognizing the beginning of one, Lizzie interrupted. “Why the sudden interest in pixies?”

“There’ve been reports on the Internet of recent pixie sightings in Georgia and Alabama.”

“Pixie sightings? The spotters must be using microscopes instead of binoculars.”

Lilly asked, “Has Mitzi been teasing you about pixies?”

“No, but she has been trolling me again on Facebook about my UFO posts,” Babs said.

“That UFO stuff is for the birds,” said Lizzie.

“No, it ain’t! UFOs is for real!”

“Little green men? Even I’m not that naïve,” Lilly said, once again underestimating her naiveté.

“Listen... I been on some real interesting UFO websites lately, and y’all wouldn’t believe what’s going on out there. The Federal government just don’t want us to know about it, that’s all. I can show y’all some of this stuff when we get time. There’s even a place within a days’ drive that—"

“So, exactly why did you invite us here for lunch today?” asked Lizzie, again forestalling another shaggy dog story.

Chapter 3

Wednesday, October 15th, 12:14 PM, EDT

The essential character of Babs and her four close friends, both individually and collectively, had long been popular subjects of gossip among residents of Thomasville. Most viewed their sometimes-eccentric behaviors as the result of freedom of lifestyle often bestowed upon those favored with wealth. That they were native-born Thomasvillians, born of native-born Thomasvillians led others to speculate a cause more interesting. Perhaps incest manifesting itself in the gene pool among the descendants of those of high-born status who tend to intermarry? Rumors relating to their unconventionality abounded as exemplified by four of the more entertaining ones, which are as follows.

1. News outlets several years ago reported a massive flood that destroyed five thousand acres of potato farmland in Germany. The week of the disaster, Lilly posted photos on Facebook of herself and the other four Casserole Ladies on vacation in Atlanta. Several of the pictures taken on the day of the flood documented their tour of an international utility's redundant control room, coincidentally located in Atlanta. Phone texts throughout Thomasville subsequently debated whether or not Babs had accidentally pushed the wrong button during their tour.
2. More recently, Facebook went offline worldwide for eighteen hours in September. Older women in Thomasville were despondent during the outage. An unnamed source on the Thomasville Police Department leaked a story that FBI and CIA personnel had interviewed five local women regarding the incident. Locals attributed the outage to Lilly and the other four dingbats.
3. Also in September, a garden shed in the Knott's backyard mysteriously blew up one night. No one was harmed. Neighbors reported hearing Babs leading other women in some sort of voodoo ritual in her kitchen at the time of the explosion. A checkout clerk at Harvey's Grocery Store subsequently told customers that Babs had bought several household cleaners on the day of the event. Babs had told the clerk it was for a voodoo ritual called a Good Luck Floor Wash. Babs' house was located in the Dawson Street Historic District next door to the Knott's house. Facebook posts commented on the probability of a voodoo ritual gone awry as the cause.

4. The juiciest gossip concerned a stunt at the annual college football game between Georgia and Florida in Jacksonville last Saturday, October 11th. Five women resembling Kardashians—although appearing to be more obese than the celebrities—ran naked across the field during the nationally televised halftime show. A Facebook poll showed Thomasville evenly split as to the identity of the streakers. Half believed the women to be the Kardashians. The other half thought Babs and the other four Casserole Ladies had streaked the game somehow disguised as the famous females. One of the beauticians at a local beauty salon told customers an interesting tidbit afterward. She admitted to having shown Lizzie three days before the game how makeup can be used to make a person resemble a celebrity.

Nothing Babs and her friends could get into would surprise anyone in Thomasville, including the reason why she invited Lilly and Lizzie to lunch at Hong Yip. Her eyes lit up as she responded to Lizzie's question. "I invited y'all here to tell y'all some really big news."

Always the wit, Lizzie asked, "Jason Statham is getting hair implants?"

"Much better than that. Y'all are gonna love what I'm gonna tell y'all. I got a call from a Hollywood producer—"

"A Hollywood producer!" Lilly said.

Babs nodded. "His name is Cordell Isler. He was a year ahead of me at FSU—one of my old college boyfriends—"

"Of which there were many, I'm sure," said Lizzie.

Babs frowned. "Anyway, Cordell said he recognized me while he was watching the Georgia-Florida halftime—"

"I knew you should have disguised yourself as Kim Kardashian instead of Kylie Jenner."

"Anyway, the big news is that he's coming right here to Thomasville to talk to all of us about staring in a reality show on TV."

"Us!? A reality show on TV! Is this Hollywood producer for real?" asked Lilly.

Lizzie asked, "Is anyone in Hollywood for real?"

"Yep. He's a real Hollywood producer. Been in the movie business ever since he graduated from FSU," said Babs.

"What kind of reality show is he talking about?"

"It would be like one of those *Real Housewives of Beverly Hills* kind of things. He wants to call it *Real Widows of Thomasville*. Sort of a take-off on our 'Widows of Thomasville' calendar. After he recognized me on TV, he did some research and ran across our calendar."

Earlier in the fall, the five women produced a risqué calendar of themselves with the help of the Thomasville Tourism Director. It was a knockoff of the famous calendar, Ladies of Rylstone, which featured semi-nude older women from the town of the same name in England. The Casserole Ladies had hoped their calendar would be noticed by older bachelors, and it was.

"The calendar has been selling well. I hear it's sold over twenty thousand so far," Lilly said.

Lizzie said, "I hear Walmart's gonna start carrying it. A reality series would be a feather in our caps."

Babs said, "Anyway, that's why I told y'all to meet me here… to hear what he has to say."

"And I thought it was for the All-U-Can-Eat lunch buffet."

"Why would anyone want to do a reality show about five old women set in Thomasville?" asked Lilly.

"Mayberry was unavailable?"

Babs said, "He was ready to air a pilot for a series called *Real First Ladies*. It was about the five living First Ladies. Had everything filmed and ready to air, but it fell through because one of the First Ladies nixed it at the last minute. So now, the network is stuck with an empty time slot that it needs to fill fast."

"I saw the ads for that *First Ladies* show," Lilly said.

"Yep. One of them just changed her mind. Said contract or no contract, she was not gonna let the show go on the air after seeing excerpts from the premier episode. She said it was too low brow—"

"Must've been pretty realistic," said Lizzie.

"Anyway, Cordell was frantic. He said he toyed with the idea of a reality show about us after he ran across our calendar this last Sunday, and then the *First Ladies* show got canceled on Monday. So, he knew right away what its replacement could be. He flew into Atlanta from LA last night and is driving down here to discuss his idea with us."

"When will he get here?"

Babs shrugged. "Should be soon. I told him to meet us here at Hong Yip for lunch. Let's just sit tight for now and enjoy the buffet and each other's company."

Lilly looked at Lizzie and asked, "How did your AA meeting go last night?"

Lizzie had recently started going to Amazon Anonymous meetings. This is a Thomasville organization, similar to Alcoholics Anonymous, but for people who have trouble controlling their excessive spending.

Lizzie nodded enthusiastically and said, "It was real good. We had some dynamite testimonies last night."

"How so?" asked Babs.

"Louise Wadkins' testimony was the best. She's been going to AA for over a year. She talked for thirty minutes about her struggles with overspending… her inability to resist a sale even though she knows in her heart the sales price is the same as the regular price… how she continually switches credit card companies even though she knows her six month zero-interest rate will be canceled out by higher transfer and annual fees… how she knows she's only going to spend the new card's extra bonus points on extra stuff she doesn't really need." Lizzie solemnly shook her head. "The balance on her Visa card would put Beyoncé to shame. Visa ought to erect a statue in their corporate headquarters in her honor."

"She can't pass a Kohl's without dropping three-to-four hundred easy."

Lizzie nodded. "Anyway, it was gut wrenching. There wasn't a dry eye in the house after she finished."

"Hasn't AA helped her?" Lilly asked.

"Oh, yeah. It has. Absolutely," Lizzie said.

Babs perked up. She asked, "How? I may have to join myself."

"Oh yeah. She said her bedroom looks much better now. She recently redecorated it. Nothing but the best—Montecito, Versace, Ralph Lauren. She showed us some pictures on her phone, which is another benefit besides texting. You get to bore people with pictures of your redecorating and your grandchildren."

Lilly looked at Babs and asked, "What's the latest gossip about us on Facebook?"

Babs quickly pulled out her phone and began keying. Presently she said, "Mitzi won't let up on badmouthing us. She's been harping how it was us that streaked, not the Kardashians." As Babs read more posts, her face got redder. "Oooh, this pisses me off!"

"What?"

"Mitzi's trying to be funny. She's badmouthing me about Area 53."

"Let me take a look," said Lilly. She pulled out her iPhone and scanned the Facebook postings.

Mitzi Merchant

Daffy and her cronies as much as admitted it was them that streaked when we asked them on Monday at the IHOP. They refused to say one way or the other, which tells me they did it. BTW, I've seen Babs sneaking around in the Plus-Size section at Belk lately. Belk's gain is Lane Bryant's loss.

Like **Comment**

Stoney Lee

It could have been the Kardashians doing the streaking. Their TV show's ratings have been slipping lately. It could have been a good publicity stunt on their part.

Like **Reply**

Penny Perdoo

A good friend of mine on the police force told me he caught Babs, Daffy, and Gidget in September performing a voodoo ceremony at midnight in Sunset Memorial Cemetery.

Like **Reply**

Toots Varnell

Don't forget the 'Widows of Thomasville' calendar. I would never have thought anyone around here would do something that crazy, but I forgot about Daffy, Babs, Gidget, Lilly, and Lizzie.

Like **Reply**

Mitzi Merchant

No way that was Kylie Jenner running across that football field naked. She don't have that much fat or wrinkled, saggy skin on her body. Babs Neauxgeaux does. It was her! Why does an old hag like her do that kind of stuff anyway?

Like **Reply**

Tammy Benedict

I think it was the real Kylie Jenner streaking, not Babs. But Khloé Kardashian did kind of look like Lilly White. Wonder if Lilly might have somehow got the Kardashians to let her streak with them?

Like **Reply**

Mitzi Merchant

Old Babsie buys her dresses at Barnum and Bailey's thrift store. I hear they sell used circus tents there. Has anyone heard if she's seen anymore UFOs lately?

Like **Reply**

Tammy Benedict

Has Babs found anymore Moons lately, or is it still only seven?

Like **Reply**

Mitzi Merchant

Who knows? Babs is a nutcase for any sort of conspiracy theory. Her latest is some sort of Internet hoax about some place called Area 53. She thinks her little green alien friends from other planets come down here in

UFOs every full moon to visit her. She thinks they stay at in Area 53, probably because they get good motel rates there. Area 53 must be the Motel 6 of space travel. They keep a light on for the aliens.

Like **Reply**

Lilly put her iPhone down and asked, "How did we ever communicate before Facebook and texting?"

"I think it was called talking," said Lizzie. "Facebook has become the primary mode of communications between the envious and the envied."

Lilly shook her head. "Don't even bother to try to explain that last sentence. I just think it's much safer to badmouth someone on social media. They can't slap your face while you're posting."

"Mitzi better quit badmouthing me on Facebook, or I'm gonna bitch slap her. Harping on about my weight and my age. That's the pot calling the kettle black. And I'm getting tired of her trying to make me out to be a UFO nutcase. She's getting much worse about it lately…" A thoughtful expression came over Babs' face. "I wonder if it's that time of the month for her?"

"She's in her sixties. Probably had her last period a decade ago."

"I'm not talking about periods. I'm talking about Mitzi's astrological karma, her emotional and psychological status. It varies depending on what your horoscope says. Sometimes a person's horoscope can be pretty depressing."

"What could be more depressing than a having period?" asked Lizzie as she looked up to see an older gentleman approaching. "Maybe a Hollywood producer? I think that's your boy coming our way."

Chapter 4

Wednesday, October 15th, 1:05 PM, EDT

The older man wore thick-lensed tortoise shell glasses reminiscent of Woody Allen's. His brown hair was cut in a medium-length shaggy style and streaked with grey. Tall and tanned, his appearance screamed Hollywood top to bottom: white Burberry T-Shirt, black Varvatos leather jacket unzipped, AMIRI skinny blue jeans, and dark grey Zegna suede Chelsea boots. A smile had been imprinted on his face after many years of playing the game with hustlers.

"You haven't changed a bit," Babs lied as he stepped up to their table.

Cordell also lied. "Neither have you." The cinematographer wheels in the producer's brain turned. *A little plumper than she was in college, especially those boobs. At least her face still has nice smooth skin. Be good for closeups showing some cleavage. Light brown hair? She was a blond when I dated her although not a true blond as I remember. Wonder if a stylist should do something about that hairdo. Maybe replace that bob cut with something more slimming. Tim's camera will love her face with the right haircut.* "I'd recognize you anywhere... even running across a football field."

"Why do you keep saying that was me?" asked Babs.

"Babsie, there are some things about a former girlfriend that a man never forgets, especially when she's naked."

Babs introduced Cordell to Lilly and Lizzie. They ordered more drinks, then Cordell discussed the overall concept of the new show. Like other reality shows, a camera crew would follow them around, filming their everyday lives. The script would include an occasional 'kink' in the narrative to enliven things. He had already hired a writer and a director and believed the show would be a ratings blockbuster. His personal fortune was at stake. Cordell emphasized they must start filming right away. He said, "I gotta know if it's a go with you ladies today. I've got some other women to talk to about an alternate series if you say no. I've absolutely got to get something on TV by Thursday, October 30th… fifteen days from today."

All three women shrieked "October 30th!" in unison.

"Yep. I've already started one of my writers working on a tentative script. I've got our legal people drafting a contract for you to sign. I can have a camera crew here this week to start filming. Unlike the other Real Housewives shows, *Real Widows of Thomasville* will have a narrator. It'll be sort of a Real Housewives-Swamp People mashup."

Lizzie said, "Our Southern accents ain't no better than those Cajun accents. You better add subtitles like they do on *Swamp People* so the audience can understand us."

"Who's gonna be the narrator?" Lilly asked.

Cordell was thinking big. "We're looking at five mature actresses. Holly Hunter, Andie MacDowell, Sandra Bullock, Julia Roberts, and Reese Witherspoon. They were all born in the South. They've got the right kind of Southern accent. They've all won Oscars. If your show goes as well as I think it will, they could be the actresses to play your parts in *Real Widows of Thomasville* movie."

"Movie! You gotta be kidding," said Lilly.

"Yep. The movie climax would be your streak of the Florida-Georgia football game."

Now it was Lizzie's turn to lie. "But that was them Kardashians that streaked that game."

Lilly motioned for silence. "Quiet. Here comes our waitress."

"Y'all like, ready to order?" the young woman asked. She took their orders, then paused as if scrutinizing them. "Like, y'all mind if I ask y'all something?"

Babs nodded. "Sure. What's on your mind?"

"Was it really y'all or them Kardashians?"

The waitress left without receiving a straight answer to her question. Cordell watched her receding fanny as he said, "By the way, there were five of you girls streaking. I'd planned on having all five of the calendar widows in the series. Where are the other two ladies?"

"Daffy and Gidget? They went on a cruise with the Marx Brothers," said Babs.

"You didn't tell me they had left town when I called you Monday night. And who are the Marx Brothers?"

"They're five old Yankee bachelor brothers that retired to live in The Villages in Florida. They saw our calendar and drove up here to meet us this past Monday. We really hit it off with them, then they called Tuesday and invited all of us to go on a four-week cruise with them. They left from Jacksonville yesterday. I wanted to go, but three of my grandchildren are having birthdays this month, and I can't miss their parties."

Cordell focused on Lizzie and asked, "What about you? Why didn't you go with 'em? It's good that you didn't." *This red hair is gonna look great on camera. Red's an awful tricky color to get right. I bet it's a professional job. This old girl must use a stylist in Tallahassee. We'll make her the Real Widows vamp. Wonder what her real hair color was before it turned grey?*

"I wanted to go most of all five of us. Those old boys are loaded and just what I been looking for. But… I got a doctor's appointment this month." Lizzie did not add that her doctor's appointment was with a plastic surgeon to have a tummy tuck. The way Cordell was staring at her, he just might be interested so she saw no sense in pointing out any of her shortcomings.

"And you?" Cordell asked Lilly.

"I'm having my shoe closet remodeled this month. It's a three-week project," said Lilly. She was an acknowledged shoe-aholic and let no opportunity pass to improve upon her extensive collection of expensive footwear. "I gotta ask… not having Daffy and Gidget here… Will you have to postpone filming until they get back?"

"Nope. We'll film the pilot and the first couple of episodes with just you three, then include Daffy and Gidget after they get back. I'll have my writer work out the script that way. Might even include these Marx Brothers at some point. Is their last name really Marx?"

"No. We nicknamed them the Marx Brothers because they are terrible dressers."

"How so?"

"They all wore the same outfits—Bermuda shorts, Hawaiian flower shirts, and sandals—the same stuff all retired men wear."

Lizzie nodded with a frown on her face. "If they hadn't been filthy rich, we would've had to turn them away. Their outfits looked like Miami Beach on steroids."

"But they wore expensive sandals. One of 'em wore Nisolo huaraches, which ain't cheap. The cheapest I've ever been able to find them at Nordstrom is $130 a pair. And that's for the women's huaraches. The men's huarache is probably thirty or forty bucks more—" Lilly said.

"Lilly sweetie, your shaggy dog story is starting to show," Lizzie said.

"Well anyway, he was wearing some expensive sandals."

Babs asked, "I thought huaraches were shoes."

Lizzie said, "That probably depends on one's footwear belief system."

"No, silly," Lilly said. "Whether huaraches are sandals or shoes depends on who's selling them. Nike calls them shoes, while Zappos calls them sandals. Most shoe retailers call them sandals. *Footwear News* is the Bible on shoes, and I've seen that magazine call them shoes sometimes, but most of the time they call them sandals….."

As she talked, Cordell thought *maybe we can develop Lilly's shoe fetish into a program segment all its own. Maybe even ongoing series of segments over several programs if we include the remodeling thing. Watch out HGTV. These women would leave Christina in their dust.*

"So, what about that one Marx Brother that wore those God-awful orange socks? Remember? He wore the weirdest things on his feet. I couldn't tell if they were sandals or shoes," said Babs.

Lilly shook her head. "They weren't sandals… or shoes. They were McGuffey slip-ons. They're more of slipper than a shoe or a sandal. They ain't cheap either. Johnston and Murphy don't make cheap slip-ons."

Babs said, "That reminds me of the time when my Momma's two sisters came to visit her. I drove the three of them to the new Walmart in Tallahassee 'cause they forgot to pack their bedroom slippers. This was when one of my girls was only six months old, and so I had to drive all the way to Tallahassee with them three old women and my six-month old baby in a tiny Toyota Corolla. Those three women wouldn't stop talking about stuff that had no business being discussed in front of a six-month old—"

"Babsie," Lizzie said, "let's make sure this story is going somewhere. I know there's a conclusion in there somewhere, but unfortunately, it's still in your brain and hasn't made it to your mouth yet."

"Y'all know how I got to tell a story just like it is in my brain, or it don't come out of my mouth right."

"But Cordell might not be that interested in your slipper story."

In fact, Cordell had been listening intently to every word the three women had said. And the more he listened, the more convinced he became these women would be perfect for the reality show he envisioned. *This kind of stuff will be dynamite on a reality TV show. Think of the ratings. Babs is as kooky now as she was in college. Viewers will eat it up*. He said, "To the contrary, I want to hear more. Please continue."

Babs said, "So anyway, they start talking about whether or not the Pope was really a Catholic, and putting a tampon in your ear, and how urine is sterile, and having sex with your husband after prostate surgery, and I had to put both my hands over my ears—"

"I thought you were driving?" Lilly asked.

"I was. Anyway, to hear your momma and her two old sisters talking about stuff like that is always so gross, especially when they go into detail on something about sex. I had to keep saying 'Happy Place' 'Happy Place.' You know the drill……."

Cordell's smile stretched ear to ear.

Chapter 5

Thursday, October 16th, 8:13 AM, EDT

The following text exchange occurred between Mitzi and her friend Stoney Lee.

Mitzi: While I was having lunch at Hong Yip yesterday, I saw a nice-looking older man having lunch with Babs, Lilly, and Lizzie. My waitress told me he's a Hollywood producer.
Stoney: A Hollywood producer! What! Why?
Mitzi: Their waitress overheard that they are going to star in some sort of a reality show on TV.
Stoney: Must be something like that show *Meerkat Manor* on Animal Planet channel with them voicing the animal characters. They'll probably be voices for five manatees.
Mitzi: We've got to figure out some way to screw this up. I don't know if I can handle seeing Babs on TV once a week. Oh wait! I just remembered something that gives me an idea.
Stoney: What is it?
Mitzi: It's that time of the month.
Stoney: ????
Mitzi: I'll explain later. No time now. I've got to make a phone call.

The three prospective reality TV stars sat on Babs' porch, sipping mimosas.

"You say he's on Facebook?" Lilly asked, referring to one of the Marx Brothers.

Babs nodded. "Oh yeah. All the Marx Brothers are. He and I 'friended' each other Monday night."

"Did he wear a condom?" Lizzie asked in jest.

"I didn't know you had to wear a condom when you were posting on Facebook," said Lilly sincerely. "What did he say?"

Babs said, "He was teasing me about letting him take the pictures for our next calendar. I told him we'd probably have clothes on if we do another calendar, and he said 'never mind' just like that woman… uh, Emily Litella, the one played by Gilda Radner on *Saturday Night Live*, although he said 'never mind' in a text. That's the thing I like about him. He has such a great sense of humor. Kind of reminds me of Avery's cousin—"

"The cousin in Waycross?" asked Lilly.

"Please, don't interrupt her any more. Let her finish, or I'll have to pee in my mimosa glass," Lizzie said.

"As I was about to say…" Babs paused.

"And?"

"I forgot. See what happens when I get interrupted—"

"Thank God."

"Oh, oh. I remember now. I was going to tell y'all about Avery's cousin from Valdosta. The one with a left foot that's a full size bigger than her right foot, and the shoe lady at Dillard's tells her to buy two pairs—one pair a size seven and the other pair a size eight—of the same style and color shoe, then mate the necessary sizes up—"

"How does Avery's cousin's odd-sized feet relate to the Marx Brother's sense of humor?" Lilly asked.

"Avery had the funniest looking toes. His toes were almost as long as his fingers. He used to say he had 'prehensile' toes—"

"What are those?"

"That's when your toes are so long you can pick up stuff with your toes like a monkey does…"

"Is that all of your story?" asked Lizzie.

"No, but I just remembered something, and I'll have to finish the story later. I gotta run pretty soon. It's that time of the month."

"Babsie, if my memory serves me, you ain't had a period in about ten years."

"No silly. I'm not talking about that. I gotta go see Madame Cassandra for my monthly reading at eleven o'clock," Babs said. The psychic claimed the ability to foretell the future and communicate with 'the other side.' Babs valued the woman's mental powers so much that she visited her every month like clockwork.

"Getting your horoscope read?" Lizzie asked.

"Nope. She's using crystals now."

"I thought she had switched to tarot cards?" Lilly said.

"She ain't used those for a long time. She dropped them and been using crystals for at least nine months now."

Lizzie said, “Her eyesight must’ve gone bad. Probably couldn’t see the marks on her marked tarot cards.”

The look of horror on Babs’ face could not have been worse if she had seen Freddy Krueger. “Don’t joke about mystical powers. That’ll get you in big trouble. In fact, she quit using Tarot cards because she said she could feel the energy surging in the crystals better than in them cards. She can hear the crystals singing to her.”

“They’re probably singing rap music.”

Lilly asked, “Crystals? Did she bring her crystal ball out of mothball? It’s been what, a decade or two since she used one?”

“No, no. Crystals ain’t the same as a crystal ball. No one uses crystal balls anymore… at least no psychics I know of. Them’s way out of date. She uses crystals. Don’t y’all ever watch any of them shopping channels on TV? It’s the same kind they sell on TV.”

Lizzie said, “Must be where Madame Cassandra got hers. If she bought them from Home Shopping Network, they probably cost her $19.95. How much does she charge you?”

“Eighty-five for a half-hour session.”

The look on Lizzie’s face said, ‘You’ve got to be kidding.’ She looked at Lilly. Lilly looked at Lizzie.

“One of us needs to go with Miss Babsie and keep her out of trouble,” Lilly said.

Lizzie asked, “Is that possible?”

The top line of the sign read “MADAME CASSANDRA”, and the line below that read “Psychic Reader and Spiritual Advisor”. Both lines were faded from many years of bright Georgia sun. That celestial body shone radiantly in the midday sky as Babs and Lilly pulled onto the gravel driveway. Madame Cassandra had long been a Thomasville fixture on State Road 122, just outside the city limits *and* the arm of local law. Her place of business occupied a house originally built in the 1930s. It was one of the old Bungalow style houses extensively built throughout the South during that period. White clapboard siding, last painted thirty-one years ago, suggested how long the psychic had occupied the house. Mold-blackened concrete steps led up to a four-column porch whose rotting wood planks flaked their grey paint worse than the deck of a war torn battleship. The old boards groaned eerily as Babs and Lilly crept over them to a door also much in need of paint.

“Didn’t you say you pay Madame Cassandra seventy-five an hour for her advice?” Lilly asked.

"Nope. Eighty-five bucks for a thirty-minute session, but I get a discount on any minutes over that. Why you ask?" Babs' sessions always exceeded thirty minutes due to her chattiness, to which Cassandra never complained.

"It looks like she's not spending any of her profits on maintenance," Lilly said.

"Oh. This is just the kind of place that attracts the spirits. They're partial to shabby chic. Madame Cassandra told me it makes 'em feel more comfortable. She says they're old and they like old houses. Spirits are more likely to come and visit with you if your place looks a little roughed up." Slick talking Cassandra could make a silk purse out of a sow's ear.

Lilly, an admitted neat freak, merely voiced reality when she said, "Shabby chic? Roughed up? I bet the spirits wear hazmat suits when they come to visit this place."

Babs shook her head in reply and rang the doorbell. They heard rattling around inside for several minutes.

"Sounds like she's moving bodies around," Lilly said. "I thought Madame Cassandra was a fortune teller."

"Spirits don't have bodies anymore. There's nothing to move. The supernatural is serious business," said Babs.

"Okay. I'll get serious and put on one of the faces I use when I'm playing monster with my grandkids," Lilly said. Her mouth formed an exaggerated frown in a caricature of someone from the supernatural world.

The door opened abruptly, and a smiling wrinkled face appeared.

Chapter 6

Thursday, October 16th, 11:05 AM, EDT

The smiling wrinkled face said, "Missus Neauxgeaux, I didn't expect you for another twenty-five minutes. Nice to see you again. Did things go the way I told you they would last month? Forgive me. Come in, come in." Lilly forgot to get rid of her supernatural face which Madame Cassandra noticed as she stepped through the doorway. The old woman asked, "Is everything all right Missus White? You looked peaked."

Lilly forced a smile and said, "It's these panty hose. They're too tight."

A multi-colored scarf tightly covered the top of Madame Cassandra's head. Long, stringy grey hair hung down over the elderly woman's shoulders and back. She wore a white blouse and a long, pleated floor-length skirt made from a multi-color floral-patterned material. Almost indecipherable faded tattoos adorned each of her wrinkled arms. One arm appeared to sport a peace sign, while the Chinese yin and yang symbol decorated the other arm. The clothes said gypsy from Romania. The tattoos said 1960's hippie from San Francisco. The Thomasville rumor mill said Wanda Warnell, aka Madame Cassandra, was born and raised in Waycross, Georgia and left that town just ahead of the police. Despite the woman's disconcerting looks, Lilly loyally followed Babs inside.

"My goodness, it's dark in here," Lilly said as they stepped into the parlor. Closed black drapes covered the room's windows. A forty-watt bulb in a faux antique Victorian ceiling light fixture above a round table in the center of the room provided meager lighting.

"Darkness is propitious for the spirits, my child," Cassandra said.

"I don't blame them. Most dermatologists say the less sunlight you get, the better. Too much sun ain't good for the skin. Especially if you have a fair complexion like me. And if anyone would have a fair complexion, it would have to be a spirit or a ghost. I was cursed with a fair complexion, and I practically got to dip myself in sunblock if I'm gonna be out in the sun too long—"

"I completely understand. I didn't expect anyone to be accompanying Missus Neauxgeaux."

"I hope you don't mind. When Babs said she was going for her psychic reading today, I thought it might be neat to tag along. I ain't been to a fortune teller since last time that traveling circus came through Thomasville. When was that? Two… maybe three decades ago?"

"The science of prognostication has changed quite a bit since then, my dear."

Babs enthusiastically nodded. "They've got all new technology nowadays. Tarot cards, stones, crystals, singing bowls, bones, dice, yarrow stalks… you name it."

"One must have the right tools for the job if one is to communicate with the other world," said Cassandra.

"Yeah, yeah… what do you call it? Me-trop-olis world?"

Cassandra smiled and said, "You mean the metaphysical world, my dear."

"Right. Communicating with the metaphysical world ain't for the faint of heart."

"The spiritual world welcomes all who seek guidance. Please, have a seat." Cassandra's arm made a sweeping motion toward the table which seemed to acquire a transcendental aura.

After the three women sat down, the faux gypsy opened a box laying on the table and extracted a bunch of rough-cut stones from it. These were her crystals. She carefully placed each one on the table in an arrangement whose meaning was known only to her. Each crystal was unique, differing from the others in color, size, shape, and surface texture. Colors included milky rose, pitch black, a shade of deep garnet, smoky brown, translucent light grey, and one that was a clash of light blue and white, to name a few. Sizes ranged from that of a lemon to a grapefruit. Their shapes and surface textures varied from smooth, round stones to rocks with crags and crevices. Two stones possessed sculpted beveled angles on multi-sided surfaces. Seventeen different crystals lay on the table after she finished.

"Ooh! Y'all got some pyrite this time!" squealed Babs, recognizing a rock she had used recently in one of her attempted voodoo rituals.

"Yes, my dear. I know how much you like it," Cassandra said. "Now, everyone please be quiet while I clear my aura."

She closed her eyes. Babs looked at Lilly, held a finger up to her lips, and softly said, "This is the hardest part for me… not talking for so long."

Cassandra grimaced as Babs spoke but kept her eyes closed and said nothing. A contemplative look returned to her face.

Babs said, "It's like she's meditating or something. I don't know what it does, but it works."

Cassandra's grimace returned. Lilly frowned at Babs, having been raised not to interrupt. Eyes closed, Cassandra remained silent but began slowly moving her hands over, around, and among the crystals. Her face morphed through a myriad of expressions during the process.

"I never know how long the aura clearing part is gonna go on. It's the hardest part for me. Oh, I think I already said that, but it is." Babs shrugged, then smiled. "The really good stuff starts after that."

After a long period, Cassandra abruptly ceased waving her arms above the stones with a theatrical flair that would have put Laurence Olivier to shame. Leaving her arms suspended in the air, she opened her eyes, looked down at the tools of her trade, and said, "The crystals are all cleared and energized."

Babs squealed, "Ooh, ooh, ooh! This is the best part! Or at least one of the better parts. It's the most exciting part at least. I'm always torn between what to do. One part of me wants to keep my eyes closed and be surprised when I open them, and the other part wants to watch and see what happens as it happens."

Ever the polite Southern lady, Lilly looked at Babs and put her finger to her lips. "Shhhhhhh."

Cassandra interrupted the interruption by dramatically lowering her arms and placing her hands on the edge of the table in front of her.

"You watch," Babs said, obvious glee in her voice. "She's gonna pick one. I just know it."

Cassandra's hands moved in a slow, indirect course. At times her hands paused over a crystal, seemingly ready to choose it, only to disappoint Babs by moving on. After several such nerve-racking instances, her hands hovered over one, held it up, and displayed it for all to see. It was an odd-shaped green crystal about the size of an orange with a smooth surface. She said, "This is the one. My lovely Aventurine"

"Sometimes it's the temperature of the crystal, or sometimes the one that she's drawn to changes color. Sometimes she sees an image in it; sometimes it sings to her," Babs said, eyes were as wide as saucers. "You never know *what* one of them crystals is gonna do to make itself be her choice."

"Babs, honey, why don't you let Madame Cassandra tell us in her own words?" Lilly asked. Amen!

Cassandra smiled. "I feel my aura is now set for the greatest good. I feel that the spirits' message will be a loving one. We are ready."

"Don't forget the gentle guidance part," Babs urged.

A grimace returned to the old gypsy's face, but she said nothing and instead reached into a drawer beneath the table. She extracted a piece of fine parchment paper and an expensive Mont Blanc pen and laid both on the table. This was when things finally got interesting.

With no apparent script guiding her, she picked up the pen and began scribbling things at random on the paper. Lilly leaned closer and silently mouthed what she saw being written. "2222 xrab34 56 dt---- ro xx........" and so forth.

Cassandra sometimes wrote seemingly meaningless gibberish. Other times, she wrote words at random. While doing so, she never said anything, her face a blank canvas, as she supposedly transcribed messages from a realm beyond the physical world. For a change, Babs said nothing and simply looked on in awe. This sort of nonsense continued for ten minutes until the paper was filled with words, numbers, letters, and symbols. Cassandra put her pen down, looked up, and said nothing. Perspiration dripped from her chin. A slight tremor coursed through her writing hand.

Lilly said, "I can't resist any longer. What does all that stuff mean? Take 'dt----' or '2222' or '2118' or 'XGttbzqnfdtkttt' or any of what you've written. What does that stuff mean?"

"Some of it means nothing..." Cassandra said. "At least it means nothing at first. The spiritual forces speak in mysterious ways. Their communications are often in code. It is up to psychics such as me to interpret what they are telling us."

"So, just what *are* they saying?" Lilly asked.

With a determined look on her face, Cassandra looked down again and focused her eyes like lasers on the parchment. Seconds passed before she said, “Babs will most definitely meet someone new, someone who will positively impact her life.”

“Ooh, ooh!” Babs squealed. “A new boyfriend?”

The faux gypsy continued looking down at her writing and shook her head. “No… no, not a boyfriend. The crystals don’t say exactly who it is. They only say that you will meet a new someone or something. What is this?” She turned the parchment around and slid it toward Babs, pointing to the phrase ‘Area 53’ on it.

Babs’ eyes got wider. “It’s a place in the Florida Panhandle.”

“The crystals exert a strong positive energy field regarding this Area 53. That is why it is written so boldly and clearly on the parchment.”

“Energy field?” asked Lilly.

“Yes. An aura that surrounds us and encompasses our chakras.”

Lilly frowned. “Chakras? You mean our cheeks?”

“No, my dear. Chakras are part of the psychic aspects of the human body. Chakras are energy centers within the human body. I sense strong positive energy flowing between Babs’ Sixth Chakra and this Area 53. The Sixth Chakra is also called the Third Eye because it governs intuition and truth.”

Babs pushed for a desired outcome. “Is the ‘someone or something’ in Area 53?”

Cassandra nodded. “The crystals also indicate this someone or something is from a place far away.” Madame Cassandra tilted her head and looked upwards.

Babs imitated the Cassandra, then raised her hand and pointed upward. She quietly said, “Outer space?”

Madame Cassandra looked down and moved her face closer to the paper. She focused on her writing for an extended period. Finally, the old woman raised her head and said, “I did feel strong energy forces when you said, ‘outer space,’ but I cannot say anything for certain at this point in time.”

“I know it. My chakra is saying that I’m gonna meet an alien. I just know it. There’s been too much about aliens on the Internet lately. I do feel something funny in my brain chakra.” Babs tapped her temple several times and nodded hopefully. Suddenly, she turned serious. “Them crystals must be saying this someone or something from far away is an alien that I’m gonna meet in Area 53.”

Cassandra’s face displayed a look of satisfaction as she said, “Anything is possible, my child.”

Lilly looked at Babs and said, "Whomever this someone or something is you're gonna meet, I'm sure you'll be happy. Can we go now? I've got an appointment this afternoon with the contractor that's gonna remodel my shoe closet."

Madame Cassandra looked at the antique clock hanging on one of the walls and nodded. "It has been thirty minutes."

While this nonsense was happening inside, malice transpired outside. Mitzi slowly cruised by Cassandra's house. Stoney Lee sat upfront beside her. Mitzi knew she would need assistance with her nefarious scheme and intended to bring someone as diabolical as herself into it.

"You were right. That is Babs' Escalade. Only a moron like Babs would go to a charlatan like Madame Cassandra more than once, much less every month. But, so what? I know you didn't ride all the way out here on this godforsaken road just to see Babs' Escalade. What's up?" Stoney asked.

"It dawned on me this morning that I could goad Babs into doing something really stupid about her UFOs?"

"Babs *is* a moron. She'll fall for anything."

"She's been posting all sorts of Area 53 stuff on Facebook lately."

"I noticed. Exactly what is Area 53 anyway?" Stoney asked.

"It's supposed to be a place somewhere in the Florida panhandle where the Federal government houses UFOs. Kind of overflow parking from that Area 51 site in Nevada… or is Area 51 in New Mexico? I can't remember. Anyway, I'm sure it's really nothing but a big Internet hoax, but Babs is a pushover for those kinds of things. She's one of the biggest conspiracy theory nuts I've ever seen."

"Okay. You've been thinking of somehow goading Babs into saying or doing something stupid about Area 53 and UFOs. So, what's this got to do with us driving by Madame Cassandra's?"

Mitzi said, "It hit me this morning while I was texting you. It's the time of the month when she goes to Cassandra for her psychic reading. Babs really believes the charlatan has mystic powers, so why not get the old bag involved? Have her come up with something in her reading about there being aliens in Area 53. Cassandra will do anything for a buck, legal or illegal. And Babs doesn't do anything without Cassandra's blessing. That's why she goes to the old bag every month. So, I called Cassandra and told her what I wanted her to do, but to be subtle about it. I don't want the old wench overplaying it and making Babs skeptical."

"Brilliant… except for the subtle part!"

"How so?"

"A dumb bunny like Babs may not get the message if it's too subtle."

"Good point. We'll come back here after Babs has left. I've got to pay the old gypsy the fifty bucks we agreed to. I'll ask her how it went and if she thinks Babs fell for it."

Stoney was skeptical but shrugged her acceptance of Mitzi's plan so far. She asked, "What's the next step in your 'something stupid' idea?"

Mitzi smiled. "Next step is even more brilliant. We get Babs to accept an Area 53 challenge on her new reality show on TV."

"What sort of a challenge?"

"Prove that it exists."

"Prove that it exists?"

Mitzi nodded. "Yep. We goad her into either trying to prove it exists, or looking like a fool or a liar or both for continually saying that it does exist if she admits she can't prove it."

"How would she try to prove it? Some sort of testimony she gets off of the Internet from some nutcase? That wouldn't be too hard to do."

"No on the Internet testimony. We goad her into saying she's going to try to break into Area 53. That's the only way."

Stoney shook her head. Getting anyone to try something like this was a stretch, even for someone as dense as Babs. She said, "An Area 53 in the Florida panhandle would be on Federal government property. That's serious business. Babs is a moron, but even she's not stupid enough to try to break into Federal property."

"Oh? Wasn't she involved in that incident in Atlanta several years ago with that international pipeline company? The one that destroyed thousands of acres of farmland in Germany? I'd say that was pretty serious."

"That was never proved. Besides, the pipeline company was a private company, not a government agency."

"Okay. Didn't she and her four girlfriends run naked across TIAA Bank football field in Jacksonville on live television last Saturday?"

"And no one's proved they did that… yet. It's still being debated whether or not it was them or the Kardashians."

"We both know they did it. You goaded Daffy into a bet, with the loser and her friends having to streak the Georgia-Florida game. She lost, and they streaked during the halftime show," said Mitzi.

"Too bad they were just smart enough to disguise themselves as Kardashians. I bet that was Gidget's idea." Gidget was considered the intellect of the Casserole Ladies quintet, but everything is relative.

The sinister look that descended upon Mitzi's face would have frightened Hannibal Lecter. "If Babs and her friends are stupid enough to get tricked into doing something as outrageous as streaking on national TV, she's stupid enough to be goaded into proving Area 53 exists."

Stoney was still skeptical but less so. "Maybe."

"Don't worry. We'll goad Miss Babsie into trying to prove Area 53 exists. It'll be a piece of cake. At the very least, we'll have fun trying."

"So, besides getting Cassandra to prep Babsie, what else are you going to do?"

"I'm gonna talk to that producer friend of hers. Put an idea in his head about an Area 53 plot for the show. A plot that will send the show's ratings through the roof, which I hate doing, but it'll be worth it to show the whole world what a nutjob Babs is."

"You think the producer will go along with your scheme?"

"He's a Hollywood producer. I bet Hollywood producers live or die by their show's ratings. I bet they'll do anything for ratings. And a stunt this outrageous would be a ratings blockbuster."

Chapter 7

Friday, October 17th, 2:33 PM, EDT

In the hours following Babs and Lilly's encounter with the other side, Facebook frothed with posts about Area 53. One of the cuter ones teased Babs about extraterrestrial romance.

Mitzi Merchant
I hear Babs has a little green boyfriend in Area 53.
Like **Comment**

Penny Perdoo
Where would Babs and her little green boyfriend go on a date? A drive-in movie on Mars? A Whataburger on Venus?
Like **Reply**

Stoney Lee
I can just imagine their reunion. He wraps his five arms around her for a little smooch, but she can't decide which of his three mouths to kiss first.
Like **Reply**

Mitzi Merchant
They'll probably rendezvous at Area 53, the Motel 6 of space travel. Or maybe she'll try to impress him by going to a tractor pull in Waycross. She'll need to make sure no one mistakes her little green boyfriend for a John Deere tractor.
Like **Reply**

Babs Neauxgeaux
Ho, ho, ho. Very funny. We'll see who has the last laugh when the Federal government admits there is an Area 53, just like they did in 2013 when they admitted there was an Area 51 in Nevada. Or was it in Utah? Anyway, Area 53 is not another conspiracy theory like you've been saying.

Like **Reply**

Ted Maybry
There are a lot of questions on the Internet about UFOs in Area 53. Are there really 37 UFOs stored there? Why did the Feds move the UFOs to Area 53? Was Area 51 too dry a climate for aliens?
Like **Reply**

Mitzi Merchant
The biggest question is when is Babs going to put her money where her mouth is and prove Area 53 exists? If she doesn't do that, then this is just another one of her crackpot conspiracy theories.
Like **Reply**

The three Casserole Ladies sat on Lilly's front porch in Thomasville's Tockwotton Historical District. Lilly and Wendell purchased the two-story antebellum house soon after they married and invested a good deal of their adult life restoring it to its present splendor. It was a labor of love even though the work was performed by contractors, and it reflected their own love for each other. A wraparound porch on three sides made it ideal for mojitos and polite conversation on a pleasant October afternoon.

"All of their Facebook posts get downright ugly. Especially the ones about me," said Babs. She wore a loose fitting, dark green silk bow blouse that performed an admirable job at hiding weight. A struggle ensued as Babs tried to blot out some mojito which she had spilled on the lengthy bow part hanging down to her waist. The bow performed the same function as a man's tie, in this case it drawing the eye to a stain. She swore, unconsciously revealing her growing dread of getting older. "Damnit. My Parkinson's again."

"Don't feel bad," Lizzie said, referring to the slanderous Facebook posts and ignoring Babs' age-induced hypochondria. She and Lilly both knew Babs' doctor had told her recently she did not have Parkinson's, somewhat to her disappointment.

"Don't feel bad? This is a $428 Halperin blouse."

"That's not what I'm talking about. I'm talking about the skanks' Facebook posts. They're not abusing you any worse than they abused their late husbands. Let's get back to what Cassandra told y'all. Was the main takeaway that you're gonna make a new friend?"

Babs stopped blotting and nodded. "Yeah, but much more than that. The way she said it was much more interesting than just saying that I'm gonna make a new friend."

"And you think the new friend she's talking about is not just some new boyfriend? Not one of those Marx Brothers?"

"No. I'm sure it's an alien," Babs said. "And he's in Area 53."

"How do you know it's a 'he'?" Lizzie asked.

"I dunno. I guess I assumed all aliens would be men. They never say one way or the other on the Internet."

"Sounds like a sexist assumption to me."

Babs squinched her nose in reply.

"Meeting a female alien would be kind of nice," said Lilly. This Southern lady did not want to say what she was thinking out loud, even in front of her closest friends. *Wouldn't it be the social event of the year to host Low Tea one afternoon for a female alien? Right here in this house. Wendel would be so proud!* She could imagine the writeup in the Thomasville Times-Enterprise the next day. *Finally, something else besides high school football in the Local Events section.* Not bad for the old ego and a chance to one-up some people. *Penny Perdoo would be sooo jealous!* Instead, she said, "The interesting part was when Cassandra wrote the words 'Area 53' on her paper. We never even mentioned Area 53! How did she know about Area 53 except from them crystals?"

"That's a question for another day," said Babs. "Cordell's production crew gets here tomorrow morning to start filming—"

An older model Cadillac turning into the driveway interrupted her.

"When is he gonna get rid of that thing?" asked Lilly. "I'd be embarrassed to ride around Thomasville in that beat up old piece of junk. Some people have no couth."

"Now, now. Don't insult Babs' boyfriend. He paid good money for it twenty years ago," Lizzie said.

"It was an old used piece of junk when he bought it."

Babs lowered her voice and said, "Shhhh. Don't let him hear you say that. He says he only keeps it because it's so old it has become a collector's car and don't depreciate no more."

Sonny Biskit exited his car, wheezing as he hobbled toward them. Visually, the sixty-one-year-old bachelor offered little to excite a female. Medium height, a weight issue evidenced by a tee-shirted belly flopping over a belt cinched in its last notch, well-worn Walmart blue jeans, combover. Residents of Thomasville viewed him in much the same way many Americans view Johnny Depp nowadays—puzzling to look at but a possible topic of conversation at a party when you run out of other things to talk about. Sonny sincerely believed women were physically attracted to him.

Babs was partially to blame for his delusion, having occasionally availed herself of Sonny's charms in some of her many moments of uncritical thinking. After all, women have needs, and the local bachelor pool was limited. The most recent occasion occurred in September in connection with their attendance at a tractor pull in Waycross. Her lapses could be excused as several other Casserole Ladies had also taken Sonny up on his advances.

At the top of the steps of Babs' porch, Sonny said, "Hey y'all. How'd I get so lucky finding three hotties like y'all here in one place all at once?"

"Probably because Babs broke a mirror, Lilly walked under a ladder, and a black cat walked in front of me this morning," said Lizzie. Sonny grinned like a Cheshire cat, thinking it a complement.

"I come over here to invite Babs to go with me to that new paintball park outside of Dothan tomorrow afternoon, but now I'm gonna invite all three of y'all. We'll have a blast." From a tractor pull in Waycross to paintball in Dothan. Sonny was upping his game.

Lilly looked back and forth between Babs and Lizzie and asked, "What is paintball?"

"It's lots of fun. You run around shooting little balls filled with paint at other people." Sonny's voice contained not a hint of sarcasm.

"Sounds like you're stretching the definition of fun, Sonny," said Lizzie.

Puzzled, Sonny guessed at the proper response. "Yeah, it will be."

"Three against one. Think you can beat all three of us?"

Sonny considered the odds and did not like them. "No problem. I'll call Dab and Squeaker and see if they can go too."

One neat thing about small towns in the South is that they love to give males nicknames if they have ordinary first names. Take Dab. His first name was Bobby but excessive use of Brylcreem hair cream in high school proved to be his undoing. For context, this was in the long-hair phase of the early 1970s. Squeaker received his appellation one night after botching a prank on a sorority at FSU. Everyone in Thomasville forgot what his real first name was decades ago.

After Sonny drove off, Babs looked at Lizzie as if her friend had suddenly grown a third eye. She asked, "Why did you accept Sonny's invitation? I thought you couldn't stand him."

"Oh, I don't mind Sonny occasionally. He's good for a laugh or two," said Lizzie.

The expression on Lilly's face looked like she had just unclogged a toilet. She said, "But paintball!"

Babs shook her head and frowned. "I dunno. From what I understand, paintball is a real physical game. It's a game for a young person, and we're too old to be running around like three kids. Especially me." Babs' increasingly tiresome dread of aging began to irritate Lilly, but she decided to let it go.

"Didn't you say Cordell's crew starts filming tomorrow?" asked Lizzie.

"Yeah."

"I can't imagine anything boosting the ratings of a reality TV show any more than filming a bunch of us old farts playing paintball."

"How about trespassing on Federal government property?" asked Lilly.

Chapter 8

Saturday, October 18th, 3:05 PM, CDT

Babs and five other senior citizens stood among a hundred acres of pine trees outside Dothan, a small Alabama town two hours east of Thomasville. Tim and Allen, two of Cordell's cameramen, walked around them, camcorders rolling.

"Welcome to Blackwater Survival Field and Axe Throwing Range," the man said. A good rule of thumb is an obese man should never wear a tee-shirt unless it's underneath a shirt which is buttoned up. The man speaking must have been unaware of this rule. The words 'Fight or Die' floated above a Blackwater skull and crossed-missiles logo on his black tee-shirt. Several rolls of fat on his protruding belly caused the two crossed missiles in the logo to wrinkle as if they had exploded in flight. The gap between the bottom of his tee-shirt and top of his blue jeans revealed two inches of hairy belly. "My name is Joey, and I'll be y'all's referee. I'm gonna go over the rules with y'all, so listen up. It might mean the difference between winnin' or losin'."

Paintball is a sport in which people shoot other people for the fun of it with pellets that explode on contact. These pellets are filled with washable but messy paint. They shoot the pellets from imitation assault rifles that look pretty scary. Players wear some protective equipment—face shields, elbow and knee pads, and chest vests. Nevertheless, the pellets sting like hell when they explode. A face shield consists of hard black plastic mask covering the entire face. The player sees through two polycarbonate clear lenses in the shield. Combined with a bulky vest covering the entire front and back of the upper body, a player resembles a character out of a *Transformers* movie.

Joey said, "Y'all selected the Black Hawk Down field as y'all's field of play. This is one of the toughest of the ten fields we got in Blackwater. Trust me, Black Hawk Down is four acres of pure hell. Girls against boys, which is what y'all decided on. That ought to make it fun. We're gonna give the girls fifteen minutes to hide first. I'll give y'all some advice on how and where best to hide while we walk over there. Then I'll come back here and get the boys ready to go huntin'. The rules is simple. No alcohol unless I don't catch you with it. Keep y'all's face shields on at all times during play. No horseplay. When I blow the whistle two times, that means it's timeout; three times, that means stop play. Either way, y'all stop shooting when y'all hear the whistle. No arguing with the referee. If you're hit, holler and I'll come over and decide if you're dead or wounded. All dead players immediately go to the dead box. Don't try to cheat by wiping off the paint; you'll only smear it on your gloves and the rest of your clothing. No real weapons permitted on the field of play, especially guns and knives. We've had some pretty awful accidents in the past. Got it?"

Out of the six heads that nodded, probably only two or three actually understood, and that was being generous. Joey asked, "Any questions before we start?"

"How long are we going to play?" Lilly asked, hoping for a short timeframe.

"Y'all rented the Blackhawk Down field for as long as it takes one of the two teams to kill off the other team. Y'all's rental package includes five hundred paintballs for each person. Five hundred paintballs typically last about two and a half hours. If it goes longer, no problem. Y'all rented the field for as long as it takes to kill off one team or run out of pellets."

"What if we have to go to the bathroom?" Babs asked. "I can't play for two and a half hours without peeing."

"Yeah, some of us have prostates you know." Sonny looked at Squeaker and Dab. "Well, at least some of us do."

Joey said, "They's porta potties on all the fields. I believe Blackhawk Down has three."

"Thank God," Lizzie said, "I can never depend on remembering to wear my Depends when I need to."

"Do the porta potties have sinks?" Lilly asked. "And soap?"

Sonny said, "I dunno. Two and a half hours. I may need to stop for a couple of carb breaks if my blood sugar gets too low."

"If any of y'all have any medical issues during play, let me know, and I'll call a timeout," Joey said. "Anything else?"

"Why do we have to wear these face shields?" Lilly asked. "I look terrible with it on."

Squeaker said, "That's not the problem. The problem is that it doesn't fit over my glasses very well. I'm wearing bifocals, and I can't see out of the bottom part of the lens. I can't even see any of the details on this gun, much less the trigger."

"It's covering my hearing aid. How am I supposed to hear someone sneaking up on me?" Dab asked.

Joey started to answer, but was cut off by Babs. "This tactical vest squeezes my boobs too much. Don't y'all have any larger sizes for a woman?"

"Try on a man's vest. That might be a better fit," Joey said.

"What? You don't have Dolly Parton size paintball vests?" Lizzie asked.

Dab said, "Don't anyone aim for my chest. It's off limits. No telling what the impact from one of those paintballs will do to my pacemaker."

Lilly complained. "This gun is too heavy."

"You can use a paintball pistol. It's lighter, but you'll have to reload more often," Joey said.

Dab asked, "Can I keep my cane? I have used it as a weapon several times. I have trouble walking without it."

"Yessir. You can keep your cane, but you have to promise to use it only for walking," Joey said.

Sonny leaned over and whispered to Babs, "Someone needs to remember to stay close to Dab if this game goes too late, and it starts to get dark. We noticed that he's started having a touch of sundowner's syndrome lately."

Dab heard Sonny's cautionary remark and nodded. "Yeah, I always want to go inside when it starts getting dark. Happens more and more the older I get."

Squeaker shrieked, "Oh, oh. Someone don't let me forget. I need to take my medicine at three o'clock sharp."

"I usually take a nap from two to four in the afternoon," Lizzie said.

Squeaker smiled. "I can help you find a nice cozy spot for a snooze if you want."

Sonny asked, "Can we take a smoke break every now and then?"

"I just hope my arthritis doesn't start acting up," Squeaker said.

Dab huffed. "Arthritis, hell! I just wish I had your arthritis. This new knee hasn't felt right ever since they put it in nine months ago."

Babs looked at Lilly and Lizzie and said, "I told y'all yesterday we're too old for this game."

Lizzie looked at Joey and asked, "Could you take a group picture of all of us before we start? Some of us may not make it through this game, and I'd like to have a picture to remember them by."

Actual play was much worse than imagined. Ten minutes into paintball, Dab's pacemaker set off a remote alert on his cardiologist's laptop. The cardiologist was on holiday in Bermuda but spotted the alert. He immediately called Dab's cell phone and told him to go to the nearest emergency room and have it checked out ASAP. Most people would have gone straight to the ER, but the boys were having too much fun shooting paintballs at the girls. Ending the game for a mere atrial arrythmia was out of the question. They played another ten minutes, stopping only after all six players—including Dab—lay gasping for breath on the ground.

Twenty minutes after the game started, all six players rode back to base camp in the bed of a Ford F-250 long bed pickup truck. No one managed to sit upright during the ride. Back at camp, Blackwater's paramedic frantically worked to alleviate everyone's ailments but to no avail. It was a bottle of Jack Daniels that eventually did the trick. Tim and Allen got everything on film.

As the group climbed into Babs' Escalade to depart, Joey reminded them, "Y'all be sure to tell all y'all's friends about Blackwater. Remember that we host weddings and bar mitzvahs here as well as birthday parties."

Chapter 9

Thursday, October 30th, 8:19 PM, EDT

Cordell and his production crew worked tirelessly twelve hours a day from Paintball Saturday until they flew back to Hollywood on Monday, October 27th to edit the video. The Casserole Ladies gathered at Babs' house Thursday night to watch the premier episode. As they waited on a batch of nachos in the oven, she said, "Sonny called me today and told me that Dab's cardiologist called him the next day. Remember how stumped the ER doctor in Dothan was? Remember how he kept listening to Dab's heart and couldn't hear anything abnormal? How he didn't see anything abnormal on the EKG?"

Lizzie and Babs nodded.

"Dab's cardiologist said there wasn't nothing wrong with his heart. It turned out to be a problem with the computer network in the beach house he was renting. Some hiccup on the network triggered the alert on his laptop."

"You mean we wasted four hours Saturday evening in the ER?" asked Lizzie.

The trip to the ER was not a total waste. On the way, Sonny and Lizzie felt like their blood sugars were getting low, so Babs pulled her SUV into the parking lot of a Buffalo Wild Wings. A few draft beers and several plates of wings resolved their issue.

"I've heard enough," said Lilly and looked at Babs. "Are the nachos ready?"

Babs checked and they were burned, so she prepared another batch. When it was finally ready, they settled down in front of her eighty-six-inch television, and she started her DVR. What unfolded on the screen defied reality.

INTERIOR SCENE: DAFFY'S PARLOR, SUNDAY MORNING

Real Widows theme song begins as camera wide shot pans across the parlor where the five women sit and chat. Camera pauses at the room's entryway. Narrator stands, unnoticed by the women, wearing a long, glistening A-list dress with a slit up one side revealing a leg Beyoncé would envy. As she begins to speak, the ladies' chatting fades. Narrator's name floats across the screen, settles on her for several seconds, then dissolves.

NARRATOR: The Widows of Thomasville live in a lovely little town in southeast Georgia. Its climate is mild, its geography relaxing. Time seems to stand still in this idyllic place. Visitors often remark how locals here are some of the friendliest they've ever met, and how they practice 'love thy neighbor' on a daily basis… [The narrator pauses, and the camera pans over to the Casserole Ladies.] For the next hour, we'll hang with these older single women and see how accurate that last statement is. [Images from 'The Widows of Thomasville' calendar are superimposed on the chatting women as narrator speaks.] Their racy calendar, Widows of Thomasville, is the impetus for this show. It says volumes about their personalities.

LIZZIE: [Her name floats across the screen, briefly settles on her, then dissolves.] I don't know about y'all, but I'm sick and tired of them low-down, sneaky Mammas. Especially that damn Stoney. She's so double-dealing they won't let her wear long sleeves at the card tables in Biloxi.

NARRATOR: [Speaks off camera] Daffy refers to the Mahjong Mammas, a group of four older women that play the game of Mahjong on a regular basis. The group includes Stoney, Mitzi, Toots, and Penny, who are in fierce competition with the Real Widows for the town's limited supply of bachelors.

BABS: [Her name floats onto her, then dissolves.] Yeah, if it don't take the cake. They're always horning in on our men. And Mitzi's badmouthing me about my age and my interest in things like UFOs and fortune telling is getting on my nerves.

NARRATOR: Thomasville is a microcosm of a dilemma in America—too many older single women and too few older eligible bachelors. Mitzi has been in a long-standing feud with Babs, heightened by competition between them for boyfriends.

LILLY: What we gonna do? [Lilly's name floats onto her, then dissolves as she speaks.]

BABS: I say we fight dirty… I know… How about slipping each of them Mammas an Ex-Lax and Grape-Nuts mickey?
LIZZIE: No, no. Ex-Lax and All-Bran. Trust me All-Bran runs rings around Grape-Nuts.
BABS: Didn't Kellogg's issue a salmonella recall on All-Bran a couple of years ago?
LIZZIE: Even better.

The camera view of the ladies' cereal discussion fades out as a close shot of the narrator fades in.

NARRATOR: Obviously, there's trouble right here in Thomasville, my friends. The Real Widows of Thomasville live in a volcano, bubbling over with backstabbing… as we'll see.

Scene of the narrator dissolves.

<u>INTERIOR SCENE: BAB'S HOUSE, LATER SUNDAY MORNING.</u>

Babs and Lilly sit at a desk in Babs' office, looking at her computer.

NARRATOR: [Speaks off camera] Babs is widely known throughout Thomasville for her pursuit of oddball things including voodoo, paranormal activity, UFOs, and magic. You name it. If it's something once featured in an episode of *X-Files*, it's probably something Babs dabbles in.
BABS: [Typing as she speaks] This is the website I was telling you about. MysteriousButRealUniverse dot org. It's a [bleeping] gold mine! Uh, oh! Did I just say that on air? Don't air that!
LILLY: One of these days, you are going to grow up. This stuff is all a hoax, a conspiracy theory.
BABS: No, this website is not [bleep]! Damn! I did it again. [Looks at camera.] Please cut that out. Anyway, just look at

this website. It's got everything. It's got stuff about ghosts, UFOs, Bigfoot, all sorts of paranormal phenomena… You name it.
LILLY: I'm not just talking about the website. Why did you want to show me this website anyway? What's so great about it? You can read about that kind of stuff in the tabloids in supermarket checkout aisle any day.
BABS: Yeah, but this website is like one-stop shopping. It's like a Walmart for paranormal phenomena. Look here! [Scene of Babs and Lilly dissolves into a closeup shot of Babs' computer screen slowly scrolling down.] See they even have webcam views of a whole bunch of things. [As screen scrolls, it shows links to websites about the Loch Ness Monster and the Popocatepetl volcano.] Let's look at that one. [Babs clicks on link to the volcano. Live video of a volcano doing nothing appears on Babs' computer screen.] Ain't that wonderful? [Scene dissolves back to a wide shot of Babs and Lilly.]
LILLY: [Shrugs her shoulders] What's so great about a webcam of a volcano?
BABS: This is a live volcano in Mexico. It's a real famous place for UFO sightings.
LILLY: [Rolls her eyes] What other kinds of webcams do they have on this website? Hopefully, something a little more exciting.
BABS: [Typing] Let's just see what else we can find. Let me go back. Yeah, here it is. They got live webcams of Leprechauns and Irish Fairies. I wonder why they call them Leprechauns. Here's a link to a webcam monitoring ghosts in Greenville, South Carolina. [Scene dissolves to a closeup of Babs' computer screen showing an empty auditorium with a whiteboard and a podium on the stage. Nothing is happening. Scene dissolves back to wide shot of Babs and Lilly.]
LILLY: [Rolls her eyes.] That's a good one. Video of something you can't see anyway. How do you see something you can't see? Ghosts are invisible, right?
BABS: Yes, you ain't supposed to see ghosts, but just because it's not showing a ghost on the screen don't mean that one might not be one in that auditorium right now. And if there is, they got it on camera. [Typing] Look, here's a link to a Bigfoot webcam, here's links to more UFO webcams—one in Wyoming, one in Colorado, and one in Idaho. I'm telling you.

This website has everything in one place. It's not just webcams. This website's got podcasts, blogs, articles, discussion forums, you name it. See, here's a discussion forum on Area 53. It's the best. I read it every day.
LILLY: Not Area 53 again? [Looks at camera.] Please don't include this in the show. People will think she's nuts.
BABS: I ain't nuts. Area 53 is for real, with real UFOs and extraterrestrials. Some bloggers even say they have transgender extraterrestrials there—

Lizzie grabbed the remote, paused the DVR, and said, "Time for a bio-break… the nachos."

Lilly asked, "Why do you think there is an Area 53? If there was, the government would say so."

Babs said, "Them Feds got all sorts of stuff they don't want us to know about. That's why they invented the Internet."

"Why would the Feds invent the Internet if they want to keep people from knowing about things like Area 53?"

After Lizzie returned, she asked, "When are they gonna show our paintball?"

"They're gonna save it for a later episode. Cordell said he wants the premier episode mostly about us… so the audience gets to know us better," said Babs, then pushed the play button on the DVR.

Chapter 10

Thursday, October 30th, 8:48 PM, EDT

BABS: Yep. There's been talk in this forum about having a rally sometime in the next year or two in Area 53 just like they did a couple of years ago at Area 51 in Nevada… or is it Arizona? Wherever Area 51 is. I forget. You do know Area 53 is in Florida, not too far from here, don't you?
LILLY: [Rolls her eyes] So, you've told me. A facility just like Area 51 with UFOs and aliens near Thomasville. You do know something like that would be hard to keep secret?
BABS: Smarty pants, Area 53 is top-secret. The Federal government ain't gonna open up a place with aliens and UFOs to the public just like it's Disneyland and sell tickets. The general public ain't ready for UFOs and aliens just yet.

Scene dissolves into a TV commercial.

Babs began fast-forwarding through the commercials. She said, "You know, I think we look pretty good on TV."

"The miracles of good makeup and expert lighting," said Lizzie.

"I wonder if it's smart to go into the Area 53 stuff too much on TV?" asked Lilly in a rare moment of clear thinking.

"Area 53 is for real," said Babs.

"Complete with UFOs and little green men from other planets who stop by for a quickie on their way to Mars," said Lizzie.

Babs took umbrage. "Y'all can be skeptical if y'all want to, but I've read things on the Internet that say that it's not only possible that there's life on other planets, but that it's probable. Something called Drake's Equation that says it's likely there's tens of thousands of civilizations in our galaxy alone. With all them planets out there, why wouldn't there be some with other life forms on them just like there's life on Earth?"

"Makes sense to me," said Lizzie, rolling her eyes. "After He created man, God probably realized He'd screwed up and decided to keep trying."

After the last commercial, Babs pushed play.

<u>EXTERIOR SCENE: A CONVENIENCE STORE/GAS STATION IN THOMASVILLE, NOON ON MONDAY</u>

Narrator stands in front of a run-down building with three gas pumps. Babs' Escalade pulls into a parking space.

NARRATOR: This is one of Cousin Cootie's Carryouts, a chain of thirty-seven convenience stores that sell gasoline in southwest Georgia and North Florida. Despite this store's outward appearance, Cousin Cootie's Carryouts are very popular around here. Why? Let's follow the Widows of Thomasville inside and find out.

Camera pans from the narrator and follows the Ladies as they walk into Cootie's. Inside, it appears to be a typical convenience store with a buffet set up next to the checkout counter. The Ladies head for the buffet.

LIZZIE: [Close shot as she leans into Lilly] Cootie's buffet has got to be my downfall. I should just have my plastic surgeon give me a fat transplant and skip the whole process of eating.
LILLY: [A serious look appears on her face.] That wouldn't be nearly as enjoyable, would it?
BABS: Nor as cheap.
LIZZIE: Tell me about it. Plastic surgery ain't cheap. I could take all my grandkids to Disney on what my lip implants cost… we'll maybe one or two of 'em anyway.

Buffet scene dissolves into a wide shot of Lilly and Lizzie sitting at a small table inside Cootie's next to the front window. They are eating from Styrofoam plates with plastic forks. Babs approaches their table, struggling with three twenty-ounce plastic bottles of Mountain Dew.

BABS: Here's y'all's Mountain Dew. [She distributes them.]
LIZZIE: Mountain Dew. The champagne of the South. [Everyone laughs.]
LILLY: So, what's on y'all's agendas for this afternoon?
LIZZIE: I got to go see my lawyer.

LILLY: What about?
LIZZIE: My alimony.
BABS: What's wrong?
LIZZIE: I haven't gotten alimony from one of my exes for the last three months.
LILLY: Your fourth husband delinquent on his alimony?
LIZZIE: No, not him. I think it's either the second or third one.
BABS: How do you get alimony from any of your ex-husbands except your last one?
LIZZIE: I get alimony from all four exes. That's always part of the divorce decree.
LILLY: How so you do that?
LIZZIE: That's why God creates lawyers, and lawyers create my meal tickets.

<u>INTERIOR SCENE: BAB'S HOUSE, TUESDAY AFTERNOON</u>

Wide shot of Babs, Lilly, and Lizzie as they sit in the living room.

LIZZIE: I got another text from Daffy this morning.
NARRATOR: [Action pauses during offscreen narration.] Daffy is an older widow that lives in Thomasville. She and another older widow named Gidget, are best friends with Babs, Lilly, and Lizzie. Together, they make up Thomasville's most notorious quintet of older single women in the market for older eligible bachelors. As we said earlier, the supply of such bachelors in this small town is very limited. That has resulted in some very nasty encounters in person and on social media between them and the Mahjong Mammas. Daffy and Gidget are currently on a Caribbean cruise with several older bachelors whom our five women have nicknamed the Marx Brothers.
BABS: What'd Daffy have to say?
LIZZIE: They enjoyed themselves the first couple of days, but it got kind of dull after that. You can only play so much shuffleboard without getting the urge to slit your wrists. The Marx Brothers have been happy as pigs in slop playing bocce ball. Daffy said they were pretty good at it.

LILLY: I wish we could've gone with them. Except for the way they dressed, they seemed like pretty nice gentlemen.
LIZZIE: We've got to be on our toes when everyone gets back from the cruise.
BABS: Why?
LIZZIE: Them Mammas is gonna try to make a run on those boys and beat our time.
LILLY: How they gonna do that? The Marx Brothers live in The Villages.
NARRATOR: [Offscreen] The Villages is a community in Central Florida for those fifty-five and over. The Marx Brothers recently retired there and saw the Real Widows calendar. It was love at first sight on their part, so they drove up to Thomasville on Monday a week ago and introduced themselves. Love blossomed, and Daffy and Gidget decided to go with them on a cruise that set sail on Wednesday of last week.
LIZZIE: Who knows what those nasty women will do. We just got to be alert. I have a feeling the old boys will be visiting us here in Thomasville on a regular basis.
BABS: I hope so. There's one of those old guys that I really want to get to know better.

Scene dissolves.

Viewing paused for fifteen more minutes as Babs made another batch of nachos. After she fast forwarded through the next series of commercials, one of the show's craziest scenes began.

Chapter 11

Thursday, October 30th, 9:05 PM, EDT

EXTERIOR SCENE: THE BIG OAK, THOMASVILLE, WEDNESDAY NIGHT 8:00 PM

The three women sit in a circle on a large light blue blanket beneath a huge live oak known locally as The Big Oak. It is pitch black nighttime. The women are the only people in the area. A black cat runs across the screen behind them, chasing a possum. Their blanket has a variety of voodoo symbols on it: a skull-and-crossbones wearing a top hat, a crudely drawn voodoo doll with pins in it, an elaborate drawing of Baron LaCroix, and another of a large python snake.

NARRATOR: [Speaks off camera] Babs is a voodoo aficionado. She visited Port-au-Prince on a cruise two months ago and stocked up on voodoo supplies. Tonight's ritual is a follow up on Lizzie's warning that the Mahjong Mammas might attempt to steal the Marx Brothers away from them. Babs selected The Big Oak as the location for the ritual due to its status as a historic landmark and the site of many outdoor weddings. Also, Lilly and Lizzie refused to go back to any cemetery at midnight for any more of Babs' voodoo rituals.
BABS: Okay. Lilly, hold the book open to the page I showed you, and Lizzie, you pass me the things I gave you as I call for them. [Lilly nods. Lizzie smirks, then nods.]
BABS: Hold the book still. Hand me the doll. [Lizzie passes Babs a small, crude burlap doll. Babs looks down at the book Lilly holds for her.] All y'all repeat after me. *o gwo lespri.*
ALL OTHER LADIES IN UNISON: *o gwo lespri.*
BABS: Hand me the powder. [Lizzie passes Babs a small jar.] All y'all repeat after me. *kite mwen jwenn yon etranje tou pre isit la.*

ALL OTHER LADIES IN UNISON: *kite mwen jwenn yon etranje tou pre isit la.*

BABS: *se konsa, mwen ka fe yon nouvo zanmi.*

ALL OTHER LADIES IN UNISON: *se konsa, mwen ka fe yon nouvo zanmi.*

[Babs tilts the jar in her hand and sprinkles a small amount of the powder from inside it onto the doll.]
BABS: Okay, that's it. That's all. It's over.
LIZZIE: I hope you didn't screw this one up like you usually do in all your other voodoo rituals. You really should take lessons in how to speak Haitian Creole.
LILLY: What'd we all say?
BABS: We said, "Let our boyfriends tell them Mammas to kiss their asses and think only about the Widows of Thomasville." [Looks at camera.] Is it okay to say asses on the air? Gee, I wish I knew what Mitzi's name is in Creole so I could've included a special hex on her.
LIZZIE: Her name in Creole would be the same as it is in English.

Another commercial interrupted, and Babs paused the DVR. She said, "I gotta go pee. Get anybody anything on my way back?" She looked around. Lizzie's head mimicked that of a bobblehead dog in the rear window of a slow-moving car riding over speed bumps as she softly snored.

"Nothing for me," Lilly said. "Should we wake her up?"

"Yeah. When I get back. I think a good part's coming up."

Ten minutes later, Babs pushed play and fast forwarded through the commercials.

<u>INTERIOR SCENE: LILLY'S BEDROOM, THURSDAY MORNING</u>

Wide shot of Lilly and Lizzie walking to a closet off of her master bedroom. Lilly opens both of the closet's double doors.

NARRATOR: [Speaks off camera] Lilly has a shoe fetish… a shoe fetish on steroids. What you see is a very large walk-in closet exclusively devoted to storage of her shoes. She has hired a contractor to remodel it.
LIZZIE: [Standing in the closet doorway and looking inside] You ever think of relocating your shoe collection to

Thomasville Regional Airport? I hear they have a couple of empty hangers.
LILLY: You know a girl can never have too many shoes.
NARRATOR: [Speaks off camera] Her clothes closet is a separate room that is connected to this one by the door in the corner. Her remodeling contractor has his work cut out for him. [Camera pans to door in the shoes closet, then back to a wide shot of Lilly and Lizzie. Behind them, several rows of four-foot-high shelves display hundreds of shoes. Each shelf and each row are labeled.]
LIZZIE: How big is this thing?
LILLY: [Shrugs] This used to be the master bedroom. Wendell used to tease me about the size all the time. He always joked that I should sublet some of it to Payless Shoes.
NARRATOR: Wendell is Lilly's deceased husband.
LIZZIE: [Camera follows Lizzie as she walks between the shelves, inspecting their contents.] When does the remodel start?
LILLY: Pretty soon, I hope. The contractor looked things over earlier this week and said it's gonna take a lot more effort than he originally thought. May be five or six weeks to complete instead of four.
LIZZIE: I see you still have them organized by shoe color.
LILLY: [Lilly steps inside.] Yeah. Reorganized them by color three weeks ago. But that's why I asked you to come over today. I just don't like this latest reorganization. I want to reorganize it again. Color ain't working nearly as good as I hoped it would. I need your advice.
LIZZIE: How did you have it organized before?
LILLY: By designer.
LIZZIE: Go back to that.
LILLY: That didn't work well either. That's why I reorganized it by color.
LIZZIE: How was it organized before designer?
LILLY: Heel height.
LIZZIE: What ways of organizing shoes are left?
LILLY: Plenty. One way would be by shoe material. You know, like a section for leather, section for canvas, and so forth. Another way would be by function—
LIZZIE: Function?

LILLY: Yeah. Function. Like shoes for formal wear, shoes for athletic wear, shoes for casual wear, shoes for special occasions—

LIZZIE: Special occasions?

LILLY: That's got a whole bunch of subfunctions.

LIZZIE: Such as?

LILLY: There's shoes for formal occasions, shoes for going to the movies, shoes for doctor's appointments, shoes for gardening, shoes for walking, although shoes for walking could also fit into the shoes for athletic wear function, depending on how fast you walk. Part of the problem of reorganizing by function is figuring out which category does this pair of shoes fit into? Sometimes it's a close call. I tried organizing by function years ago but gave up after I bought a pair of boots. I figured they overlapped three different functions and couldn't decide which one to use, so I went back to Dillard's and bought two more pair. Got home and said to myself, 'Lilly, y'all are gonna be buying a lot shoes at this rate.' And Christian Louboutin boots ain't cheap either! Organizing by function ain't easy.

LIZZIE: I hate to think of making all the labels.

LILLY: [Vigorously nods] That's the reason I wanted you to come over here and help me decide on which way to reorganize this mess.

LIZZIE: [Shakes her head] Okay. Let's go over the other ways of organizing shoes.

LILLY: [Looks at camera.] How much time do we have?

Scene dissolves.

Chapter 12

Thursday, October 30th, 9:44 PM, EDT

INTERIOR SCENE: MANICURE AND PEDICURE SALON, THURSDAY AFTERNOON

Babs, Lilly, and Lizzie sit in adjacent salon chairs at Ngo's Nails getting their weekly pedicures.

BABS: I think Lizzie's right. We have got to deal with them Mahjong Mammas somehow before they get to the Marx Brothers.
LIZZIE: Maybe your voodoo ritual will work… for a change.
BABS: Cordell told me last week that he wants to work Mitzi and the others into our show.
LILLY: Why?
BABS: He says the intergroup tension will add spice to the show. Help ratings.
LIZZIE: He's the expert.
LILLY: I don't like the idea of them floozies getting publicity on our show.
BABS: Yeah. There ain't that many eligible bachelors running around here nowadays, and we don't need to be giving them [bleeps] any more attention. I know one thing. We ain't gonna let those four floozies get to first base with our boyfriends.
LIZZIE: [nods] We need to give some thought as to exactly what to do.

Scene dissolves.

Lilly looked around as the next scene came into focus. Babs had nodded off.

INTERIOR SCENE: LOCAL RESTAURANT, FRIDAY
Medium shot of the ladies sitting in a booth. All are looking at their iPhones as they talk.

NARRATOR: [Speaks off camera] It is Friday, and the Real Widows meet at a local restaurant for lunch. Their conflict with the Mammas is fast reaching a boiling point.

BABS: [Looking at her phone] It's Mitzi again. She's really been pickin' at me on Facebook for days. Trash talk about Area 53. Trash talk about my age…
LILLY: [Looking at her phone] That woman! I'd love to pull her hair out by the roots.
LIZZIE: [Looking at her phone] Good idea. That way, we can find out what her real color is.
BABS: [Looking at her phone] They're just asking for it.
LILLY: [Looking at her phone] It's as if Mitzi is obsessing over this Area 53 stuff.
NARRATOR: [Speaks off camera] Let's see just what it is on Facebook that's got our heroines so upset.

As the narrator explains that Harvey's is a southeastern chain of grocery stores, scene transitions to an enlargement of an iPhone screen that scrolls through a series of Facebook postings.

Mitzi Merchant
One of the checkout girls at Harvey's said she heard from a local cop that he saw Babs, Lilly, and Lizzie filming some sort of voodoo ritual at the Big Oak Wednesday night. Can y'all believe it? Must have been Babs' idea. How nutty can you get?
Like **Comment**

Toots Varnell
Babs is a senile nutjob. Lilly's ditzy. Daffy's oversexed. Gidget's a nerd. Lizzie's a gold digger. They're all perfect for each other.
Like **Reply**

Stoney Lee
Next thing you know, Babs will probably be trying to drag all of them to Area 53. She says it's close by in Florida.
Like **Reply**

Mitzi Merchant
It is. It's inside Disney World.
Like **Reply**

Penny Perdoo
Yeah. Area 53 is the newest Disney theme park. It's between the Magic Kingdom and EPCOT.
Like **Reply**

Mitzi Merchant
It's a shame that all five of them have gotten so senile in their old age. Babs' dementia is really starting to show. More so than it usually does.
Like **Reply**

Toots Varnell
She's either senile or sniffing too much of that powder she uses in her voodoo rituals.
Like **Reply**

Scene transitions back to the women sitting in the booth.

BABS: I'm getting sick of Mitzi insulting me about my age. She's the same age as I am.
What a bunch of [bleep].
LIZZIE: Too bad they'll probably bleep that last word out. Those old bags have been getting real vicious lately. I bet it's because Daffy and Gidget are on a cruise with some new boyfriends, and they're jealous.
LILLY: On top of that, we're doing a reality series on TV.
LIZZIE: Don't forget our calendar.
LILLY: What do we do next?
BABS: I'd love to make them eat their words about Area 53. Can you imagine how stupid they'll look? One day…
LIZZIE: The Mammas have maxxed out on looking unattractive, but they do have some room left on looking stupid.

Scene transitions.

INTERIOR SCENE: ANTEBELLUM MANSION OUTSIDE THOMASVILLE, FRIDAY NIGHT

Wide shot of twelve older women sitting at three card tables inside living room. As the women chat, the camera pulls back to include the narrator in the shot. She stands beside the room's fireplace.

NARRATOR: Every other Friday night, the Real Widows of Thomasville play bunko with some other older women. Let's listen in.

JOYCE: [Camera focuses on Joyce and several other women engaging in conversation.] I saw Toots wrapped around Sonny Biskit earlier in the week. Talk about disgusting.
NARRATOR: [Speaks off camera] Sonny Biskit is a local bachelor whom the Real Widows have occasionally passed around amongst themselves.
DOTTIE: That's for sure. You'd think neither of 'em ever had sex before.
LIZZIE: That's probably true in Toots' case.
LILLY: I overheard Toots in the Flower Shop the other day say how they're planning another cruise and how Sonny is invited. She made sure I heard it.
GINGER: Who else is going?
FANNIE: Probably Mitzi and the rest of the Mahjong Mammas.
LIZZIE: I didn't know Visiting Angels ran a cruise line. [All players laugh.]
BABS: Visiting Angels does provide dementia care which would mean that Mitzi could go. [more laughter]
DOTTIE: [Camera focuses on Dottie and several other women engaging in conversation.] My neighbor told me that one of the clerks at Harvey's told her that her sister told her that Georgina at the dry cleaners told her that Alicia at the beauty salon said that [name bleeped out]'s cancer is getting worse.

GINGER: Sounds like Odell is gonna be on the market soon.
CHARLENE: Wonder who'll be first at his door with a casserole when he becomes a widower?
LILLY: I'd bet money that Penny Perdoo will be first in line. Her problem is that Rodney handled all their finances when he was alive. The rumor is that Penny's having money problems now that Rodney's gone.
NAN: I remember Augusta told me the funniest story one time about what she told Odell about his, shall we say 'less than ideal looks.'
BABS: Odell *is* one of the ugliest men in town. [Looks at camera.] Please delete what I just said.
LIZZIE: It's amazing how having a lot of money can improve a man's looks. I always thought Odell looked pretty good myself. What did Augusta say about him?
NAN: Augusta and I were having cocktails at The Distillery two years ago, and she said she and Odell got into an argument the week before. You know how you hope that if your spouse ever remarries after you divorce, it's not with some ugly old piece of [word bleeped out]. I mean what does that say about you if you married someone that couldn't find someone decent looking after you? [Heads nod.] Augusta told Odell that he'd never have to worry about her running off with an uglier man than him because one didn't exist. [Explosive laughter.]
DOTTIE: Speaking of ugly, I heard that Sonny Biskit is thinking about running for mayor next year.
BEVERLY: That would be a natural transition for him. Unemployed ne'er-do-well to employed ne'er-do-well.
TRUDY: [Looking at Babs] What does Toots see in him anyway?
LIZZIE: What she sees in him is called Viagra.
EVIE: [Camera focuses on Evie and several other women engaging in conversation.] Speaking of which … [Evie looks at NAN.] I hear Cootie stopped by your pharmacy yesterday with a prescription for some Viagra. Wonder who the lucky girl is?
NAN: You know I can't talk about things like that… even if it wasn't true.
BABS: I bet the lucky girl is Mitzi.
LIZZIE: I heard she wanted Sonny, but now that he's hanging with Toots, she's after Cootie again. Especially now that he's had his Viagra refilled.

BABS: Cootie and Viagra and Mitzi! Don't that sound exciting? Talk about a night to forget.
GINGER: That's about as exciting as having sex while listening to Ray Conniff. [Camera pans to Charlene who is talking to Dottie.]
CHARLENE: My late husband, God bless his soul, was terrible about passing gas in his sleep. He could've inflated a Goodyear blimp every night.
FANNIE: [Camera pans on Fannie and several other women engaging in conversation.] I think some of these computerized things are getting a little too big for their britches.
LILLY: How so?
FANNIE: Last Monday, I wanted to find out what the latest college football rankings were. You know my smart TV has that Alexa in it, but I made the mistake of asking Siri on my iPhone what the latest college football rankings were, and she says, 'Alabama is number one, Georgia is number two, Ohio State is number three,' and so on. Well, Alexa also heard my question and says, 'Georgia is number one, South Carolina number two, Ohio State number three.' But then Siri says, 'No, no. That is not correct' and starts repeating her rankings. Then, they both got into an argument. It got downright dirty. They were calling each other names, even cursing at each other. I ws scared they'd get violent.
LILLY: How'd it turn out? I hope they didn't get physical with each other.
FANNIE: No, it didn't get that bad… They are both ladies after all. It turned out that Siri was quoting the AP poll, while Alexa was quoting the CFP rankings. It was all just a misunderstanding.
LILLY: Did they kiss and makeup?
FANNIE: No, but I did make them apologize to each other.

Scene dissolves.

<u>INTERIOR SCENE: MITZI'S LIVING ROOM, SATURDAY AFTERNOON</u>

Wide shot of the four Mammas sitting on furniture. They sip cocktails as Narrator stands in a corner of the room.

NARRATOR: We've seen what the Real Widows think of the Mammas. Let's find out what the Mammas think of the Real Widows.

TOOTS: I feel so sorry for those poor old guys from The Villages. Getting taken in by a bunch of floozies like 'The Real Widows.' What a joke. What could any man see in a fat old hag like Lizzie anyway?

MITZI: Same thing a man would see in an old flabbo like Babs—an easy lay, especially in the parking lot at a tractor pull. Did y'all hear about all of them going to play paintball with Sonny and his cronies? Only someone as nutty as Babs would come up with something like paintball for going on a date. I'm surprised she didn't take them to visit Area 53. Oh, I forgot… She can't because there is no Area 53. It's just another one of them conspiracy theories on the Internet.

PENNY: I wonder where her Escalade's GPS would have taken them if she had asked for directions to Area 53?

STONEY: Where else? It would have given them directions to Disney World.

MITZI: Nope. Directions to Chattahoochee.

NARRATOR: [Speaks off camera] Mitzi refers to the town of Chattahoochee, located forty miles west of the state capital and site of the Florida State Hospital, which served as an insane asylum from 1876 until 1947.

MITZI: Sooner or later, Babs is gonna have to put up or shut up on this Area 53 garbage.

PENNY: Babs shut up? That motormouth? The motormouth?

MITZI: We can't let those [bleeps] get away with… whatever they're getting away with. We've got to do something…

[Sound fades as camera pans from the women to the narrator.]

NARRATOR: We'll leave the Mahjong Mammas to their scheming as we wrap up our first episode of the *Real Widows of Thomasville*. Maybe Thomasville isn't quite the idyllic small town we imagined it to be. Some here are not as friendly as we were led to believe. Some don't always practice 'love thy neighbor' quite as much as they should. Do unto others before they do it to you seems to be the philosophy in Thomasville.

You must look beneath the surface and get to know a town's real people. Once you do, you often find that small towns are just like big towns. Jealousy, lust, and competition thrive everywhere. Tune in next week and find out more. Goodbye for now.

Credits begin scrolling across the screen as ending music plays.

By now, Lilly also snored. After the credits ended, the DVR kept playing the recorded program until it timed out and went into a blank screen. It was after midnight before the three women woke up and went to bed.

Most of Thomasville also watched the premier episode of *Real Widows of Thomasville*, including Mitzi Merchant. She went to bed extremely pleased with herself. That Isler fellow had included several of her suggestions. Mitzi had managed to pull Babs' chain a couple of times during the show—Babs' weight problem, UFO craziness, and best of all the gossip about her having sex with Sonny in the parking lot at the tractor pull in Waycross. Everyone in Thomasville joked about that. Things were going better than anticipated.

Chapter 13

Friday, October 31st, 8:31 AM, EDT

The *Thomasville Times-Enterprise* headlined with a story titled "Thomasville Reality Show Premiers on National TV."

By Ellen Campbell

Thomasville — Three local women became national celebrities last night. Babs Neauxgeaux, Lilly White, and Lizzie Sherbert starred in the pilot episode of *Real Widows of Thomasville*. The show is set in Thomasville and chronicles day-to-day antics of the two widows and four-time divorcee who are the Real Widows. A major network chanced a reality show based on their lives after the quintet's risqué calendar became a regional sensation in September. Many in Thomasville believe the trio to be part of the notorious streaker quintet at the Georgia-Florida game in earlier this month, disguised as Kardashians.

Humor abounds in the show, much of it lowbrow as in the lunch scene at one of our Cootie's Carryout's. A hilarious guided tour inside Lilly White's massive shoe closet documents her obsession with footwear. I personally laughed five minutes non-stop at the one-liners delivered during a Bunko game with several other local women, although some of it was a bit over the top.

Local residents will appreciate the attention the show paid to Thomasville's most celebrated feud. The Real Widows and four other local notables collectively nicknamed Mahjong Mammas have quarreled since the late 1970s. This timespan surpasses the twenty-eight-year long Hatfield-McCoy feud. Trash talk between the two groups both in dialogue and on Facebook added tension throughout the show. This was very much the case with the long running animosity between Babs Neauxgeaux and Mitzi Merchant.

The biggest criticism of the show lies in its potential to leave a negative impression of Thomasville with viewers. Much of this is due to Babs Neauxgeaux. Several scenes in the pilot episode revealed her many eccentricities, implying this kind of weird behavior is common down here in the deep South. Most locals know her to be smitten with the occult arts. The rest of the country now knows it after her voodoo ritual scene set beneath The Big Oak at midnight.

In several other scenes, Babs reiterates her belief in the latest Internet hoax—a conspiracy theory about a secure compound called Area 53 located on Federal land in northwest Florida. This facility supposedly houses UFOs and aliens from other planets. DoD and NASA have repeatedly debunked this myth. Despite this, Babs Neauxgeaux repeatedly insists that it does exist throughout the pilot episode. One only hopes that viewers did not assume this kind of nonsense to be commonplace thinking in Thomasville.

Aside from this, the show can be an entertaining Thursday night diversion. If nothing else, it puts Thomasville on the reality TV map.

The Casserole Ladies celebrated the morning after the pilot over breakfast at Q Café. Cordell told them before he left town that he would call Babs with the audience share numbers as soon as he got them Friday morning. "They're gonna be dynamite," he said. His crew was supposed to arrive back in town that afternoon to film the ladies' Halloween activities that night. Cordell intended to be there as well.

Babs made the mistake of ordering the most popular item on the menu, the main component of which was a cathead biscuit, so named because it was as large as a cat's head. "I just know Cordell is gonna say it's a megahit," Babs said. A mouth full of cathead biscuit rendered everything after the word 'know' indecipherable.

Lilly looked at her as if she had a daffodil growing out of her ear. "What did you just say about Cialis surging in whose groin?"

"She's talking about her last date with Sonny Biskit… reliving old memories," Lizzie said.

Babs swallowed as she shook her head. "No, no, no. I said I know that Cordell is gonna call with news that *Real Widows* is megahit."

"You did bring your phone, didn't you?" Lilly asked, looking at Babs.

Babs nodded as she asked, "Does any grown woman in America with at least one ear and one hand not have an smart phone with her at all times?"

"They should graft these things onto our ears at birth," Lizzie said, not looking up as she scrolled on her phone.

A puzzled look came over Lilly's face. She touched one of the diamond studs adorning her ears. "But where would we put our earrings?"

"I see a lot of women with nose rings lately."

"Not to be a party pooper," said Lilly, "but did anyone read Ellen Campbell's article in this morning's *Times-Enterprise*?"

Lizzie nodded. "Yeah, but I wasn't gonna mention it."

"What's it say?" asked Babs.

"It was generally positive, but it slammed you."

Babs attempted to ask 'how so', but a mouth full of biscuit yielded, "Mousa."

"It slammed your voodoo and said your Area 53 stuff was a myth. Said you leave viewers with a bad impression of Thomasville. Like we're nothing but a bunch of kooks," said Lilly.

"At least they have an accurate impression of us," said Lizzie.

Babs gulped the mouthful of biscuit and said, "That's Ellen Campbell for you. Miss Debbie Downer. She and Mitzi are real tight, so you can bet Mitzi had a lot of input into the article. I know one thing though. Slamming voodoo ain't very smart. And, Area 53 ain't no myth. She's gonna look like a fool when the government finally admits it does exist."

"That's three things. Not one," said Lizzie.

Lilly smirked. "Whatever. The story *was* mostly positive about the show."

"*Tallahassee Today* talked about our show this morning." Babs referred to a morning show on one of the regional TV stations.

"They loved the voodoo ritual but thought the Area 53 stuff was just more conspiracy theory junk."

"You probably wouldn't have talked about Area 53 so much if Mitzi hadn't been goading you. She's been especially meanspirited about it lately," said Lizzie.

"Let's change the topic before I blow a gasket. Anyway, I hope Cordell calls soon. I've got things to do, and we're burning daylight," said Babs.

"What you got going today… other than the Masquerade Ball tonight?" Lilly asked.

"Quarterly Sawgrass Bank Board of Directors Meeting this morning at ten o'clock. I'm Vice Chair, and without Daffy there to chair the meeting, I've got to somehow keep eleven men, all over seventy-years old, awake for two hours straight."

"Try going topless," Lizzie said.

"Don't forget that I'm sixty-three." Babs shook her head then looked down. "The only way men would notice these saggy girls is if they dispensed draft beer."

"Eleven old men and you and Daffy. Why y'all got such a large board?" Lilly asked.

"Blame it on Royce. It was a good old boy network. Daffy says he wanted to keep all his longtime friends happy and a few politicians in his pocket. What are you gonna do today?"

"I'm going to a grand opening today. There's a new home décor store opening up in Waycross."

"Oh, I hadn't heard about that. What's the name?" Babs asked.

Lilly beamed. "Dorothy's Décor Boutique. Sounds scrumptious, don't it?"

"How'd you hear about it?" Lizzie asked.

"I was listening to a Valdosta radio station earlier this week and caught the tail end of their commercial. They said that they have lots of goodies women will enjoy. And free shipping."

"Will you be able to make it back in time tonight for the Masquerade Ball?" Babs asked, horrified at the thought of missing one of Thomasville's biggest social events of the year.

"It's only a two-hour drive to Waycross. I'll head out as soon as we finish breakfast. There'll be plenty of time to go there and back.

Besides, there's no way I'm gonna miss out on a costume party at Preble Hill." Lilly referred to a Thomasville landmark, an old plantation whose history goes back to 1825, now used as a venue for social occasions. "What about you, Babsie? What're you doing today?"

Babs shrugged. "Nothing really. Just going down to Tallahassee to pick up my costume for the Ball tonight."

"What are you going as?"

"I'm not telling. It's gonna be a surprise… and a doozie of a costume if I do say so myself. I'm gonna beat Mitzi for first prize."

Lizzie said, "I think Mitzi's reserved that honor for herself. How many years in a row has she won top prize… two or three?"

"Not this year. I found a great costume at Costumes Galore in downtown Tallahassee. They had to alter it, so it'll fit. Was a little too long for me. It's the only one like it. One of a kind."

Babs looked at Lilly. "What about you? What are you going as?"

"I'm not gonna tell either. It'll have to be a surprise. I can give you a hint. It's based on a nursery rhyme."

"She's probably going as Wee Willie Winkie," Lizzie said.

"I hope it's nothing too risqué, lest the Cultural League take offense," Babs said. Twenty-three of Thomasville's wealthiest and most uptight matrons ran the Thomasville Cultural League. That organization originally began in 1895 as the Thomasville Cultural Club. It swapped 'League' for 'Club' in 1983 after *Karma Chameleon* became a megahit for the band Culture Club. The organization has sponsored the annual Thomasville Halloween Masquerade Ball for the last fifty-seven years. High society in Thomasville considers it to be one of, if not, *the* most prestigious social event of the year. "What about you, Lizzie?"

"I was going to see a hypnotist at one o'clock today, but I think I'll cancel my appointment and go with Lilly to the open house. She can use the company, and a grand-opening sounds like much more fun. You always get good bargains at grand openings."

"Why were you going to a hypnotist?"

"To see if I can get my spending addiction under control."

"I thought Amazon Anonymous was working for you," Lilly said.

"It was, but I had a relapse Tuesday during Lollapalooza Cutlery Night on one of them home shopping networks on TV."

"Another relapse? That's four relapses since you started AA a month ago. What did you buy this time?"

"A set of sushi knives."

Babs frowned. "But you don't eat sushi."

Lizzie frowned as she nodded. "Yeah, I don't. But the set was half off."

The other Ladies shook their heads in pity. Lizzie said, "I know. I know. As soon as I hung up the phone, I realized I had relapsed and needed some sort of intervention. Everyone at my AA meeting Wednesday night agreed with me. One of the ladies suggested I go to a hypnotist that she's been seeing for six months for her spending addiction."

"If she's been seeing a hypnotist for six months, it doesn't sound like the AA meetings are working very well for her," Lilly said. "Nor the hypnotist for that matter."

"Everyone knows overspending is one of the most powerful addictions there is. It's almost as bad as online video gaming." After Lizzie finished rationalizing, she looked at Lilly. "Anyway, this home décor grand opening sounds like it might be fun. Count me in. I'll even drive."

Babs said, "You two be sure to get back in time for the Masquerade Ball. I don't want to be there without y'all."

Chapter 14

Friday, October 31st, 9:45 AM, EDT

Lilly and Lizzie sped off shortly after breakfast in the latter's Lincoln Nautilus SUV. They reasoned they could complete the two-hour drive to Waycross in time to get to Dorothy's before all the freebies and the best bargains were gone. US 84 is a straight shot from Thomasville to Waycross, so getting lost is virtually impossible, even for these two. The primary road hazard on the trip is falling asleep at the wheel. Seeing nothing but pine trees for a hundred and six miles is better than taking an Ambien.

"What do you want to listen to on SiriusXM?" Lizzie asked as she touched the Lincoln's audio screen.

"Anything so long as it's one of them stations where you can understand the words they're singing."

An hour into their trip, the ladies crossed Interstate 75 in Valdosta. Lilly noticed something. "Look at that. That adult store up there off of I-75 wasn't there last time I came this way. That must've been about six months ago."

"The porn business must be booming. There must be dozens of those adult stores all the way up and down I-75 in Georgia and Florida."

Lilly shrugged, pulled out her iPhone, and began checking her texts. She shouted, "Got a text from Babs! Looks like our show was a megahit! Ratings through the roof. Higher than any of the *Real Wives*' series. They want more shows."

"Never doubted we'd be a hit. Maybe a hit show like this will help buck Babs up."

"What do you mean?"

"Haven't you noticed? She's been fretting about growing old more and more lately. I'm getting tired of it."

Lilly scrolled through Facebook posts. She said, "Well, here's part of the reason why she's moaning about getting older. The Mahjong Mammas are all over Facebook insulting us and last night's show. Mitzi called Babs a wrinkled old hag. She says Babs should enter Area 53's alien lookalike contest. Says with Babs' old, wrinkled face, she's sure to win."

"Slamming Babsie about Area 53 is bad enough but about getting older is not what she needs right now."

Lilly squinted at her phone. "I don't get this. Mitzi says that Babs is jealous that she, that is Mitzi, is going on a cruise because the last cruise Babs took sunk on an iceberg. What does she mean by that?"

Lizzie smiled. "Ever hear of the Titanic?"

Lilly's scowl would have shamed Grumpy Cat. She said, "Mitzi is one to call Babs old."

"Mitzi is older than dirt. I heard the only reason Leonardo da Vinci painted the *Mona Lisa* was 'Mitzi Lisa' didn't have the right sound to it."

"Now that you mention it, Babs has been whining a lot about her age lately. Wonder why? What's happened to make her start worrying about growing old all of a sudden?"

"Who knows? Growing old is harder on females than men. As men age, they get more tolerable. As women age, we just get more raggedy."

"But we get older all our adult lives. Why did Babs start worrying about it right now?"

"I don't know." Lizzie shrugged. "You look in the mirror one morning, see things you didn't notice before, and realize there's an old person looking back at you."

"Babs *has* been harping for months about the crepey skin on her upper arms, age spots on her hands, skin tags on her neck, bags under her eyes. I guess that's why she puts on a half-dozen creams every night for all her different age-related maladies."

"I remember the first time I felt like I was growing old was when I was sixty-two, and Jenny turned forty. I thought, 'My God, my oldest child is middle-aged. What does that make me?' It's a sobering feeling," said Lizzie. "I just hope Babs can pull herself out of this funk."

"Babs' oldest did turn forty… what two months ago? And, don't another one of her kids turn forty next year? That'll make two forty-somethings by her sixty-fourth birthday."

"Another thing that makes you feel like you're getting old is getting back up from getting down."

"What do you mean?" asked Lilly.

"You know… Like when you squat down to get a pan out from a lower kitchen cabinet, then when you go to get back up, it ain't that easy to get back up. That makes you realize you're old."

"Now that you mention it, Babs did have a devil of a time getting back up off that blanket after she finished the voodoo ceremony the other night. You could hear her joints creak."

"She wasn't the only one moaning and complaining as she was getting back up that night. Yours truly whined a bit too," Lizzie said. "Husbands usually aren't very helpful during the aging process either. My last husband used to call me his old lady. I wanted to punch his lights out every time he said it, but he was bigger than me. Avery didn't help Babsie either. He was real good at pointing how old she was getting. But she loved him and never told him to go screw himself like I would have."

"I never had that kind of problem with Wendell."

"Wendell was a pussycat. Several of my exes tried to bully me. All of 'em cheated on me, but I never put up with it. Wonder which of us was the smarter of the two—me or Babsie? At least she had one man until the end."

Lilly looked up from her phone. "Talking about the show last night, Stoney says that all of us have faces for radio. Penny says you need to find a drug rehab center that caters to seniors with dementia. Toots said that the Federal government's gonna start requiring hazardous waste labels on my casseroles—"

"The EPA must've gotten your casserole recipes mixed up with mine. What else?"

A smile replaced Lilly's scowl. "Toots called you an oversexed gold digger, and Mitzi gave it three thumbs up."

A sure sign of a healthy ego, Lizzie said, "Every once in a while, one of the Mammas gets something right."

Fifteen minutes outside of Waycross, Lizzie asked, "By the way, what's the address of this place… what's the name?"

"Dorothy's Décor Boutique. It's on US 84, so we don't even have turn off onto any other streets."

"What's the number?"

Lilly's brow furrowed as she said, "I don't remember exactly… it had several numbers in it… like ones, twos, and threes. It was on a Valdosta radio station, so the reception wasn't the greatest. All I remember was Dorothy's Décor Boutique… Grand Opening… lots of goodies women will enjoy. Free shipping… Prizes… They said that it was on US 84 as you come into Waycross. You know my memory has always been bad."

"At least now your age gives you an excuse. Hopefully, Dorothy's will have their name on a sign out front that's easy to see. Wish I hadn't forgotten my glasses again. Let's ask my GPS for the address and let her guide us there." Lizzie's navigation system was enabled with SYNC 3 technology. It had voice recognition and an intelligent user interface that allowed it to interact with humans to an amazing degree. Lizzie pressed the system's touchscreen and said, "Find a POI." She leaned in and whispered to Lilly, "That's a point of interest."

"How would you like to search?" SYNC 3 asked with a pleasant female European accent. "Please say 'by name or by category'."

"By name."

"Where would you like to search? Please say 'Nearby, along my route, near my destination, or in a city'."

"In a city."

"Please say the name of the city."

"Waycross, Georgia."

"Please say the address or name of the business."

"Dorothy's Décor Boutique."

SYNC 3 briefly processed Lizzie's request then said, "Dorothy's Décor Boutique is at 1537 Oak Avenue in Panama City, Florida."

Lizzie frowned and said, "Damn it, quit fooling around. What is the address of Dorothy's Décor Boutique in Waycross, Georgia?"

"Dorothy's Décor Boutique is at 1537 Oak Avenue in Panama City, Florida."

Lizzie's anger increased. She said to no one in particular, "What in the hell good are these damn GPS systems when they can't even give you directions to a simple business."

SYNC 3 said, "Maybe if you would give me a valid business name in Waycross, I could help you."

Lizzie said, "I gave you a valid business name. Dorothy's Décor Boutique. You stupid bitch."

"Please refrain from using profanity."

"Don't you tell me what to do! I'll use whatever language I want to when talking to you! You work for me, you know!"

“You sound hostile,” SYNC 3 said. “Maybe you should breathe slowly and consider the reasons for your anger.”

Lizzie shook her head in disgust. In a rare intentional attempt at humor, Lilly said, “Maybe she’s attempting an intervention in your overspending addiction.”

SYNC 3 said, “Please do not interrupt. I am speaking with the other female who is having some anger management issues right now.”

“Don’t you get uppity with my best friend!” Lizzie said. She added the phrase “Stupid slut,” under her breath.

“Please temper your language. Hostility never accomplishes anything.”

“I don’t need no dumbass like you telling me how to act!”

“Maybe you should look for positive ways of channeling your anger.”

“I’ll channel my anger any damn way I please!”

“Are you menstruating?” SYNC 3 asked.

“No! I ain’t menstruating! I ain’t had a period in twenty years!”

“How long have you felt this anger?”

“Just since I touched your damn touchscreen!”

“Perhaps we can work together to resolve your problem. Let us first try to identify what is really causing your anger.”

“I’m pissed off because you won’t give me directions to Dorothy’s Décor Boutique!”

“Maybe you should consult a psychiatrist or seek some sort of psychological counseling.”

“I don’t need no damn psychiatrist or psychological counseling! What I need is a damn navigation system that can tell me how to get to friggin’ DOROTHY’S DÉCOR BOUTIQUE!!”

SYNC 3 did not respond immediately. It was as if the software was thinking. Finally, it said, “Perhaps you should take some anger management classes. Here is a list of such classes in your area.”

Lilly and Lizzie watched as a list of nearby anger management classes scrolled down the SYNC 3 touchscreen. Lizzie reached over and viciously navigated a series of menus. The touchscreen finally displayed ‘Audio Off’ on its screen before transitioning back to the Main Menu.

Lilly said, “My goodness. And I thought my GPS navigation system was pushy.”

“That’s okay. We don’t need her anyway. All we need to do is stay on US 84 till we see a Dorothy’s Décor Boutique sign. If we don't find it, we'll go to Sapps instead," Lizzie said, referring to another home décor store in Waycross. "Make lemonade out of lemons I always say. You know, it just dawned on me that we should have brought Babs with us."

"Why?"

"She could've drove her Escalade. It's got a lot more cargo space for our purchases." Overspending addiction is like alcoholism—the more you consume, the more you want.

Most of the roads into Waycross are pretty boring unless you have a thing for pine trees. Dorothy's Décor Boutique itself was definitely not visually boring. The hot pink adobe (or 'tabby' as they call it in South Georgia) house screamed 'Notice Me!'

"I guess that must be it," Lilly said. "I see the 'Grand Opening' sign."

"Wish I'd remembered my glasses. All I see is a parking lot full of cars." Lizzie slowed down. "Good Lord. Everyone in Waycross must've come to Dorothy's."

"I've never seen this many SUVs in one place in South Georgia. Must be close to a hundred. I hope we can find a vacant space."

Lizzie put on her turn signal just as a Nissan sedan sped out of the parking lot in front of them. Its driver appeared not to care about his rudeness.

"Wonder what's stuck in his craw?" Lizzie asked as she pulled into the lot. She pointed to the sign on the tabby house. "That certainly don't say 'Dorothy's Décor Boutique' does it? What does it say?" Lizzie asked.

The look of shock and awe on Saddam Hussein's face during the invasion of Iraq never came close to the look on Lilly's. She said, "Don't ask."

Chapter 15

Friday, October 31st, 11:53 AM, EDT

Lizzie stopped the SUV and looked at her passenger. "I'm asking."

Lilly hesitated, reluctant to read what her eyes saw. "Dorothy's… Dorothy's Amour Boutique."

"Sounds like I need to apologize to my GPS. Must be a play on Dorothy Lamour, the actress that starred with Bing Crosby and Bob Hope in those old 'Road' pictures. Dorothy's Amour Boutique. Does sound kind of like Dorothy's Décor Boutique. What does it say below that?"

"Adult Toys. Adult Movies. Sexy lingerie. Goodies Men and Women Will Enjoy. Does this mean what I think it means?" Lilly asked.

Lizzie nodded. "It's an adult store. Just like the ones on I-75."

"Let's go to Sapps."

After a moment of quiet reflection, Lizzie began slowly cruising the parking lot. She looked for a vacant space while contemplating something she probably should not have contemplated.

"Come on. Let's go to Sapps," Lilly said.

"I've got an idea—"

"Let's go to Sapps."

Lizzie said, "Hear me out. You know how obnoxious those Mammas have been lately. Especially Mitzi. I don't know what's gotten into her, but she's been a downright bitch. She's insulted Babs about Area 53 and getting older way too much lately. It's gotten on my nerves, and I normally don't pay Mitzi no never mind."

Lilly nodded her agreement. "But—"

"We could buy some stuff in this place and embarrass the hell out of them. Things really gross. You said they have free shipping, so we anonymously mail each of them something so disgusting… like it's something they had to order online to keep it secret. We mail it to a place where someone else is sure to see them open it."

"Such as?"

"We'll figure that out as we go," said Lizzie. Action over deliberation anytime.

It usually took some effort for Lizzie to convince Lilly to embark on a new misadventure. The latter said, "I've never been in an adult store before. You sure it's safe? Might be all sorts of perverts in there."

Lizzie grinned, picked up her Coach handbag, and ostentatiously held it aloft. "Don't worry. I brought my Glock with me today."

"Okay, but only if we make it quick. I've got to get back in time for my hair appointment."

Lizzie found one of the few vacant parking spaces and led Lilly to the store's entrance. As they opened the door, two men brusquely stormed out past them without so much as a 'by your leave.' Both men grumbled at no one in particular.

"More angry men leaving this place. There must be something inside men don't like. Wonder what it could be?" Lilly asked.

Lizzie smiled. "Shopping? Women wearing bras? Light beer? With men, who knows what they get upset over? The little darlin's. Come on."

Inside, both ladies stopped dead in their tracks at the sight before them. In a rare moment of silence, neither said anything. No men were to be seen. Dozens of women of all ages pushed and shoved in search of bargains. Everyone seemed to be talking at the same time. A debate in the Japanese legislature over whether Godzilla or Mothra was the better monster would not have been as raucous. The scene resembled a half-off rug sale at crowded Turkish bazaar.

Once the initial shock wore off, Lilly and Lizzie got their bearings. The old tabby house appeared to have been gutted and converted into one large room with many aisles, each of which was full of sexually oriented wares. A cashiers' counter located close to the front entrance was staffed by three busy clerks. Nonstop sounds emanating from cash registers on the counter implied a booming business. Lizzie began barging her way through the crowd with Lilly in tow.

First stop—Aisle 3, Videos. Lizzie squeezed into a gaggle of ladies, all examining videos and talking. A Millennial in a leopard print blouse carefully inspected a DVD—*Gloria Goes Gaga for Georgia Guys.*

"Gloria never dated anyone from Blackshear," said a middle-aged brunette with a Bob Cut.

“How about this one,” said a Boomer with platinum blonde hair as she held up a video. “*Vicki Visits Vegas.*”

Lizzie rolled her eyes. “Sounds enticing. Where y’all from?”

“The four of us are from Blackshear,” said Bob Cut.

How did y’all find out about this place?”

A middle-aged woman with a Poodle Perm said, “On the radio. Sounded like a Bed and Bath knock-off called Dorothy’s Boudoir Boutique.”

Another Millennial in a tunic top shrugged. “We thought it was home décor store until we pulled into the parking lot. We almost turned around and left, but… y’all know how it is. It’s hard to pass up a sale… even when it’s this kind of place.”

All heads nodded simultaneously.

Lizzie said, “We’re looking for something really gross—”

“Gifts for some people we really don’t like,” said Lilly.

“Any ideas?”

Poodle Perm said, “You can’t go wrong in here if you’re looking for something disgusting. It’s kind of like walking into a picked-over Dollar General store that’s going out of business… just not quite as bad.”

All heads nodded simultaneously.

Bob Cut said, “Look in the S&M aisle.”

Poodle Perm shook her head. “Nope. The Technology aisle.”

“I thought the Handhelds aisle had some pretty disgusting things,” Boomer Blonde said.

A Gen Z with a Pixie Cut and purple side-swooping bangs said, “Just walk down any aisle with your eyes closed and start picking up stuff.”

All heads nodded simultaneously.

Poodle Perm said, “The good thing is that today only, they have free shipping. How can you pass that up?”

“I’d even buy pink lawn flamingoes if they came with free shipping,” Bob Cut said.

“Ladies, it’s been nice talking to you, but I’m looking for something this aisle don’t have,” Lizzie said as she moved off.

Second stop—Aisle 4, S&M. Lizzie and Lilly waded into a crowd of women oohing and ogling a variety of menacing-looking devices. An older lady wearing a floral print pullover top was waving a riding crop back and forth over her head. She said, “Give me a few minutes with this and Horace, and he’ll never complain when I serve boiled okra again.”

After the laughter died down, Lizzie said, "My daddy always said, 'Check your boots after you eat boiled okra.'"

More laughter. Floral Print said, "My daddy used to say the same thing about boiled peanuts. Where y'all from?"

"Thomasville. We thought this place was gonna be a home décor store."

"We're from Alma. We thought it was gonna be an antique shop—Dorothy's Décor Antiques," said a young woman wearing a gold top.

Lizzie nodded. "I'm Lizzie and this here's Lilly. This must be the *Fifty Shades of Grey* aisle."

"Yeah. There's stuff here that would put Christian Grey's Red Room to shame," said a Gen X brunette.

"A Red Room is like a circus," Lizzie said.

The other women stared at Lizzie. A Boomer with a grey feathered bob asked, "Why is a Red Room like a circus?"

"It's a fun to watch, but you don't want to join it."

Once the laughter subsided, Feathered Bob asked, "Y'all looking for anything in particular?"

Lilly said, "Something really, really gross."

Gold Top picked up a blindfold. "What about one of these?"

"I could've used that with my third husband. It was kind of tough to look at him with his clothes off," Lizzie said.

"Stuff on this aisle is kind of tame. Try Aisle 5," said Grey Feathered Bob.

Third stop—Aisle 5, Love Dolls. This aisle mostly contained cheap inflatable female dolls, but all the women crowded around a life-size silicone male doll. Thick jet-black hair on top, faded down the sides and back. A slim body clad in tight black leather pants that bulged at the crotch. Tattoos. Body piercings. Pure punk.

"I don't know if I could take him home to meet momma," said a Silent Generation woman.

Lizzie said, "He reminds me of my last husband, but without all his weight… and he didn't have any of this guy's piercings… also, he didn't have any hair… on his head at least. But the last husband did have a sleazy look, although not like the sleazy look that this doll has."

Lilly asked, “Does he talk?”

Silent Gen nodded. “Yeah, but he doesn’t say the things most husbands say like ‘Where’s my underwear?’ or ‘What’s for dinner?’ God, how I got tired of hearing that.”

Lizzie said, “So long as he doesn’t say ‘Let’s have sex’ before he’s showered after he’s mowed the lawn.”

A woman with a Layered Bob haircut turned to Lizzie and said, “You and I must have been married to the same man.”

“Probably. I been married four times.”

“There’s a problem with having a life size sex doll like this one. How would you fit it in with the décor in your home?” Silent Gen asked.

Lilly nodded vigorously and said, “It’s not like putting a piece of pottery on a shelf or a lamp on a table.”

“What room would you put it in?” asked a woman with salt-and-pepper hair.

“Why not store it in your closet when you’re not using it?” asked Pixie Cut.

Lilly frowned. “That sounds cruel. What if he’s claustrophobic or afraid of the dark?”

“How about in a rec room or a mancave?” Silent Gen asked.

Salt-and-Pepper said, “My husband would probably cut him in two at the waist and mount the top half on the wall with all his deer heads.”

“Where are y’all from?” asked Lizzie.

“Screven. We heard a commercial on the radio for an open house at Dorothy’s Glamour Boutique and came here thinking we’d get our hair and nails done.”

“You ladies seen anything really gross and disgusting? Lilly and I are looking for some really gross things to give some special people.”

Silent Gen said, “You got to be careful giving gifts, you know. I have one friend that’s got a touch of dementia. She forgets what I give her, sometimes regifts it, and gives it back to me.”

Salt-and-Pepper vigorously nodded. “Tell me about it. I always give those people a good wine. That way, I get something I can drink when I get it back.”

Layered Bob pointed. “Y’all want to check the next aisle over, Aisle 6. They got some humdingers in that aisle.”

Fourth stop—Aisle 6, Handhelds. More women crowded this aisle than any other in the store. Every one of them held a piece of merchandise in their hands, carefully bending and squeezing it as they evaluated its pros and cons. With great difficulty, Lizzie and Lilly pushed their way in.

"What's going on?" Lizzie asked. "It looks like half of Georgia is in this aisle."

A young woman wearing a black Nike tank top said, "Yeah. My girlfriends and I are from Homerville. We heard this commercial for Dorothy's Aro-ma-tiques and drove over here thinking we'd check out their perfumes and candles."

Her older companion sported an auburn Beehive hairdo. She said, "Not what we expected, but you can't beat the prices... I guess."

"At least they finally rehabbed this house. It's been an eyesore for years," said an older woman with a short shag hairstyle.

A Boomer wearing a drifter shaker sweater sneered. "Turning a dilapidated old house like this into an adult store really isn't an improvement. It's like turning a pawn shop into a vape store."

"Or a tattoo parlor," said Beehive.

"Or a payday lender," said Short Shag.

Lizzie asked, "Anyone seen anything really gross in this aisle? I mean disgustingly gross. We're looking for something really sickening."

Lilly became embarrassed at the thought of others thinking she would buy a vibrator for herself. "Not for ourselves. For gifts."

"Giving a gift from this aisle is like giving a Life Alert fob for a Christmas present," said Shaker Sweater. "Says what you really think of the recipient."

"How about this?" Short Shag asked, holding up a weird looking device. "It's called a Rabbit."

"Who designs these things?" Tank Top asked.

"Lagerfeld? Michael Kors?" Short Shag sarcastically asked.

"Michael Kors didn't design that thing. You can spot Michael Kors designs a mile off," said Lilly.

"Yeah. You can't miss that 'MK' logo. Where would you put the MK logo on these things?" Beehive asked. "If they put it in the wrong location, you're going to visit the ER."

Lilly said, “I always go with a great designer whether its clothes, shoes, or furniture. It’s worth the extra money you pay.”

“I don’t know if I’ll ever be able to do Easter with my grandkids again,” Beehive said as she closely examined the Rabbit before handing it to Lizzie.

Lizzie shook her head. “Not revolting enough.”

Short Shag held up an even weirder device.

Lizzie said, “Keep that thing away from me. It looks like a prop from *Aliens*. On second thought, hand it to me.”

Beehive held up another device. “This one here’s called a—”

“You don’t have to read the label on the package. Just hand me one.” Lizzie accepted the device with two fingers as if she was picking up a toad.

Shaker Sweater held up an extremely slimy-looking device and turned it on and off. She asked, “What the heck is this thing anyway?”

“I don’t know, but it reminds me of one of those creatures you see in one of those terrarium cages in the Okefenokee Swamp,” said Short Shag.

“It does bring new meaning to the word ‘ugly’,” said Tank Top.

“How would you clean that thing after you used it?” Lilly asked.

“It looks like cleaning it wouldn’t make any difference anyway,” said Short Shag.

“I’d hate to have someone open a drawer in my house and see that thing staring at ‘em,” said Tank Top.

“Hand me one,” Lizzie said.

“How about this?” Beehive held up a twelve-inch-long, green and red cylindrical device covered with many small nodules. A series of protruding ribs spiraled upward around it.

“It kind of reminds me of a candy cane,” Lilly said.

“It looks more like one of Yoda’s body parts,” said Tank Top.

Shaker Sweater nodded her agreement. “I wouldn’t put that thing inside my body for a million bucks.”

“Hand me one,” Lizzie said then turned to the women. “That’s enough. Nice meeting you ladies, but Lilly and I gotta check out. We got a costume party to go to.”

Short Shag said, “Looks like you two will be wearing some very interesting costumes tonight.”

Chapter 16

Friday, October 31st, 6:10 PM, EDT

Babs watched Sonny Biskit's aged Cadillac pull into her driveway. She opened her front door to find Mister Potato Head smiling at her. She said, "The spud of my dreams."

Head encased in the full body costume, Sonny ogled her before mumbling, "The 'I don't know what' of my dreams. What the hell are you supposed to be anyway?"

"Zoran the Alien. Who else?"

Babs wore a costume guaranteed to attract notice. A combination of several sci-fi and monster movie creatures. The top of the creature's green head billowed as if its skull had been inflated like a balloon. Dozens of small bumps covered it. Three oversized eyes bulged above a combination nose and mouth. The creature had a floppy furry ear on each side of its face. A green baggy uniform shirt extended down to its waist. It had three arms, two of which worked, one was just for show. Below the uniform shirt, dozens of thick green tentacles extended down to the floor. They emulated a Hawaiian grass skirt and hid her short, real legs.

Lilly and Lizzie milled inside Babs' parlor, having agreed beforehand to meet Sonny and Babs at her house and carpool to Preble Hill. Parking would be tight for the crowded Masquerade Ball. Lilly wore an outfit consisting of tight pink boddice, short puffy sleeves, and pink polka dot chiffon skirt. A pink bonnet complemented her rouged cheeks. She held a long crook.

Sonny asked, "Do you rent out for children's parties?"

"Lilly Bo Peep, if you please," said Lilly.

"I'm voting for Babs for best costume tonight."

"What about me?" the speaker wore a gorilla costume complete with head piece.

"Lizzie, I'd recognize you anywhere."

"Just call me Queen Kong."

"I'm switching my vote for best costume."

"Let's get rolling," said Babs.

Preble Hill Plantation sits on three thousand acres five miles south of Thomasville. Several venues for social events exist there. The most lavish of these, the Main House, is reserved for only a few special occasions. One of those is the Thomasville Cultural League's Annual Halloween Masquerade Ball. The Main House includes 16 bedrooms, 19 bathrooms, and 24 fireplaces. Its largest room, the Big Room, is elegantly furnished with priceless antiques and art. It can accommodate well over a hundred people.

Babs' Escalade pulled into the long driveway in front of the Main House before six-thirty. They waited ten minutes for valet parking as many cars and SUVs had arrived before them. Lilly Bo Peep alone suffered the least trauma exiting the vehicle as the others' costumes were very bulky. After shuffling and waddling inside, they found the Big Room packed. Although its antique furniture had been removed, the room's dark walnut paneled walls still displayed irreplaceable art including priceless paintings by Gilbert Stuart and Frederic Remington. Expensive 12x15 Persian rugs from Tabriz, Kashan, and Mashhad littered the floor.

Over a dozen gleaming mahogany serving tables displayed silver trays with an overabundance of heavy *hors d'oeuvres* and desserts. They included delicacies such as Oysters Rockefeller, smoked salmon, Bayonne ham finger sandwiches, and Wagyu beefburgers. Pie offerings were a cardiologist's nightmare—chocolate cream, cherry, blueberry, coconut meringue, and lemon icebox. Several open bars served a variety of alcoholic beverages including cocktails and heavily spiked punches.

Anyone who was anyone in Thomasville was there. The town's City Council and their spouses showed up in costume. Mayor Joy Flamingo appropriately wore a pink flamingo costume. The other four Council Members included Ted Maybry dressed as Mister Peanut, Chastity Knott as Cruella de Vil, Troy Seconell as Lieutenant Woof of *Star Trek* fame, and Toddie Wurlitzer as Wilma Flintstone.

The Police Chief and his wife dressed as a Keystone Cop and his prisoner in a black-and-white striped prison uniform. Thomasville's Georgia State Representative wore a Wonder Woman costume, while her husband appeared as Casper the Ghost. Squeaker and Dab of paintball fame somehow managed to get invitations. Squeaker wore a full body sheep's costume. He stood next to a fat man wearing a skimpy dress, enormous blonde wig, heavy pancake, and garish eye makeup. It turned out to be Dab, dressed as Fay Wray, star of the original *King Kong*. The duo made a beeline for Lilly and Lizzie, having coordinated costumes with theirs beforehand.

Many local merchants, wealthy members of society, and other local celebrities and notables also attended. The media were present. News crews from local CBS and Fox television stations filmed onsite interviews with guests. Cordell supervised a film crew from *Real Widows*. A reporter from the Thomasville newspaper roamed and took notes.

Babs, Lilly, and Lizzie mingled for several hours eating and drinking. Contact between them and the Mahjong Mammas was limited at first. Stoney wore an Elvira, Mistress of the Dark costume. Elvira was a 1980s character who hosted campy B movie horror films at midnight on TV. Stoney's costume began with an enormous jet-black wig. Its bouffant crown peaked half a foot above her forehead. Long tresses of straight hair framed both sides of her face and extended down below her breasts. White pancake makeup gave her face, neck, and cleavage an embalmed look. Her eyebrows were severely darkened, and their arches exaggerated. Her lips were blood red and full. Overdone eyeliner completed the vampire effect. She wore a floor-length tight, slinky black dress whose V neckline ended just above her navel. Her pal Mitzi wore a similar costume only it included a black headpiece with two long curved horns. She dressed as Maleficent of *Sleeping Beauty* fame. Due to Mitzi's plump frame, her overall effect failed to match Elvira's.

It was inevitable that the Casserole Ladies and the Mammas would eventually clash. The first run-in occurred shortly after eight o'clock. Fueled by alcohol, Mitzi barged into a group that included Babs, got into her face, and said, "Y'all know that this is gonna be my Best Costume win two years in a row. Why didn't you wear a costume Babsie? I guess you *are* a little too old for such things." Toots, dressed as a ballerina, and Penny, costumed as a penniless hobo, belittled the first episode of *Real Widows* in front of Lizzie and Lilly. Penny said, "It should be called Real Weirdos, not Real Widows." However, the *pièce de résistance* occurred when Babs and Mitzi got into an argument in front of Batman and Robin as well as the local CBS affiliate's news crew and Cordell and his film crew. Their quarrel lowered the bar for poor taste.

“Only an idiot would wear a costume that stupid,” said Mitzi. “If your little green boyfriend can make it past all those legs, he’s gonna find the payoff is not worth the effort. I bet y’all are going to the Motel 6 in Area 53 for some cheap sex later on.”

“Sex in a Motel 6 would be a lot better than sex in the backseat of a car with you.” Babs turned to the CBS news crew and said, “Mitzi always keeps a towel handy in the backseat of her car just in case she picks up a hitchhiker on the way over to Valdosta.”

“Only a senile old nutjob like Babs the Zoran here would believe in an Area 53.” Mitzi turned to look into the *Real Widows*’ camera as she spoke. The smile on Cordell’s face said ‘dynamite footage.’ He nodded a ‘keep it up’ signal to Mitzi. She said, “Babs just says those Area 53 lies for ratings. She don’t believe a word of it, elsewise she would volunteer to prove Area 53 exists. If she does believe it, it only shows how bad her dementia has gotten. They got homes for old women like Babs.”

By midnight when Best Costume winners were announced, everyone had consumed a lot of alcohol. This greatly contributed to what subsequently happened. It began when Mayor Flamingo strode to a microphone to present awards for Best Costume. She was one of the five judges in the best costume contest. It was widely known that she and Mitzi were close friends. Joy Flamingo had sided with Mitzi throughout the Babs-Mitzi feud in high school. After thanking the Cultural League and brown-nosing various notables in the audience, Mayor Flamingo said, “Third place goes to someone widely known throughout our fair city, Sonny Biskit or Mister Potato Head as he is known tonight.”

Sonny staggered up to the microphone and accepted his trophy. He said something no one could recognize due to his entire head being encased in the top of the costume. Excessive alcohol consumption also contributed to his incoherence. Lieutenant Woof and Mister Peanut stepped up to steady him.

Mayor Flamingo said, “Second place goes to a long shot—Mistress Elvira.”

Stoney stepped forward, an obvious frown on her face at not winning first place. As she approached, Mayor Flamingo said, “It was a tough call for the judges.”

Stoney made a lame acceptance speech, then stepped back from the microphone. Mayor Flamingo’s expression turned sour as she said, “First place goes to a visitor from Area 53, Zoran the Alien, also known by her Earthling identity, Babs Neauxgeaux.”

Zoran tipsily zigzagged to the microphone, took the trophy, and hiccupped.

During Babs' trek to the microphone, Maleficent Mitzi began mimicking the theme to *Star Wars*, "Dum dum… dum de de dum… dum… dum de de dum… dum… dum de de dum." When Babs hiccupped, Mitzi began singing an altered version of the chorus to Elton John's *Rocket Man.*

She's not the girl they think she is at home
Oh, no, no, no
Babs the rocket girl
Rocket girl, of air-re-ah fif-ty three not one

During the second repetition of the chorus, Lilly Bo Peep leaned into Queen Kong and said, "I didn't know Mitzi had any musical talent."

During the third repetition, Mitzi suddenly stopped and shouted, "There ain't no damn Area 53. What a bunch of bullcrap. It's just another conspiracy theory in Babs' peewee brain. She still believes in the tooth fairy."

Slurring her words, Zoran Babs said, "You're one to talk. You leave cookies for Santa Claus and carrots for the Easter Bunny. There *is* an Area 53 with aliens in it. The government has been catchin' aliens and puttin' 'em there for years."

Very intoxicated, Maleficent Mitzi leaned on a nearby *hors d'oeuvre* table for support and said, "Aliens in Area 53! What hogwash! Another ridiculous conspiracy theory on the Internet! The only reason you said that Area 53 crap was for ratings for your stupid show! You know that alien nonsense is a bunch of BS. You're just lying for ratings."

"I ain't lying. There is an Area 53, and they got aliens stored there."

"Put your money where your mouth is, you lying sack of shit. Prove there's aliens in Area 53, or go back home with your tail between your stumpy fat little legs."

Also very intoxicated, Zoran's mouth got ahead of her brain. "I'll show you, you bitch. I'll go to Area 53 and bring back pictures and shove 'em up your butt, Mitzi Moron."

Truth hurts. Hearing the humiliating nickname others called her in high school was the straw that broke the camel's back. Maleficent Mitzi waddled over to the nearest dessert table, picked up a chocolate cream pie, and heaved it at Zoran Babs. She saw it coming and ducked. The pie missed but hit Mayor Flamingo. Standing next to Zoran, Elvira Stoney ducked, her Elvira wig toppling into a bowl of blueberry rum punch on a nearby table. Several nearby attendees were soaked. Elvira Stoney grabbed a handful of Swedish meatballs and chunked them at Zoran Babs who along with the Bride of Frankenstein and Mayor Flamingo received a meatball shower.

An honest-to-goodness food fight broke out. The Grinch threw a lemon icebox pie at Zoran, hitting her and Queen Kong. Queen Kong tossed a large smoked salmon, covering Cruella de Vil, a giant Lobster, and Wonder Woman. The latter pitched a blueberry pie that hit Batman and Robin. Some of the same pie also splattered a Remington painting. Kobe beefburgers thrown by Space Woman hit a member of the local NBC affiliate's camera crew and R2D2. Maleficent heaved a chocolate lava cake that hit Lilly Bo Peep's face. She sprayed Elvira with a Coke explosion from a shaken can. Mister Peanut threw a cocoanut meringue pie that ruined a Persian rug from Tabriz. Maleficent received an assortment of *petits fours* in her face, thrown by Chewbacca. Maleficent returned fire with a cherry pie but missed. It coated Casper the Ghost's white linen-and-silk costume. He in turn lobbed artichoke dip, covering Fay Wray and Zoran. A Klingon randomly tossed pink gooey shrimp dip at targets of opportunity. Wilma Flintstone hurled a chocolate cream pie that missed everyone but the subject of a John Singer Sargent portrait hanging on a wall. Maleficent and Zoran concentrated on bombarding each other with a variety of pies and *hors d'oeuvres* to great effect. Both became unrecognizable, so covered were they in blueberry pie and guacamole dip. Wonder Woman coated Mister Peanut's head with a bowl of blueberry rum punch. He reciprocated with a bowl of lime sherbet punch. The sherbet turned Wonder Woman's costume into an interesting shade of green.

Over one hundred of Thomasville's elite participated in what the local newspaper headline next day titled 'Cultural League Food Fight.' One sentence in the article summed it up. "Thirty minutes into the melee, food and drink covered three quarters of the guests, thirteen Persian rugs, and four priceless paintings." It praised Preble Hill staff for their dedication, noting they replenished *hors d'oeuvre* trays and pies as soon as ammunition was expended. The article mentioned how camera crews from both area TV stations and *Real Widows* caught everything on film. It did not report that Cordell watched and smiled the entire time.

Chapter 17

Saturday, November 1st, 12:10 PM, EDT

Harvard Medical School recommends several remedies for a hangover including fluids, carbs, aspirin, coffee, zinc, and a lighter-colored hair of the dog. The Casserole Ladies unsurprisingly chose the last one. They met at The Plaza Restaurant and Oyster Bar for Bloody Marys in the lounge as soon as it opened at noon. Michael, the owner of the Plaza, walked up to their table, looked at them, and said, "Rode hard and put up wet comes to mind to mind, Ladies. I heard about youse guys."

His accent identified Michael as a transplant from Brooklyn. He left sixteen years ago before the exodus from the Big Apple began in earnest. He had to work Friday night so he missed last night's fun.

Lizzie said, "It's more like 'rode hard and trailered to the glue factory.'"

Michael smiled, shook his head, and headed off to oversee their order.

Cordell joined them fifteen minutes later. "Ladies, ratings for the pilot episode *Real Widows of Thomasville* set a record in television history for a new reality show, but those ratings will pale when we air the footage from last night."

Lilly's face froze in horror. He might as well have asked if she was going to wear Crocs to church on Sunday. She asked, "You're not gonna put *all* the video from the Masquerade Ball in our show? Not the food fight stuff?"

"You bet your sweet bippy I am. I told my editor this morning to work the footage from last night in with stuff from previous filming. That food fight was dynamite. *Keeping Up with the Kardashians* better look out."

"Could we talk about something that requires less exertion of my brain until after we've gotten our first round of Bloodies?" asked Lizzie, rubbing her temples. "That blueberry rum punch last night should have come with a warning label."

"A lot of important people around here may not be too happy showing the food fight on national TV," said Lilly, ever cautious.

"Screw 'em. Their idea of exciting TV is watching reruns of *Bill Nye the Science Guy* on PBS."

"I don't care who gets their panties in a wad. Both the Cultural League and Preble Hill signed our contracts and have no editorial say-so on the show's content. All they saw was free publicity on national TV," said Cordell. He emphasized the publicity part during his sales pitch. "You girls won't believe the feedback the network has been getting on your show."

"What kind of feedback?" asked Babs.

"Email feedback, feedback on the network's Twitter accounts, phone calls. Hundreds of thousands of emails and tweets. It got the network execs' attention."

"How so?"

"A whole lot of people loved Lilly's shoe fetish. I'd say we got the most feedback on the shoe closet scene."

The slick Hollywood producer stumbled with his off-the-cuff remark. Lilly's angry expression rivaled that of Clark Griswold receiving his jelly of the month club membership. She said, "I do *not* have a shoe fetish. Shoes are an important component of any lady's ensemble. What I try to do is make sure that component is optimally outfitted and organized."

Lizzie snickered and said, "You mean obsessively outfitted and organized."

Cordell said, "I apologize, but I do want to make your remodel project a recurring piece… probably one remodeling scene every week. We'll have to make sure there's some sort of remodeling problem every week."

Lilly's expression worsened at that idea. Lizzie asked, "What else did you get a lot of feedback on? Please don't tell me it was lunch at Cooties."

"Interestingly enough, we got a whole lot of feedback on Area 53."

"How so?" asked Babs.

"A lot of viewers are into this UFO stuff. Believers and skeptics. Want to hear some of it?"

Four heads nodded.

Cordell pulled a piece of paper out of his coat pocket, unfolded it, and began reading. "Here's a tweet from Myra in South Carolina. 'Babs is spot on. The Feds are covering up Area 53 just like they coverup everything.' Here's an email from someone that wouldn't give their name. 'That Area 53 stuff is just a bunch of bull… you know what.' You can fill in the blank. It goes on. 'Babs is either a nutcase or a liar or both about Area 53 nonsense.' I'll skip the rest."

"I bet Mitzi tweeted that one," said Babs.

"We even got an email from a lawyer offering his services pro bono if you do try to break into Area 53. Someone called the network's feedback line to say that she agrees with you and thinks the Feds won't tell us about Area 53 because they think the American public is too stupid to handle it. Here's a tweet from Barbara in Des Moines. 'Babs is right on. Go Girl, Go.'" Cordell looked up from his paper and directly at Babs. "Stan from Cleveland wonders why someone hasn't done an intervention on your behalf. A lot of viewers think you might be lying about the Area 53 just to get ratings."

Babs frowned. "They've been saying that kind of stuff on Facebook all morning."

"Why don't you enlighten us?"

Babs pulled out her phone and began scrolling. "There's a lot of stuff here. It begins with trash-talk about the Masquerade Ball."

Lizzie smiled. "I gotta hear that. Don't leave out a word."

Babs nodded. "First off, Mitzi says, and I quote, 'Lilly's costume looked like she just got back from street walking the strip at Vegas.' I guess she didn't notice what she and Stoney wore. Here's what Toots says about Lilly. Quote, 'Lilly should wear costumes with necklines high enough to cover up her turkey neck.' Here's what she said about you. 'That gold digger Lizzie could have saved money on the gorilla suit by not shaving her underarms, legs, and facial hair for a week.'"

"Why didn't I think of that?" asked Lizzie. "Renting that costume cost me seventy-five bucks."

Lilly had also accessed Facebook on her iPhone. She slammed it down on the table and said, "Penny 'Liked' Mitzi's post and replied that even someone as feebleminded as me won't go for breaking into Area 53. She's getting a bunch of 'likes' on that."

"What are you folks gonna do about them insulting y'all?" asked Cordell. Who said Hollywood producers are not Machiavellian? Answer: no one.

Lizzie shrugged. "What can we do? I don't think we'll get anywhere replying to them with insults. It'll just give them the publicity they want."

"I'd like to pull out their hair… starting with Penny," said Lilly.

Babs looked up from her iPhone. "It gets worse. Mitzi has a poll on her page."

"What kind of poll?"

"She's asking all her Followers to vote on whether each of us is stupid enough to sneak into Area 53. Looks like she has 3,128 Followers, and 2,978 have voted so far."

"What are the results?" asked Cordell.

"100% think I *will* do it. 83% think Daffy would do it. Lizzie, 78% think you'll do it. 23% think Gidget would do it. Lilly, you're low man with only 4%. Looks like Penny was right about you… not breaking into Area 53 that is."

"Feebleminded Lilly thanks you for the clarification," Lizzie said.

The ladies steamed in silence until Cordell looked at Babs and asked, "You're not going to let Mitzi get away with that, are you?"

"What you mean?" Babs asked.

"She's called you a liar. She said you're making up this Area 53 stuff to get ratings. She challenged you to break into Area 53 and take pictures of aliens. And now, she put out a poll that reinforces her challenge. You've got a national audience that is split on whether you are lying about Area 53. What you going to do about it?"

"What can she do?" Lilly asked. "The Mammas are just trying to goad us into doing something we'll get in trouble for. It's just like they did on the streaking bet. They're just a bunch of jealous old hags."

Cordell smiled. "Let's prove her wrong. Let's visit this Area 53 and get it on video. Even if there aren't aliens in Area 53, it'll make for a blockbuster *Real Widows* episode. We'll hype the episode answering the existence of Area 53 question big time before the show airs."

Lilly looked up from her phone. "Mitzi just posted something again. Quote, 'If Babs don't put her money where her mouth is and prove there are aliens in Area 53, 2978 people are gonna know she's full of you know what.' End quote."

"It gets worse," said Lizzie, reading from her iPhone. "Stoney replied that she bets Daffy and the rest of us are gonna leave Babs to break into Area 53 all by herself."

"Y'all can't let Stoney get away with that," Cordell said.

Lizzie shook her head. "Let's don't be too hasty. Stoney is just trying to goad us into doing something irrational, just like she did with the streak at the Georgia-Florida game."

"I agree," Lilly said. "We just barely managed to get away with that."

"I say we go to Area 53 and make the Mammas eat our dust," said Cordell.

Babs hesitatingly said, "I… I don't know. I feel bad that so many people that watched the show think I might be lying. I'd love to rub Mitzi's face in it by proving her wrong. But Area 53 is a federal government facility. They ain't gonna just let us walk in. And breaking into it would be a federal crime. I can't drag all y'all into that. This ain't like streaking the football game."

"But wouldn't it be great to get a selfie with an alien?" joked Lizzie.

"The Mammas would look like fools if you could do that," said Cordell. "You could accept their challenge on this Thursday's episode."

"Get this…" Lilly said. "Mitzi just posted that Babs a senile serial liar."

The thought of someone insulting her friend's intelligence finally sank in. Lizzie exclaimed, "Calling Lilly feebleminded! Penny makes Homer Simpson look like Einstein… It would be very satisfying to show them bitches up."

"I could film an Area 53 break in attempt so it would do exactly that… make them look like fools… even if we *can't* get inside," Cordell said. "I can picture it now. We video security personnel confronting you in front of a government facility. Then, we overlay them denying existence of Area 53 with voice over narration," Cordell's voice shifted from normal to that of an imaginary newscaster. "'Government officials issued similar denials about Area 51 until they admitted it did exist.' What do you think?"

Babs shook her head. "How could we break in? Security there would be too tough."

Cordell looked at Babs. "Let me worry about that. We'll at least get some great video for the show. It all comes down to this. You've been telling everyone for some time that there is an Area 53 with

UFOs and aliens in it. Did you really believe what you were saying?"

Babs remained silent. Had she let her ego get ahead of her?

Lilly sighed. "I remember that we backed Daffy up when she went out on a limb with that streaking bet. Whatever else we are—feebleminded, senile, gold diggers, you name it—we are best friends and loyal. Babsie, I want you to know that I'm one hundred percent behind you, whatever you decide to do. And as to how to break in, I do wish we had Gidget here to handle the planning for that just like she did for the Georgia-Florida game. Her planning was a masterpiece of genius."

"That alligator was brilliant," Lizzie said, referring to Gidget's use of Oscar, an iconic alligator from the Okefenokee Swamp in Waycross, as a diversion while the five ladies ran naked across the field.

"That's the spirit," Cordell said.

Babs shook her head. "I… I donno. I'm too old to be doing this kind of stuff. Streaking. Breaking into Air Force bases. I ain't no spring chicken, you know. Besides, this is a federal crime we're talking about."

Cordell put on his Churchill face. "I promise I'll put the entire weight of the network behind this thing. I'll get their lawyers to work right away on how to handle the legal aspects of this thing. I'm thinking some sort of journalistic defense if we get caught. Freedom of the press kind of thing. What right does the Federal government have to keep information about aliens from the public? And, if we do get caught, that's even better for ratings. Think about it. Are they going to throw five older women in jail for exercising their right to find out what's been going on in Area 53? I love to see them prosecute that in court." No politician could have said it better.

Babs said, "I… I have to think about it."

"Think quickly. I want to film your acceptance of Mitzi's challenge and air it on this Thursday's episode. That way, we can get our exploration of Area 53 on the third episode."

Babs' response was delayed as the wheels in her brain turned. "I'll let y'all know Monday afternoon after I see someone."

Cordell scrunched his face in consternation. “Why can’t you see this ‘someone’ today?”

“She don’t work Saturday afternoons or Sundays.”

Chapter 18

Monday, November 3rd, 8:15 AM, EST

Babs and Lizzie cruised down State Road 122 on their way to an eight-thirty appointment with a person that did not work on Saturday afternoons or Sundays. Thunderclouds produced dark skies, and heavy rain that pelted her windshield. Babs complained about driving in those conditions. She slowed and said, “This is as bad as driving at night. You can’t see a thing. The older I get, the harder it is to see in the dark. They should have a driver’s license for old people like me that prohibits us from driving at night or in the rain.”

“Why stop there? How about limiting old people to only driving Hoverounds inside Walmart?” Lizzie referred to powered wheelchairs often seen in those stores. She regretted accepting Lilly’s suggestion that someone accompany Babs to Madame Cassandra’s. Lizzie was a late riser. “I don’t want to drive anything this early. My eyeballs are still looking at my brain.”

“How about your eyeballs start looking for Madame Cassandra’s sign? I can hardly see it’s so dark.”

“Why don’t we turn this behemoth around, go back home, and wait out this deluge over mimosas?”

Babs shook her head. “It ain’t smart to piss off Madame Cassandra. I had to beg her to see me this morning. Her schedule was full, and she don’t start seeing people until nine o’clock.”

“You and that old snake charmer. What do you see in her?”

Lizzie might as well have asked what her friend saw in voodoo, Tarot, magicians, or hypnotism. Babs’ obsession with things offbeat had been lifelong. Take her belief that seven moons orbited the Earth. This came from her childhood, sitting with her family after supper in their backyard. Her father explained the various phases of the moon—full, half, quarter, waning gibbous, waxing gibbous, waning crescent, and waxing crescent. She naively mistook these to be seven distinct moons. This kind of broken, mystical logic pervaded her thinking throughout her life.

"She has powers few people have," Babs said. "She can talk to the dead, tell the future… which she did last time I was here. She said I was gonna meet someone new in Area 53—an alien."

"And so, you're going to see Cassandra again so she can repeat that before you decide whether or not to actually try to get into Area 53?" Although phrased as a question, Lizzie knew the answer.

Babs nodded. "I've had enough of Mitzi's insults. She's gone over the line this time, telling all Thomasville that I'm lying about Area 53. Saying that just for ratings. I've gotta show everyone that she's the fool, not me."

"But what if it turns out that there is no Area 53 and no aliens?"

"That's why it's so important to find out from Madame Cassandra whether there is or isn't. She sensed strong positive energy flowing between my Sixth Chakra and Area 53. There must be something to Area 53, but I don't want to take all y'all there and get arrested only to find out that it don't exist. I *got* to hear her tell me for sure that it does exist before we go."

"I don't trust Cassandra. You should trust your gut instinct and go with that. No need to do what some charlatan says."

"She ain't no charlatan. She'll know what I should do."

Lizzie rolled her eyes. "I'm on pins and needles. How was your date Saturday night?"

"Wonderful. Sonny and I went to another tractor pull in Waycross. Hyper Harvester was there," Babs said.

"What's that?"

"It was Limited Pro Stock Champion in the Wisconsin Tactor Pullers Association last year. Trust me, Hyper Harvester is one mean tractor."

"Sorry I missed it. I guess you really can't appreciate a tractor pull until you've been to one." Lizzie tried to keep her eyes from rolling again but failed.

Babs nodded. "It came all the way down from Wisconsin to compete with a bunch of local and state tractors. Tore the treads off of 'em. Real embarrassing to Waycross. What did you do?"

"Lilly and I watched *The Irishman* on Netflix."

A short period of silence—a long period of silence would be impossible with these two—before Babs said, "I just keep wondering if maybe Mitzi's right. Maybe I am getting old. Maybe I'm getting too old to be doing these kinds of crazy things like paintball, streaking football games, breaking into federal government property…"

"Kiddo, you're not too old. You don't even collect Social Security. The only time you're getting too old is when the elopement alarm in the nursing home goes off, and you don't realize it's because you set it off."

Babs shrugged. "Yeah, maybe. Oh… Here it is."

Babs turned into Madame Cassandra's driveway.

"What is Cassandra using now? Cards, or did she go back to a crystal ball?" asked Lizzie.

"She uses crystals."

"She used cards when I used to see her, but that was years ago," said Lizzie.

"Cards?"

"Yeah. She had been using a crystal ball but switched to cards right before I started seeing her."

"I wonder why she switched?"

"She was just getting started in the psychic business. I heard she'd moved all of a sudden-like from Waycross. The first year or two, she was trying different things. Trying to find her mojo so to speak," Lizzie said.

"I never heard that."

"You gotta get plugged in, Babsie. Yeah, she tried a couple of fortune telling tricks in her early days—killing goats and looking at the poor things' entrails, telling the future with rods, that kind of nonsense. I never saw her do any of that stuff, although I talked to a couple of people that did. The entrails thing didn't last long. It didn't exactly draw a crowd in Thomasville back in the seventies… although it might nowadays."

"You saw her back in the seventies?"

"Yeah, I think it was sometime in that decade. Maybe the eighties… maybe the nineties. I only saw her for a short time. It was… what was it? It was my first or second husband, so it must've been in the seventies or eighties. I suspected the SOB was fooling around on me, so I went to Cassandra to get her read on whether he was or was not. She was cheaper than hiring a private detective, and I was just starting out. Hadn't made my fortune yet."

"What did she say?" asked Babs.

"Cassandra, Sibyl as she was known at that time, said that he *was* fooling around. Gave me exactly what I needed to sue for divorce."

"How so?"

"During the court hearing, I used Cassandra's psychic reading as proof of his infidelity. Helped me get the settlement I was looking for."

"The judge accepted a psychic reading as proof of infidelity?"

Lizzie nodded. "Yep. Judge Rothwell was one of her regular customers. He said that she was always right on the money and that it was all he needed to know."

"Your poor husband. I guess he didn't know what he was up against."

"Yeah. He was too stupid to think about seeing Cassandra himself, or he'd have found out I was fooling around on him at the same time."

"Now I know I gotta hear what she says about Area 53." With that, Babs threw open the Escalade's door and sprinted toward Cassandra's porch.

Chapter 19

Monday, November 3rd, 8:29 AM, EST

The old boards on Madame Cassandra's porch groaned in misery as Babs and Lizzie walked to the door. They heard a commotion inside after Babs rang the doorbell. The mystic's smiling wrinkled face finally poked out of the doorway. She said, "Oh Babs, it's you. Pardon the mess inside. I don't normally see believers this early. I see you brought a friend again."

The psychic wore a turban made from a multi-color scarf atop her head. She had pushed some of her grey hair up under the turban. Some of it hung down on either side of her face in a style reminiscent of an Afghan Hound. She wore a white lace blouse and a paisley floor-length skirt secured at the waist with a wide brown leather belt. Lilly and Lizzie stepped inside.

Lizzie's head swiveled horizontally and vertically as she took in the room's interior. She said, "It's a lot darker in here than the last time I was here. But that was quite a while ago. You know they invented electric lights since then, don't you?"

Inwardly, Cassandra stewed. *This would be a lot easier without her here. The old gold digger is pretty sharp. I hope she doesn't blow it for me*. She chuckled perfunctorily. "My dear Lizzie, always attempting humor. Why are you here today? Another divorce you need help with?"

"Not now. But give me a couple of weeks."

"You should come back more often, my friend. If you did, you'd remember that darkness is propitious for the spirits."

"Propitious for the spirits *and* my face—makes it harder to see the wrinkles Botox missed," Lizzie said. "Hope you don't mind me sitting in on this."

Babs said, "Yeah. I asked her to come. I got something important that I need to get your advice on. I need your… uh expertise on the… uh metropolis women again."

"You mean the metaphysical world, my dear," said Cassandra.

"Right. Metaphysical world. I can never remember that term. I ought to get it tattooed on the back of my hand. Anyway, I need to see what it says about Area 53."

Perfect. "The spiritual world should be able to provide you with guidance. Please, have a seat." Cassandra's arm made a sweeping motion toward the table.

After the three women sat down, Cassandra opened a box laying on the table and extracted seventeen crystals. She carefully arranged them on the table.

"I see y'all got pyrite again," Babs said.

"Yes, my dear. Pyrite is a very powerful medium. The spirits are attracted to it," Cassandra said, "which makes it a very good medium to communicate with their world." *As well as a good medium to give a sucker what she wants.* "Now, everyone please be quiet while I clear my aura."

After Cassandra closed her eyes, Babs looked at Lizzie, held a finger up to her lips, and softly said, "This is the hardest part for me—not talking."

Cassandra grimaced but kept her eyes closed and said nothing. A contemplative look returned to her face.

Babs said, "She's meditating… sort of. I don't know what it does, but it works."

Cassandra's grimace returned. Eyes still closed, Cassandra silently began slowly moving her hands over, around, and among the crystals. Different expressions including worry, contentment, fear, and enlightenment slowly drifted across her face during the process.

"This aura clearing part is the hardest part for me. Did I already say that?" Babs asked.

Lizzie silently nodded.

Cassandra finally ceased waiving her arms above the stones with a theatrical flair that would have put Norton in the *Honeymooners* to shame. Leaving her arms suspended in the air, she opened her eyes, looked down at the tools of her trade, and said, "The crystals are all cleared and energized."

"Energized? Wish I'd have brought some marshmallows for roasting," Lizzie quipped.

Cassandra shot her a nasty look, then lowered her arms and placed her hands on the edge of the table in front of her. After a while, she began moving her hands in a slow, random course. Every so often, her hands settled over a crystal as if ready to choose it, only to disappoint Babs before moving on. At one point, her hands lingered over the pyrite. An obvious look of satisfaction descended on Babs' face only to be dashed as the old gypsy's hands moved on. This sort of nonsense lasted a couple more minutes. Finally, her hands lingered over one stone before carefully holding it up for her audience to see. It was a multi-sided crystal about the size of a jar of mustard. The rough, craggy surface glowed a subtle shade of pink. She said, "This is the one. My lovely Rose Quartz."

"Sometimes it's the temperature of the crystal, sometimes the one that she's drawn to changes color, sometimes she sees an image in it," Babs whispered to Lizzie. "You never know *what* one of them crystals is gonna do to make itself be her choice."

"I feel my aura is now set for the greatest good. I feel the spirits' message will be a loving one. We are ready," Cassandra said.

"Don't forget the gentle guidance part."

Cassandra forced a smile, then reached into a drawer and extracted a piece of fine parchment paper and an expensive Waterman pen.

"This is where things get really interesting," Babs said.

"Don't tell me," Lizzie said. "The crystals are gonna form up into a rock band and play '*We Will Rock You*'."

"Ooh, I loved that song. I remember seeing Queen when they came to Atlanta."

Cassandra ignored the distraction and began scribbling on the parchment. Babs and Lizzie leaned in to see what she was putting on the parchment. Some things were crude pictures—birds, weird-looking machines, flowers. Some were simply doodles—curlicues, figure eights, and so forth. A lot of numbers, letters of the alphabet, and nonalphanumeric characters such as %% 2222 ysbc45 87 mn**** fo zz 2118. She continued scribbling meaningless things like this for ten minutes, never saying a word, filling up the parchment, including the words 'Area 53' and 'XGttbzqnfdtkttt'." When she finally put her pen down and looked up, perspiration dripped from her chin. Her writing hand shook with a slight tremor.

"What does it mean?" Babs anxiously asked.

"It is very propitious," Cassandra said. "The spiritual forces speak powerfully today. They are aroused."

"What do they say about Area 53? I saw you write that down. And what do they say about aliens in Area 53?"

A subtle expression, one resembling a crocodile's smile before eating its victim, inched its way over Cassandra's lips. *It's like shooting fish in a barrel with Babs.* "The spirits do not communicate in that way. I cannot tell you anything absolute. I cannot say 'yes' or 'no', 'this' or 'that'. The gulf between the other world and ours is such that direct communication is impossible. The spirits can only communicate feelings. As you can see, the spirits communicated something to me through the crystals about Area 53, which accounts for it being written on the parchment. I again got strong positive feelings from the spirits when you just said the words, 'Area 53'. Exactly what these feelings mean, I cannot say. The spirits speak in code often times."

Babs looked at Lizzie and said, "Madame Cassandra is never wrong. She predicted I'd meet someone or something new. It must be connected with Area 53."

"Exactly how do you get feelings from that stuff you drew on the paper?" Lizzie asked. This was why she wanted to accompany Babs—to be a force of reason for her naïve friend. Lizzie pointed to something Cassandra had written on the paper. "What kind of feelings do you get from that 'X-G-t-t-b-z-q-n-f-d-t-k-t-t-t' for example? Is it some sort of code?"

The psychic looked down where Lizzie pointed and seemed surprised, as if she had just read something unexpected. She kept her eyes on the parchment, at a loss for words. Finally, she said, "As I have said many times, spiritual forces speak in mysterious ways. Their communications are often in code. It is up to psychics, such as myself, to interpret what they are telling us. I can tell you that the spirits are invigorated. They wanted me to write X-G-t-t-b-z-q-n-f-d-t-k-t-t-t just as they did Area 53."

"Maybe this xgtt thing is some sort of code that has to do with Area 53?" Babs asked, hope springing eternally in her voice.

Lizzie rolled her eyes, looked at Cassandra, and said, "What about this *Fons Iuvenis* you wrote right after 'Area 53'? What does that mean?"

The old gypsy looked down at the parchment and scrunched her face. *Did I write that? I don't remember writing that. Did I forget to take my Prevagen again?* "I cannot decipher its meaning at this time, my child. It is obviously some sort of coded message from beyond this world to Missus Neauxgeaux."

Lizzie persisted. "Do your spirits say that Area 53 exists and that there are aliens in it?"

Cassandra slowly moved one hand over the Rose Quartz and the other over the pyrite, stalling for time. Her mind debated what to do. *If I say yes, it will probably come back to bite me in the ass after Babs goes on a wild goose chase and comes back empty-handed. But Mitzi is paying good money. If I don't deliver the goods?* Cassandra mulled over the consequences of that as she looked up. "Yes, to both of your questions."

Babs looked at Lizzie. "See, see. Area 53 is for real."

Cassandra nodded. "Yes, my dear. Your quest for truth about this Area 53 is valid."

Babs looked at Lizzie. "I've heard enough. I'm telling Cordell that we're gonna go to Area 53."

Cassandra looked at the antique clock hanging on one of the walls. *Better quit while I'm ahead.* "Where has the time gone? It's almost nine o'clock. I must prepare for my nine o'clock appointment."

The psychic closed the door after Babs and Lizzie stepped onto the porch and immediately picked up her phone. She dialed a number and said, "It went as you requested."

She listened then said, "She is going to call someone named Cordell and tell that person that they are going to go to Area 53. That is what you were looking for, isn't it?"

Cassandra listened then said, "I expect to be compensated better this time. I let you know right after she called, didn't I? I went out on a limb big time. Don't forget, I want my payment in cash. No checks. I'm a cash-only business."

On the other end of the call, Mitzi hung up.

Chapter 20

Thursday, November 6th, 8:12 PM, EST

The Casserole Ladies gathered at Lilly's to watch Episode 2 of *Real Widows of Thomasville*. Lilly fired up the DVR.

<u>INTERIOR SCENE: BABS' BEDROOM, FRIDAY EVENING, HALLOWEEN</u>

Title sequence with opening credits scrolling across a long shot of Babs trying to get into her alien costume with help from her two granddaughters.

NARRATOR: [Voiceover] This is a big night for the Real Widows. The Thomasville Cultural League is hosting its Annual Halloween Masquerade Ball at Preble Hill, a magnificent antebellum plantation near Thomasville. Anyone who is anyone in Thomasville will be there, including the Real Widows. Babs is having some difficulty getting into her costume with the help of two of her granddaughters, six-year-old Amelia and three-year-old Charlotte.
BABS: [Medium shot of Babs and her granddaughters.] Okay, y'all come over here… Amelia, you take this side. [Babs offers Amelia one side of the legs part of her alien costume. Amelia grabs it.] Now, Charlotte honey, you take this here other side. [Babs holds the other side out for Charlotte.]
CHARLOTTE: [The three-year-old stands frozen and vigorously shakes her head.] No! No!
BABS: Come on, baby girl. Hold this side for Nanna.
CHARLOTTE: No! [The three-year-old shakes her head even more vigorously, steps back, and says something unintelligible, fear clearly in her voice.]
BABS: Honey, it ain't gonna hurt you. It's just a costume. You'll be wearing a costume yourself when you go trick-or-treating tonight with Amelia and your momma.
CHARLOTTE: No. [Close shot from second camera as the three-year-old turns and scoots under the bed.]
BABS: [First camera medium shot as Babs looks at Amelia.] Sugar, I guess you and I will have to do this all by ourselves. [Fast motion of Amelia holding one side of the legs portion of

the costume as Babs climbs in, then back to normal motion. She looks at herself in a full-length mirror before turning to Amelia.] Sugar, hand me that shirt over there on the bed. [Second camera wide shot as Amelia runs to the bed and returns with green baggy uniform shirt part of the costume.]
AMELIA: [Medium shot of Amelia looking on as Babs pulls the uniform shirt over her head and onto her torso.] Nanna, you got three arms!
BABS: It's supposed to have three arms, Sugar. It's supposed to be an alien's uniform. This one is fake. [Babs begins flipping the fake third arm up and down.] Now, I'm gonna need your help putting the costume head on. It's pretty bulky. [Babs walks over to her bed.] Is Charlotte still under the bed?
AMELIA: [Lays on the floor, looks under the bed, then stands.] Yessum.
BABS: That's okay. Leave her be if she's happy. [Babs reaches onto the bed and lifts up an oversized green orb covered with dozens of small bumps. Two floppy fur ears hang down, but one flops open as Babs turns the head over, revealing a disgusting looking inner ear. Three large holes have a thin ring of fur around each, while a larger hole is surrounded by dark black lipstick. Silicone molded to look like slimy goo drips from the mouth.] Here take hold of this head and help me put it on.
AMELIA: No! No! [The six-year-old rapidly backs up several feet.]
BABS: Come on, Sugar. It ain't gonna hurt you. It's part of Nanna's costume. Here… take this end.
AMELIA: No! No! [Begins crying.] I don't wanna. It's… it's too scary. [The six-year-old scrambles under the bed.]
BABS: [Slips alien head on, gets down on her hands and knees, and looks under the bed.] Y'all come on out now. It ain't gonna hurt y'all. Nanna's here.

Scene fades.

As a scene of Lilly and Lizzie sitting in the beauty salon transitioned onto the screen, Lizzie said, "Babsie, you might want to be on the lookout tomorrow for Child Protective Services to show up on your porch. That was definitely a scene of child abuse."

"Their momma told me the next day they both had nightmares," said Babs.

They watched beauty salon scenes as well as each of the other two Casserole Ladies getting ready for the Ball, none as entertaining as Babs'. After the last of those and some commercials, the episode transitioned to the fun scene.

EXTERIOR SCENE: PREBLE HILL, FRIDAY EVENING

Wide shot of a stream of cars driving up to valet parking in front of the Main House. Each car stops, and its costumed occupants exit and hand car keys to a valet.

NARRATOR: [Voiceover] It is almost six-thirty, and the Masquerade Ball is well underway. Dozens and dozens of elite Thomasville society are already here, with over one-hundred and fifty guests expected to attend. As I said, anyone who is anyone in Thomasville will be here. No *hoi polloi* allowed. If it can be said that Thomasville has an aristocracy, it is here tonight. Speaking of which, one is arriving right now.

Scene transitions to full shot of BMW M850i pulling up. Valet opens the passenger door, and Elvira Stoney steps out. Valet freezes, awestruck at her low-cut dress.

NARRATOR: [Voiceover] It looks like a Mahjong Mamma has arrived. Looks like the valet is mesmerized by her costume. [Close shot of valet, mouth open, staring at Elvira. Scene fast forwards through several more cars pulling up to valet parking. Babs, Lilly, Lizzie, and Sonny exit vehicle.] Looks like the Real Widows have arrived with a date. [Transition to medium shot of another valet opening front passenger door. Mister Potato Head tries to exit the vehicle.] It looks like her date is Mister Potato Head. A Cadillac Escalade is a big vehicle, but I'm still surprised how he could fit in with that bulky full-body potato costume. The cream of the crop has indeed arrived.

Valet laughs as Mister Potato Head struggles to exit, then hobbles over to Zoran who has circled to his side of the Escalade. They attempt to link arms, handicapped by Mister Potato Head's short arms and big hands. Scene fades with them holding hands and walking to the Main House, followed by Lilly Bo Peep and Queen Kong.

<u>INTERIOR SCENE: BIG ROOM, MAIN HOUSE, PREBLE HILL, FRIDAY NIGHT</u>

Wide shot inside Big Room, packed with costumed partygoers.

NARRATOR: [Voiceover] It's after seven-thirty. All of the Real Widows have arrived and enjoyed food, drink, and polite company for an hour. Lilly Bo Peep engages in conversation with one of her Lost Sheep and She-Hulk, who is actually the city's Superintendent of Schools, as Velociraptor looks on.

Scene transitions to close shot of Lilly Bo Peep, Lost Sheep, Velociraptor, and She-Hulk standing next to a table with alcoholic beverages.

LILLY BO PEEP: [Leaning in and looking closely at She-Hulk's costume. Slurs] How you gonna get that green makeup off your skin?
SHE-HULK: [Slurs] Same way you're gonna get that white pancake off yours.
LOST SHEEP: [Slurs] Excuse me, but I gotta go pee. Tell you what. If I can't find a bathroom close by, I'll find Cruella or one of the other Mammas and pee on her. [Lost Sheep abruptly staggers off.]
LILLY BO PEEP: [Shakes her head.] He told me he had a few beers before he came here. I told him all that beer wouldn't go very well with an enlarged prostate.

Lilly paused the DVR and asked, "That peeing scene reminds me. Anyone need a bio-break?"

Lizzie and Babs stood to head for the bathroom.

Walking with them, Lilly said, "I can't believe I said that on national TV. Thank God I was wearing that costume. Who was that guy standing with us in the raptor costume? I don't remember him. I must've really been bombed."

Lizzie said, "That was Reverend Morris. You told him he could make a fortune panhandling in that costume in Times Square."

"He probably could."

"He probably will... now that you gave him the idea," said Lizzie.

After everyone returned, Lilly pushed play.

Scene cuts to Queen Kong talking to the president of one of Thomasville's banks who wears a Sasquatch costume.

NARRATOR: [Voiceover] Another hour has passed. Queen Kong Lizzie appears to have met her match costume-wise in the president of a local bank, dressed as Sasquatch, also called Bigfoot, the never-captured ape-like creature purported to live in the forests of the northwestern United States.
QUEEN KONG: [Slurs] I've been looking for you.
SASQUATCH: [Slurs] Hasn't everybody?
QUEEN KONG: No, no. Not the way you're thinking. I've been wanting to talk to you about refinancing my mortgage at a lower rate.
SASQUATCH: Lizzie, you've never had a mortgage. Your first husband gave you the house mortgage free as part of the divorce settlement.
QUEEN KONG: No more bourbon for me. Guess I'll have to switch to gin.

Lilly looked at Lizzie and asked, "Don't you remember? You already took out an equity loan with Sawgrass Bank a year ago."

"Oh, yeah. You're right. I forgot about that. That was right after my last divorce, and I needed the money for a butt lift."

Chapter 21

Thursday, November 6th, 8:27 PM, EST

Scene transitions to wide shot of the Big Room for a few seconds before transitioning to a medium shot of Space Woman and Mister Peanut talking to Wolfman and LavaGirl as Elvira, Zoran, Lieutenant Woof, Queen Kong, Dolly Parton, Freddy Krueger, and Maleficent Mitzi look on.

NARRATOR: [Voiceover] Space Woman and Mister Peanut talk to Wolfman. He owns several Cadillac dealerships in South Georgia. His date, LavaGirl owns twenty-thousand acres of pecan groves.
LAVAGIRL: [Slurs as she looks at Zoran.] What's this I hear about you breaking into Area 53? Ain't that a federal offense?
SPACE WOMAN: [Slurs as she looks from LavaGirl to Zoran.] Probably… but I don't think she's going to do it.
WOLFMAN: [Slurs as he looks from LavaGirl to Zoran.] I know Babs, and I'd bet odds that she does.
MISTER PEANUT: [Slurs] What kind of odds could you get? We don't got a bookie here in Thomasville.
WOLFMAN: No, but we do have illegal gambling.
MISTER PEANUT: Whereabouts? I been missing out.
WOLFMAN: In the Thomasville Senior Center. The Merry Mallwalkers play rubber bridge there every Thursday night for a penny a point. [Laughter]
LAVAGIRL: [Points to the Maleficent and looks at Zoran.] Mitzi here has been going around saying that you're gonna *have* to break into Area 53 and prove there's aliens in there… or else get outta town.
MALEFICENT: [Looks at Queen Kong Lizzie and speaks with a snotty tone.] Yeah! That's right. By the way, are y'all gonna have one of them weird-looking aliens from Area 53 be a guest on y'all's show?

QUEEN KONG: [Points to camera and slurs.] Yeah, we are. Look into that camera over there and say hello.

Scene transitions to a commercial.

Lilly began fast forwarding through the commercials. She said, "It's almost 9 pm, and I'm fading fast. How about we skip the awards and go straight to the good part?"

The nice thing about being a senior citizen is being able to go to bed early without shame. The others nodded their heads in concurrence, and she fast forwarded to the food fight.

INTERIOR SCENE: BIG ROOM, MAIN HOUSE, FRIDAY MIDNIGHT

Medium shot of Queen Kong and Elvira standing next to *hors d'oeuvre* table. Maleficent stands on other side of table.

NARRATOR: [Voiceover] Looks like tempers are rising. Too much alcohol mixed with long-simmering animosities is a deadly combination.

QUEEN KONG: [Slurs] Those dumbass Mammas don't know their ass from a hole in the ground. [Remainder is sung the tune of "Wheels on the Bus."] Dumbass Mammas don't know their ass from a hole in the ground, hole in the ground, hole in the ground. Dumbass Mammas don't know their ass from a hole in the ground, hole in the ground, hole in the ground... Dumb as rocks.

MALEFICENT: [Slurs] Who're you calling a dumbass?!

ELVIRA: [Slurs] Who do you think, dumbass? Us! [Maleficent picks up a chocolate cream pie and throws it at Queen Kong, misses, and almost hits Elvira, who ducks. Pie misses and hits a Pink Flamingo. Elvira's wig falls into a bowl of punch. She grabs a handful of meatballs and throws them at no one in particular. Meatballs hit Bride of Frankenstein, Pink Flamingo, a Grinch, and a Witch.]

Scene transitions to wide shot of food fight in Big Room.

NARRATOR: [Voiceover] Looks like an honest-to-goodness food fight in the Big Room at Preble Hill has broken out. I see blueberry and chocolate cream pies being thrown by Wonder Woman and Fred Flintstone. Chewbacca is getting hit in the face with a plate of *petits fours*. I believe the pie that just hit Peter Pan was a lemon cream pie thrown by a Ghostbuster. Now, it looks like Peter Pan is shaking a bottle of champagne and spraying Popeye and Olive Oyl. Uh oh…one of the Remington paintings got spattered with artichoke dip. And there goes Funshine Care Bear running through the crowd throwing chocolate truffles at everyone…

The Casserole Ladies watched another four minutes as the Narrator described the food fight scene before it transitioned to a commercial. Lilly paused the DVR for another pit stop. After everyone had returned, Lilly hung her head and said, "I can't believe they just showed that on national TV. How embarrassing. We look like clowns."

"Wasn't everyone in that video wearing a costume?" asked Lizzie.

"Yeah. So?"

"All the viewers saw was people in costumes having a food fight. They can't identify any of us."

Lilly pushed play.

<u>EXTERIOR SCENE: MAIN HOUSE, PREBLE HILL, FRIDAY 1:30AM</u>

Wide shot of the Main House as exhausted partiers stand in line waiting for their cars.

NARRATOR: [Voiceover] Guests, most of whom are covered in foods like blueberry pie, avocado dip, and a variety of dipping sauces, wait for their cars. A little too much of the bubbly. It certainly has been quite a Masquerade Ball. I'm sure the Cultural League will have something to say next week.

Scene fades to black.

INTERIOR SCENE: STONEY LEE'S LIVING ROOM, TUESDAY MORNING

Wide shot of four Mammas seated and frowning.

NARRATOR: [Voiceover] This group of women has earned the sobriquet 'Mahjong Mammas' or simply the 'Mammas'. They are upset and have a challenge for the Real Widows. [As she speaks, each of the names 'Stoney', 'Mitzi', 'Penny', and 'Toots' floats across the screen and settles on its respective owner for a few seconds before de-materializing.]
STONEY: [Close shot] There ain't nothing too low that them Real Widows won't stoop to. I'm the Chairwoman of the Tourism Board. They had a FedEx package delivered there that I opened, thinking it must be something tourism related. Right in front of a bunch of the employees. And this is what was in the package. [Holds something that is XXX'd out.] I could've died right there on the spot. It was supposedly sent from a 'friend' who wanted to remain anonymous and is postmarked in Waycross. I know who sent it. It was Lizzie and her pals, and we're gonna teach those [bleeps] a lesson.
MITZI: [Camera pans to Mitzi.] There was a similar package for me Sunday morning at my church when I had Altar Guild. [Holds something that is XXX'd out.] I opened it right in front of the other Altar Guild members, thinking it was unleavened wafers. This thing has Babs written all over it.
PENNY: [Second camera close shot of Penny, holding something that is XXX'd out.] Mine was FedEx'd to my country club, where I opened it at Sunday brunch with several of the ladies from my Sunday school class. Everyone knows we always eat the buffet lunch there after church.
TOOTS: [Camera pans to Toots.] Y'all are lucky. Mine went to my mother-in-law's house. [Holds up something that is XXX'd out.] I made the mistake of opening it up there instead of taking it home. I thought I'd die. She never believed me when I said I didn't know a thing about it… that it was just a Halloween trick being played on me by one of them Real Widows. She just kept repeating over and over, "It's good my poor son ain't alive to see this."
MITZI: [Close shot as she looks directly into the first camera.] We know who did this, who sent these disgusting things to

embarrass us. But we are gonna have the last laugh when Babs and the other Real Widows cannot prove there are aliens and UFOs in Area 53. It was all a bunch of lies to boost ratings for their stupid show. Only someone as old and senile as Babs would believe a conspiracy theory as crazy as Area 53. [Pause as second camera medium shot shows other Mammas smiling and nodding their heads, then back to first camera close up of Mitzi who resumes speaking.] I personally challenge you, Babs Neauxgeaux. Prove that Area 53 exists! Prove there *are* UFOs and aliens there in Area 53! Either that or give up now before you get yourself in big trouble. Admit your old age is getting the best of you. Babsie, it is no shame to acknowledge your dementia. You are getting old, and it has affected your thinking. Either that, or you have been lying to your nationwide audience for ratings. If that is the case, admit it and move to Waycross where you belong.

Camera fades.

<u>INTERIOR SCENE: BABS' LIVING ROOM, TUESDAY AFTERNOON</u>

Wide shot of Babs, Lilly, and Lizzie sitting and fidgeting.

NARRATOR: [Voiceover] Blood runs in the streets of Thomasville. Accusations are hurled—lying for ratings, FedExing embarrassing sex toys. Losing the Halloween costume contest results in a food fight for the ages. Hell hath no fury like a woman losing to her worst enemy in an alien costume. Jealousy rages in Thomasville. Reputations are on the line. Amid the turmoil, will the Real Widows rise to the challenge?

BABS: [Close shot of Babs.] I just want to say to the whole world that I ain't no liar. I would never lie to anyone, especially our audience, just for ratings. I don't like using profanity, but as far as I'm concerned, Mitzi and those Mammas can go [bleep] themselves. I… [Babs looks around at

her companions.] *We* accept the Mammas' challenge. There is a real Area 53, and we are going there. We are going to prove there are aliens there. And excuse me for cursing, but sometimes it just gets to me. [Wide shot of Lilly and Lizzie clapping.]
NARRATOR: [Voiceover] You heard it. The Real Widows of Thomasville have accepted the challenge. Is there actually an Area 53? Do aliens live there? Are the Real Widows up to the task of proving Babs' assertions? Be sure to tune in next week to find out.

Ending credits scroll across screen as the Casserole Ladies remain seated, clapping.

"What have we gotten ourselves into?" asked Lilly after she stopped the DVR.

The glum expression on Babs' face would have rivaled Rodney Dangerfield's mug. She said, "We're in a no-win situation. No matter what we do… whether we chicken out or break into Area 53, we sure ain't gonna come outta this smellin' like roses."

"Don't sweat it," said Lizzie. She was on her fourth margarita. She had made the last two rounds, and they were potent.

Lilly said, "Babs is right. The flowers we *are* gonna smell like are lilies. Like the kind they put on caskets... our caskets."

"No way. The flower we're gonna smell like after this is over is Baby's Breath."

"Baby's Breath. Why Baby's Breath?"

"Because of what Cassandra wrote."

"Huh?" asked Babs.

"Remember when she wrote that phrase *Fons Iuvenis* on that piece of paper during her séance? Although I flirted during most of Missus Polhemus' Latin class in high school, I did recognize that Cassandra had written something in Latin. So, I asked Alexa, and she said *Fons Iuvenis* is Latin for Fountain of Youth. So, the flower we're gonna come outta this smellin' like is Baby's Breath."

Chapter 22

Friday, November 7th, 10:00 AM, EST

All major papers across the nation carried the story the next morning. *The Washington Post* ran it above the fold under the headline "Air Force Denies Existence of Area 53."

> Washington (AP) — Pentagon spokesman Kirby Johnson categorically denied existence of Area 53. Johnson said today, "Rumors that the United States Air Force maintains a secrete facility code-named 'Area 53' in northwest Florida are false. Also false is the idea that this facility would be used by the Air Force to house UFOs and aliens from other planets." Johnson went on to remind reporters that the reality show *Real Widows of Thomasville* is just a reality show on television and not a reliable source of information on Air Force extraterrestrial research. After the show's episode Thursday night, the Pentagon was flooded with phone calls and emails from people wanting to know why the Air Force continues to cover up existence of such facilities.
>
> These denials are reminiscent of previous denials by Federal authorities of existence of Area 51, the common name of a highly classified facility located in Nevada. This facility was widely suspected for decades of containing Unidentified Flying Objects or UFOs as well as alien beings that landed on Earth in UFO spacecraft. It was not until June 25, 2013, that the Central Intelligence Agency publicly acknowledged existence of Area 51.......

The Thomasville Times-Enterprise carried the *Post* article in the morning edition. Many Thomasville residents had either read it or heard about it by mid-morning when the City Council met for its regular meeting. It was the first item on the Council's agenda. Councilmembers smarted from negative publicity generated by their contemptable behavior at the Masquerade Ball. Typical politicians, they used the meeting as an opportunity to shift attention onto someone else.

Mayor Flamingo said, "I call this meeting of the City Council to order. Will the Recorder please note that the following are present: Councilmembers Toddie Wurlitzer, Dr. Ted Maybry, Troy Seconell, Chastity Knott, and myself, Mayor Joy Flamingo. We will dispense with the previously published agenda as I'm sure everyone has read this morning's article in the Times-Enterprise. I watched *Real Widows* last night and was disgusted at the negative portrayal of our Annual Masquerade Ball, an event that benefits several local charities. Also, I was surprised, to say the least, at some of the assertions made on that program. It just so happens that other Thomasville residents were as surprised and upset as I was that our fair city had become associated with what I would call conspiracy theories. One of the residents, Mitzi Merchant called me and asked to speak to us about this issue. Ms. Merchant, please approach the microphone and make your presentation."

Mitzi sat in the front row of audience with other Mahjong Mammas. She ceremoniously stood, walked to the microphone, and began reading from a prepared statement.

"Thank you, Your Honor and Members of the City Council for this opportunity to address you on a matter of utmost importance concerning the reputation of our fair city. As you know, Babs Neauxgeaux and the other Real Widows have made some outlandish statements on their TV show, *The Real Widows of Thomasville*. This show is an embarrassment to the town of Thomasville. It portrays the residents of Thomasville as being nothing but a bunch of ignorant, low-class hicks. All Thomasville residents should be ashamed of this show."

"Last night, Babs went over-the-top when she made more ridiculous statements. She claimed Area 53 exists and is located somewhere close to Thomasville. She said Area 53 is where the United States government keeps UFOs and aliens from outer space hidden." Mitzi paused for effect, heightened by an eye roll. "According to Babs, some of these extraterrestrials are transgender. She said she will go to this Area 53 and prove that it does exist. Babs Neauxgeaux has gone too far. I've known her ever since kindergarten. She's always been… to put it politely, eccentric. But lately, she's really gotten bad with this kind of nuttiness. I believe that her behavior is caused by dementia. She's gotten old and doesn't think very well nowadays. She needs an intervention to put a halt to this kind of behavior.

The *Real Widows of Thomasville* made our beautiful town look ridiculous last night. After last night, people must think Thomasville is populated with drunks and a bunch of conspiracy theory wackos. The rest of the country must think that we all need to be committed to an insane asylum if we all believe in Area 53s and UFOs and aliens. Why would anyone want to come visit Thomasville if the residents are wearing tinfoil hats?"

The women starring in that show as well as their friends Daffy Belvedere and Gidget Smurfitt have been an embarrassment to the town for decades. I don't need to remind everyone of the many stunts they have pulled in the past such as crashing Facebook, going to a nudist colony, and so on.

"For this reason, I ask the City Council to approve a motion to censor Babs Neauxgeaux, Lilly White, Lizzie Sherbert as well as Daffy Belvedere and Gidget Smurfitt… who are no telling where… for their outrageous behavior, both in their TV show and off screen as well. By off screen, I mean their streak at the Georgia-Florida football game in October in which Daffy Belvedere and Gidget Smurfitt also participated. I also ask the Council to approve another motion that Thomasville does not believe Area 53 exists and that there are no UFOs and aliens being hidden in this Area 53 and that this is just a hoax… another one of them conspiracy theories on the Internet. Thank you for allowing me to present these motions."

Mayor Flamingo said, "Thank you. As y'all just heard, Mitzi Merchant has proposed a motion to censure Babs Neauxgeaux, Lilly White, Lizzie Sherbert, Daffy Belvedere, and Gidget Smurfitt. I call for discussion, beginning with Councilmember Toddie Wurlitzer.

Wurlitzer said, "I agree with Mitzi. Everybody knows about Babs' obsession with weird stuff. She's been into strange stuff ever since she was a little girl. I remember when she was into them poltergeists after she saw that movie and had that man from Tennessee come down here and 'smudge' her house."

"Smudge? What is that?"

"He put this awful smelling stuff in a bunch of pots and placed them on her lawn all around her house and set them on fire. They smoked everything up. He said it cleansed her property of the poltergeist."

Dr. Maybry asked, "Did it work?"

"How the hell would I know? All I know is it stunk up my house for days, and I live two doors down across the street."

Mayor Flamingo said, "Councilmember Ted Maybry."

Dr. Maybry said, "We all know that Babs is eccentric. Take her belief that the Earth has twelve moons. And she runs around all the time talking about her Zodiac. Give me a break. Her Facebook page has a new conspiracy theory every week. Before she got her TV show, most people in Thomasville thought she was just an eccentric old woman. Now she's spouting all her weird notions in front of the rest of the country. I sadly have to agree with Mitzi. She is an embarrassment to Thomasville."

"Councilmember Troy Seconell."

Seconell said, "I have it on good authority that Babs has been investigated by the CIA, the FBI, and the National Security Agency for several run-ins with the authorities. Everyone knows that Babs and those other Real Widows were the cause of the recent Facebook outage. She supposedly did something when she was touring the Colonial Pipeline Worldwide Backup Distribution Control Center that destroyed the potato crop in Germany a couple of years ago. This woman is a menace to society and an embarrassment to Thomasville. The idea that there is an Area 53 with little green men is preposterous."

"Councilmember Chastity Knott."

Knott said, "Babs Neauxgeaux has gone too far this time. I can only imagine what the rest of the country must think about Thomasville. It shames me to think that this woman represents our fair city on national TV. The fact that she visits a fortune teller every month says all that needs to be said. Why Daffy and the others associate with her is beyond me. My garden shed mysteriously blew up one night about a month ago. I cannot prove it, but I believe it was the result of one of Babs' voodoo rituals. She even had the gall to perform one of her voodoo rituals on that first *Real Widows* show."

Mayor Flamingo said, "We just heard a lot about Babs Neauxgeaux's kooky behavior, and having known her all my life, I believe all of it is true. Except for the part about Babs and the others streaking the Georgia-Florida game. I watched that game, and to me it looked like it *was* the Kardashians running naked across that football field. Although I wouldn't put it past the Babs and the other Real Widows to do something like that. Beyond that, these five women have been associated with so many wacky stunts over the last decade that I think it is appropriate to consider Missus Merchant's motions. Anyway, would someone like to propose a vote on Mitzi's two motions?"

Councilmember Maybry said, "I would, Your Honor. I propose the City Council censure Babs Neauxgeaux, Daffy Belvedere, Gidget Smurfitt, Lilly White, and Lizzie Sherbert for the shame brought on Thomasville by their past outrageous behavior and their TV show *The Real Widows of Thomasville*."

"A motion to censure the Thomasville residents Babs Neauxgeaux, Daffy Belvedere, Gidget Smurfitt, Lilly White, and Lizzie Sherbert for their outrageous behavior and for their TV show *Real Widows of Thomasville* has been proposed. These residents include. Each member of the council will now vote by saying either Yea or Nay. Councilmember Toddie Wurlitzer."

"Yea."

"Councilmember Ted Maybry."

"Yea."

"Councilmember Troy Seconell."

"Yea."

"Councilmember Chastity Knott."

"Yea."

Mayor Flamingo said, "I also vote Yea which makes the motion unanimous. We will now vote on Mitzi Merchant's second motion to affirm that the City Council of Thomasville rejects the idea that an Area 53 exists and is used by the Federal government to hide UFOs and transgender aliens. Would someone like to propose such motion?"

Councilmember Maybry said, "Your Honor, I propose that this City Council emphatically reject the idea that the Federal government hides UFOs and aliens in an Area 53 and that an Area 53 in fact does not exist."

"Each member of the council will now vote by saying either Yea or Nay beginning with Councilmember Toddie Wurlitzer."

"Yea."

“Councilmember Ted Maybry.”

“Yea.”

“Councilmember Troy Seconell.”

“Yea.”

“Councilmember Chastity Knott.”

“Yea.”

Mayor Flamingo said, “And I also vote Yea which makes the motion unanimous. Accordingly, the Real Widows of Thomasville have been censured and the City Council rejects their assertion that Area 53 exists. Next agenda item.”

Chapter 23

Friday, November 7th, 11:35 AM, EST

Babs finished reading the rest of the *Post* article aloud then put her iPad down. The Casserole Ladies ate lunch at Henderson's, unaware that City Council had just voted to censure them. Lizzie said, "Looks like the Federal government knows about us. No telling what they're gonna do to us."

People sometimes make hasty decisions which they later regret. This appeared to be the case with these ladies. As the wise man said, "And he who hurries his footsteps errs." [Proverbs 19:2] These ladies' decision-making process now resembled a sixty-meter sprint.

"I look awful in horizontal stripes," Lilly said.

"Remember how Gidget told us that studies have shown horizontal stripes actually make you look thinner," offered Lizzie.

"Then why do I have so many vertical-striped clothes?"

Lizzie shook her head and said, "You don't have to worry about wearing stripes in jail. They wear solid orange in Federal prisons."

"Shoot! That don't do me no good either. Orange ain't in my personal color palette. They should give prisoners a choice among several colors of jumpsuits."

Babs had been semi-tuned out during this exchange. A sad look came over her face. "Spending my last days in jail ain't the way I planned on spending my senior years. I don't have that many years left. You know, when I was thirty, I'd jump in and out of the shower, blow dry my hair, and I was ready to go in ten minutes max. Nowadays, it's like a major construction project. After I get out of the shower, I got to put Aveeno body lotion on most of my skin, then I got to put CeraVe on the heels and soles of my feet, then Guerlain face cream for my face. And if I got hemorrhoids that day, I got to put Preparation H in my butt. Finally, there's Nu Derm for the liver spots on my hands. What used to take ten minutes nowadays takes over thirty—"

"What's your daily lotion routine got to do what to wear in Federal prison?" asked Lizzie.

"I… I forget where I was going with it. That happens to me more and more nowadays. I guess it's just another sign of approaching senility… It just that takes so much longer to shower nowadays than it did when I was thirty… because of having to put on all them creams and lotions. Oh, yeah… that's where I was going. It takes so long to shower and all that nowadays, and I bet they don't give older prisoners like me nearly enough time to do what I gotta do to make myself presentable like I do now, so it ain't really gonna matter whether I wear orange or stripes…"

Lizzie nodded sarcastically. "Oh, the horror of not being presentable in the Federal pen."

Lilly put her phone down. She had been reading the Post article. "Notice something a little fishy about that article?"

"Yeah, that guy Johnson should have mentioned that even though *Real Widows* is not a reliable source of information, it is a reliable source of gossip."

"No, not that. They denied existence of 'Area 53 in northwest Florida.' No one ever mentioned the location of Area 53 in last night's episode."

"You're right!" Babs said. "Then there must be something in northwest Florida, or why would they mention it when we didn't?"

"How are you coming with your planning on getting into Area 53?" Lizzie asked.

"I meet with the show's program director and the editor at four o'clock today. They're flying in from Hollywood," Babs said.

The door to Henderson's opened, and Mitzi and Stoney walked in. They had heard Babs, Lilly, and Lizzie were having lunch there and wanted to be the first to tell them about the City Council's resolutions. Mitzi intently looked around, spotted them, and beelined to their table with Stoney in tow.

"I'm surprised y'all are showing your faces in public after what just happened." Haughtiness dripped from Mitzi's words.

"I'm surprised you're showing your face in public," said Lizzie. "They have laws against public nuisance, which your face definitely is."

Mitzi said, "At least, *we* haven't been censured by the Thomasville City Council."

"Give the Council a little time. You know how slow bureaucracies are in doing the right thing. What nonsense are you talking about now?"

Stoney said, "The City Council just unanimously censured the three of you and Daffy and Gidget."

"What for?" asked Babs.

"What do you think?" asked Mitzi. "For the embarrassment brought down on Thomasville by all y'all's past antics and that stupid show. They also unanimously rejected your stupid idea that Area 53 exists. They want the rest of this country to know that Thomasville don't believe there's UFOs and transgender extraterrestrials in Area 53!"

Lizzie shook her head. "You can always count on politicians doing something dumb."

Chapter 24

Sunday, November 9th, 11:59 PM, CST

Thus, it came to pass that the Casserole Ladies sat in Babs' Escalade outside Elgin Air Force Base in northwest Florida at midnight. A six-foot high chain link fence topped with razor-sharp concertina wire and posted with ominous warning signs faced them. The brooding black forest beyond the fence signaled danger with menacing animal sounds. Only fools would enter such peril. To make matters worse, they were about to embark on the boldest misadventure they had ever undertaken *without* Daffy and Gidget, the brains of the quintet. But assertions had been made, and reputations were now at risk. To not undertake this misadventure would expose all of them to shame and ridicule. These women were Southerners, for whom reputation is paramount. Nevertheless, gloom pervaded the air like a thick fog. It is often easier saying something beforehand than doing it when the time comes.

"How we ever gonna get over a fence with that many volts in it?" Babs asked.

"I knew this was a bad idea from the git-go," Lilly said.

"Not according to Madame Cassandra," Babs said. "She gave me the green light on this… uh what did we decide to call what we're gonna do tonight?"

"I think it starts with the word 'cluster' and ends with a dirty word," said Lizzie. "We're going to have to accept looking like fools and liars, tuck in our tails, and get this tank back on the road to Thomasville."

"Better that we look like fools and liars than go to jail," said Lilly. "Besides, orange ain't in my color palette."

"It's not too late. If y'all want to bail on me, I'd understand," said Babs. "Orange ain't my favorite color either, but after what the Thomasville City Council did to us Friday, ain't no way I'm not going over that fence."

Lizzie's smile disappeared as she said, "We could do some serious jail this time, Ladies. How did I ever let myself get into this kind of a… this kind of a snafu?"

"I know I just said that it's better to look like fools and liars than to go to jail for breaking into a top-secret facility like this one here," Lilly said. "But I'm starting to agree with Babsie."

"Agreeing with Babs? You sure you feel okay?"

"I feel fine except that I'm pissed off… sorry, I forgot myself. I'm mad now that I think about the City Council's resolutions censuring us last Friday. We can't let that stand without at least trying to prove whether or not Area 53 exists. If we don't at least try to prove it, everyone will think Babs, and by inference you and me, were all lying for ratings."

"I wasn't lying for ratings. Area 53 does exist. And the feedback from someone at the Council meeting was that Mitzi says I'm saying this stuff because I'm old and I got dementia." Babs sighed and wistfully said, "Maybe she's right."

Lizzie rolled her eyes. "Look, maybe we at least somehow sneak in, take a few videos, then sneak back… real quick. We could even admit on the next episode that there was no Area 53 with UFOs, but because we truly *believed* it existed, we tried to break in and document it on film. That will at least show the City Council and Thomasville that we believed what we said on our show Thursday night and weren't lying just for ratings. The more I think about that censure, ain't no way I'm *not* going over that fence with you Babsie."

Babs nodded. "We will look like grifters if we don't at least try something after what was said on TV."

"But I do look awful in orange," Lilly said.

"Anyone have a Xanax?" asked Babs, then added. "I am getting too old for this sort of thing."

Lizzie said, "Me too. Here we are in the middle of the night when we could be asleep at home in our own beds instead of looking at nothing but pure pitch blackness with God knows what kind of varmints out there—"

Startled by sudden rapid knocking on the window, the ladies screamed. It was Cordell. So busy fretting, they failed to notice his approach. He asked, "Are you ladies gonna gab all night, or are we making a TV show? Tim and Allen are almost ready to start filming."

Parked next to Babs' Escalade was a Ford panel van. The two cameramen busied themselves prepping their equipment as they stood outside the opened side-doors of the vehicle.

Lizzie rolled down her window. "Well, we were just shooting the breeze waiting for y'all to let us know when to start."

"Where are Kim and Alexis?" asked Babs. They were two female members of the *Real Widows* four-person camera crew.

"They're with the Jailbirds," Cordell said, referring to the ladies' thirteen cellmates, with whom they spent a night in Duval jail after their streak a month ago. "They just texted me that everyone's at the main gate and just about ready to start. Hop on out. We want to get some video of y'all getting ready to go snipe hunting."

"Don't you dare call this a snipe hunt," Babs said, indignant at the reference to an old practical joke. It was sometimes pulled on naïve people who were left in the woods at night by themselves to catch a nonexistent animal called a snipe. "We *are* gonna meet an alien. Madame Cassandra foretold we would."

"Since we can't call it a snipe hunt, it is okay if we call it a unicorn hunt?" asked Lizzie.

Cordell looked at Tim and Allen. "I want both of you to get low angle shots of each of the girls stepping down out of this gargantuan." He then turned to the ladies. "Each of you exit, one at a time. As you step down, look at the camera as if you mean business. You're ready to go hunting."

Tim positioned himself to film those exiting from one side of the Escalade, while Allen did the same on the other side. Babs climbed out first, speaking to Cordell, "We knew we had to look our best on camera, so we drove over to Cordova Mall in Pensacola earlier today and went shopping. They got a Dillard's."

"Good thinking," Cordell said. Nighttime darkness prevented Babs from seeing his eyes roll upward.

"We've been having second thoughts about doing this," Babs said, stepping down and looking like a model for a *Duck Dynasty* fashion show. She wore a White + Warren Camouflage Hoodie that combined light and dark shades of grey with black for a subtle camouflage look. It coordinated with her Sketchers camo sneakers. Both hoodie and sneakers used a traditional Woodland camouflage pattern. However, Babs lost points on her choice of leggings. Color-wise they complemented the other components of her ensemble, but their MARPAT digi-camo pattern did not. Score: 6.0 out of 10.

Cordell said, "Ladies, please calm down. We're gonna pull this thing off. This will break all records for audience share for a TV reality show. I'm expecting an Emmy out of this episode."

"We won't be able to watch the Emmys if they don't have TV in prison," Lilly said as she stepped down from the mammoth SUV. Unlike her companions, she avoided any attempt to blend in with the nighttime forest environment. Instead, she chose clothes complementing her personal color palette. Her camouflage Marella top mixed maroon, coral pink, and sage green over a light pink background. She mated that with leggings containing hot pink, carnation, and magenta in a similar camouflage pattern. Although her Sperry Saltwater boots had no camouflage pattern in them, their solid Rose Oat color perfectly complemented the rest of her outfit. Score: 7.8 out of 10.

"There's no way the network's lawyers will let y'all go to jail. It's like I said before—no way five older women are going to jail for exercising their First Amendment journalistic rights," said Cordell.

"Even if they can't arrest us for breaking into a classified facility, they'll probably lock us up on a crime of fashion charge," said Lizzie wearing a Salvatore Ferragamo camouflage shirt. Although she did not particularly like the shirt, Lizzie could not resist 45% off. Her crime of fashion arose from a mishmash of colors. The shirt combined periwinkle and sky blue with black and a color the price tag labeled as asparagus green. The four bold blues in her Nike Camo leggings clashed terribly with the colors of the shirt, especially its asparagus green. She chose Skechers Max Cushioning shoes in delightful colors of blue and lavender that unfortunately failed to rescue her overall color choices. Score: 4.7 out of 10.

Cordell laughed politely at her unoriginal 'crime of fashion' joke and said, "Calm down, and take some deep breaths. Y'all will be fine." Cordell looked up from his phone. "Kim just texted. They've started the protest."

The gameplan included a diversion. Gidget's Oscar the alligator diversion at the Florida-Georgia game in October worked so well—except for all five ladies getting caught and arrested—that the producer wanted to use another diversion for their Area 53 break in. This consisted of having the Jailbirds stage a demonstration in front of the main gate to Elgin Air Force Base, the supposed location of

Area 53 in northwest Florida. This would cause security resources to be diverted from other areas of the base to assist in controlling the protestors. Accordingly, security personnel would likely be less prevalent in those areas the ladies would be hiking. Cordell also figured the protest would make a good secondary storyline.

The Jailbirds agreed to the risky task primarily for two reasons. First, the ethnically diverse women had bonded with the rich old white women during their short prison time together. The Casserole Ladies' sincerity, a trait all too uncommon, won them over. More importantly, Lilly got all of them out of jail as the Sheriff of Duval County was one of her old college boyfriends.

"I wish we could see them," Babs said.

"You can. Everyone, come over here," Cordell said as he led them to the van. With both side-doors opened wide, he pointed to an array of TV monitors and control panels inside. "We've got feeds from all four cameras into these monitors. Look at those two, and you'll see Kim's and Alexis' camera feeds. Let me turn up the sound."

They saw a fifteen-foot high by thirty-foot wide solid dark grey wall sporting the stylized Air Force logo atop the words 'United States Air Force' and below that 'Elgin Air Force Base'. Below that in smaller letters, the words 'Main Gate' appeared. This wall flanked the gate itself—in reality a four-lane roadway—while a similar wall flanked the other side of the road. Four uniformed Air Force Security personnel, each armed with M-16 assault rifles and 9mm automatic pistols, stood guard. They did so behind a series of three-foot high concrete Jersey wall barriers anchored in the four-lane road leading to the gate. Anchored in a staggered pattern, incoming traffic had to slow down and maneuver through them to enter the base.

"Look, there's Kanesha," Lilly said, pointing to one of the TV monitors.

Kanesha held up a professionally printed sign 'FREE THE ALIEN' while leading the other Jailbird protestors among the Jersey wall barriers. Behind her, Brianna strutted with the sign 'ALIEN RIGHTS' swaying back and forth. Behind her shouting protest slogans, Latonya, Ebony, Isabella, Pink, Jada, Frigerator, Angie, Peggy, Delphine, Butterfly, and Juanita each carried one of the following signs:

NO ALIEN IS ILLEGAL

DON'T GITMO AREA 53

ALIEN AMNESTY

WE ♡ ALIENS

MAKE ELGIN A SANCTUARY BASE

ALIENS ARE DREAMERS TOO

SUPPORT ALIEN RIGHTS

ADOPT AN ALIEN

AREA 53 TRANSPARENCY

WELCOME MISTER ALIEN

AMERICANS FOR ALIENS

Cordell said, "After he and Babs finished their plan on Friday, my producer flew into Jacksonville yesterday to meet with the Jailbirds. All of them were eager to help you girls. He rented an RV, bought a case of Colt .45 malt liquor, and drove them here today. Had those signs printed at Office Depot. Aren't they great?"

"The Air Force doesn't know what it's up against," said Lizzie. She left her thoughts on the wisdom of any plan in which Babs had a hand unsaid.

Lilly said, "I wonder if any of them Jailbirds would like to trade places?"

Chapter 25

Monday, November 10th, 12:20 AM, CST

"I wonder how Pink gets that dye job without an EPA permit." Lizzie referred to the Jailbird's pink spiked hairdo.

Babs nodded. Referring to another Jailbird, she said, "Looks like Frigerator has put on a few more pounds since… What's it been, almost a month since we spent the night in jail with them?" The woman's width almost matched her height.

"I wouldn't want to be an MP trying to arrest her," said Lilly.

"That's one of the reasons I hoped she would be able to make it. I just love Frigerator. I remember she was the first to accept us," said Babs.

The Casserole Ladies-Jailbirds interactions during their night in jail together were a sociologist's dream come true. Initially, the thirteen hardened criminals bullied the five newcomers. Kanesha called them a 'bunch a raw meat.' All the Jailbirds exhibited menacing behavior toward them until Brianna made a disparaging reference to Frigerator's excessive weight. Babs, naturally sympathetic to other people with weight problems, expressed empathy with the large black woman. This caused a seismic change in Frigerator. She immediately accepted the newcomers as fellow cons, thereby making it okay for the other Jailbirds to do so. The Casserole Ladies regaled the Jailbirds throughout the night with humorous stories about their quest for male companionship. By the time all were released the next morning, both groups of women had become lifelong friends.

Two monitors carrying the camera feeds showed several Air Force vehicles pull up and unload more security personnel. They dispersed, making a perimeter around the protestors who continued their shouting and marching without missing a beat. The security personnel took no further actions and simply remained in place.

"I bet they are waiting for reinforcements before taking any action," Cordell said.

Babs nodded. "That's the way we planned it. Your producer figured the Air Force would be sensitive to protests, especially from these folks. They can't just start hauling them off. They don't know that we told the girls to get back into the RV and leave the minute it looks like the MPs are gonna take them into custody. Your producer expected security would draw personnel from around the base, enough to deplete the remote areas like this one."

"And we need to take advantage of it while we can. Listen up. Tim and Allen will be carrying backpacks with extra flashlights, rope, an extra handheld GPS, spare camcorders, and some other tools you might need to get into Area 53. They'll be filming most of the time y'all are walking. The gameplan is that Tim will stick with Babs like glue and film her as she's the one this whole thing is about. Allen will film Lilly and Lizzie. For God's sake, don't get separated. Stay together. This is some pretty wild country with dangerous creatures, so you don't want to get separated. Tim and Allen have pistols."

Babs opened an Alfie Leather Bag and pulled out a Sig Sauer P238. "Me too."

"Better keep that pistol in your hand. I bet all the lizards out there are gonna try to mate with that handbag." Lizzie's comment alluded to the bag's glossy green patent leather color.

"You're one to talk," Babs said, firing back at Lizzie's Small Solfernino Shoulder Bag. Its spotted leopard calf hair and YSL monogramed clasp made a statement, although one not suited to the current situation. "I bet every bobcat in these woods is gonna be after you."

"Let 'em come. I got my Defender," Lizzie said. She opened her bag and extracted a snub-nosed revolver. This revolver's cylinder was chambered for five rounds of either .410 shotgun shells, .45 caliber bullets, or a combination of the two.

Not to be outdone, Lilly reached into her very large Longchamp Crossbody Hobo bag and pulled out a small pink .38 caliber automatic pistol. "I got mine."

"Tsk, tsk. Your pistol doesn't match your handbag," Lizzie said referring to the bag's cognac color.

"I know. I was in such a hurry to leave Thomasville that I couldn't find one of my pink handbags."

"I'm sure Tim and Allen feel a lot more secure knowing all you ladies are packing," Cordell said.

A sudden movement in the darkness thirty feet away caught everyone's attention. Lilly and Babs screamed, the latter unintentionally dropping her Sig Sauer P238. A large being approached from the direction of the fence line, zipping up its pants. As it moved closer, its hairy arms, thick neck, and wide belly became distinguishable. It wore a black T-shirt imprinted with a fluorescent skull-and-crossbones and in large fluorescent letters 'Eat or Die' and 'Cootie's Carryout' below.

As the being approached, its identity became apparent. Unable to mask the disgust in her voice, Lizzie said, "Oh my God!"

"Hey, y'all!" called Sonny Biskit.

Cordell said, "I hired an ex-Special Forces guy that I've used on other TV projects to help you get through these woods, but he broke his ankle jumping off a roof yesterday. I was frantic to find someone to take his place but couldn't get any of other special ops people on such short notice. My producer was on his way to the Thomasville airport to catch his flight to Jacksonville when he stopped off at Cootie's for a Coke and saw Sonny there. He told Sonny about our dilemma, and Sonny volunteered to help you girls get to Area 53."

"And just how is he going to do that? I didn't know they made a four-wheel drive Hoveround," said Lizzie.

"Hey now—" said Sonny.

"Hold on," interrupted Cordell. "Calm down. Sonny told us that he spends a lot of time in the woods hunting and fishing and can make his way through just about any kind of terrain."

"Cordell, the man barely made it through twenty minutes at the paintball range. How's he gonna hike for hours through that stuff?" Babs pointed at the fence.

Lizzie asked, "Even more important, how are *we* gonna hike hours through that stuff?"

"Ladies, y'all may not last a hundred yards after you cross over the fence. It doesn't matter. Tim and Allen will get enough to piece together a jungle expedition to impress the average viewer. Have a little faith in Hollywood film editing. Come on. Let's get you girls over the fence," Cordell said.

Lizzie shook her head. "Getting my lard butt over that ain't gonna be easy."

Cordell laughed, turned, and led them to the only other vehicle parked nearby, a flatbed tow truck. A small Genie bucket lift sat on the flatbed. These are often used by tree trimmers, firefighters, painters, and such when they must work in high places. The lift consisted of a bucket into which two people could stand, attached to a set of long articulating arms. The arms were attached to a motorized turret mounted on a small four-wheel chassis. Cordell signaled to the driver of the flatbed, and ten minutes later the bucket lift sat in front of fence.

"Our driver is going to lift each of you over the fence and place you on the ground on the other side. After he's done that, he's gonna load the bucket lift back onto the flatbed and high tail it out of here. He's going to park in one of the strip malls in Niceville until I phone him to come back here to pick you up. Any questions?"

"Babs wants to ride over in the bucket with Sonny," Lizzie said. "It'll be like a date on the Ferris wheel at the county fair. They want to get married on the ride back over the fence."

"But that fence is electrified, ain't it?" asked Lilly.

Cordell said, "We've insulated the articulating arms so that if they do touch the razor wire, no current will be transmitted to the lift. Remember, I'll be here in the van the entire time monitoring y'all on the camera feeds from Tim and Allen as well as Kim and Alexis. Y'all can call me at any time if you need to. Everyone remembered to bring their phones, I hope."

Stunned at his last statement, Lilly said, "You gotta be kidding. Two things a woman never leaves home without are her phone and credit card."

Cordell shook his head. "My bad. Any questions?"

Lizzie asked, "How are we gonna know which way to hike? I mean, we don't even know if there is an Area 53 somewhere in there."

"Why do you think I was so eager to have y'all accept the Mammas challenge? The special operations guy I planned on sending with you inside Elgin used to go on training exercises here. Army Rangers and Green Berets conduct training exercises on this base year-round," said Cordell. He did not add that the Army chose the base as a training location precisely because of its dense jungle and wildlife that included snakes, panthers, and wild boar hogs.

"But which way do we go inside the woods to get to Area 53?" asked Babs.

"My guy tells me there is a highly classified area inside Elgin officially designated as the Near Earth Object Detection and Holding Compound. It's part of the new Space Command. He has some contacts from his Army days that work on base. They tell him this compound is known on base as Area 53. It's approximately five acres in size with a chain link inside a perimeter fence topped with concertina. He faxed me a map of the base. He annotated the most likely location of Area 53 as well as the route he recommends you follow." Cordell unfolded a map and laid it out on the top surface of the turret. He began pointing to sections of the map. "Area 53 is located here. Here's the way you'll be going to get there. You folks need to stay together. I don't want any of you getting lost."

"And you expect Sonny to lead us all the way to Area 53?" Lizzie's expression said it all.

"Y'all forget that I practically live in the woods come deer season. Turkey season too," said Sonny. He neglected to mention that most of this time was spent sitting twelve feet above the ground in a tree stand, waiting for deer and turkeys to come to him. "I think I can find my way around in anything."

"Can you find your way inside the Tallahassee Mall?"

"Oh, that's funny. I think Cordell's Special Forces guy has got a pretty good route mapped out for us."

"Maybe we'll get lucky and get captured early on," said Lilly.

"And as a bonus, we'll get three hots and a cot," Lizzie said referring to the old military slang for three meals and a bed, "for seven to ten years, courtesy of Leavenworth."

"It's like I told you. I've got the network's lawyers on speed dial. The network is not going to let their three hottest stars on the highest rated TV reality show spend one night in jail," Cordell said. "And if you do get caught before getting into Area 53, Tim and Allen will at least get some good video for the next episode. It'll be dynamite on TV. Any more questions before we lift you gals over the fence?"

"Do you have an EMT on speed dial? My heart is probably gonna stop halfway over that tall fence," said Lizzie.

"Do you have a hairdresser on speed dial?" Lilly asked. "This night air is ruining my hairdo."

After the group was deposited on the other side of the fence, Cordell watched until they disappeared into the woods. The tow truck driver returned his bucket lift to the flatbed and drove off to Niceville. Cordell climbed into the back of the van, closed both doors, and began watching the monitors. Fixated for the next twenty minutes, he never heard noise outside the van until its doors were suddenly flung wide open. Two men stood outside, both wearing identical black suits, white shirts, and black ties. One sartorial accessory stuck out. Each held a submachine gun, pointed at Cordell. He froze, his mouth too dry to say anything.

One of the men said, "Don't do nothing stupid."

Chapter 26

Monday, November 10th, 1:05 AM, CST

The forest looked intimidating from inside Babs' Escalade. It turned out to be worse as the ladies walked through it. Scattered pine trees rose amidst scrub oaks and saw palmetto bushes. Saw is in the plant's name for a reason; it has sharp, hard leaves that can easily puncture a person's skin if not careful. Scrub oaks also offer their own form of misery to travelers. These are small bushy oak trees whose low gnarly branches produce a lot of narrow, stiff leaves that make maneuvering among a cluster of them difficult. The *Real Widows* group contested a tight forest canopy from the ground up. The scrubby flatlands of northwest Florida also provide an ideal environment for wild animals. It provides them with ample cover in which to hide from both predators and prey.

Elgin's grounds maintenance crew kept ten yards between the fence and the woods clear-cut for security reasons. The ladies traversed that part easily, but once inside the dense foliage, their expensive tops and spandex leggings took a beating. What looked great in the store did not work so well in the woods. Shortly after entering, disaster struck.

"Ow!" Babs said. "These palmetto bushes are ruining my leggings."

Two other voices rang out, shouting in unison, "Mine too!"

"Camouflage doesn't give us much protection from palmetto spikes, does it? I'm beginning to question our wardrobe choices," Lizzie said. Sometimes, better late than never is not true.

Tim and Allen filmed the carnage. They used full spectrum night vision camcorders, allowing them to videotape in total darkness by means of infrared light. Think *The Blair Witch Project* filmed using technology unavailable in 1999.

Sonny led the expedition while Babs and Tim brought up the rear. Tim walked around her as he filmed. Allen did the same with Sledge and the other four ladies. Both cameramen had a difficult task given the thick brushy understory.

Allen focused on Lizzie and said, "Don't forget to smile."

"Smile yourself," said Lizzie. "And while you're at it, kiss my—"

A loud screech preempted her obscenity.

"What was that?" asked Lilly.

“I don’t know, but I’m getting my gun,” Babs said.

Nighttime darkness amplified the sounds made by latches and zippers of three designer handbags being opened simultaneously.

“I knew we never should have come on this wild goose chase,” Lilly complained as she frantically rummaged in her Hobo bag.

“This ain’t no wild goose chase,” Babs said. “Madame Cassandra told me that the spirits spoke in my favor.”

“Cassandra stole that line from Bullwinkle,” Lizzie said, referring to the bit where the cartoon character appears as turbaned psychic reading a crystal ball.

The *Real Widows* group continued to grumble like this for the next twenty minutes. Afterwards, the serious whining began. Lilly said, “I didn’t realize it was gonna be this tough. I wish I’d stayed home.”

Lizzie nodded her agreement. “It’s like I said before. We should be home sleeping. Or maybe streaming *The Crown* on Netflix right now… and sipping Crown Royal.”

“What. You don’t like walking with snakes and panthers?” Babs said in a good example of when not to use sarcasm.

“I wish you hadn’t said that,” said Lilly.

“Ow!” Lizzie yelled after bumping into one of the pointed ‘teeth’ on a saw palmetto bush. “This stuff is downright dangerous.”

Babs said, “I wish we could’ve just driven onto this base.”

“And I thought you had camped out in the woods before.”

“Camped out? I never said I had camped out. I wouldn’t ever dream of camping out in my backyard, much less these or any woods.”

Lilly said, “Oh yes you did! You said you’d camped out before. You said on Friday that the woods around Area 53 probably wasn’t any worse than any of the other woods you’d camped out in Florida.”

“I never said I’d camped out in Florida.”

“Yes, you did. We all heard you.”

Babs said, “I believe what I said was that I had roughed it in Florida. Y’all was talking about how bad the woods around the base here might be, and someone said they’d never even camped out before, and I said I’d roughed it before… down in Florida.”

“So, exactly how did you ‘rough it’ in Florida if you didn’t ‘camp out’?” asked Lizzie.

“I was thinking about when Avery and I took the kids on that Jungle Cruise ride at Disney World in Orlando. Y’all know, the one where they take you and a bunch of other people on one of them small boats on that river that goes through a man-made jungle. That jungle stuff looks pretty realistic, you know. You see elephants that spray water at the boat from their trunks, pygmies, headhunters. There’s a rhinoceros chasing a couple of people up a totem pole. There’s crocodiles… Lordy, them crocodiles were so realistic looking that they scared the daylights out of little Mitchell. He was only three or four at the time. It was about ten years or so after Disney World opened up down there…” Babs paused her story, slowed her walking pace.

Babs’ abrupt pause prompted Lilly to ask, “What? Why’d you stop your story? Do you see anything in the woods?”

Don’t stop her from stopping a shaggy dog story, thought Lizzie, then looked around to see if something was following them. Seeing nothing, she said, “Why did you stop your story? Did you see something in the woods?”

“No, I didn’t see anything,” Babs said. “I… It just reminded me. That was almost forty years ago. Mitchell’s middle-aged now. It reminds me of how old I am. I’m getting too old to be doing crazy things like walking in these woods out here like this. Too old…”

Melancholy dripped from Babs’ words. Lizzie realized an intervention was needed before her friend fell into a fruitless death spiral of self-pity about her age. She said, “Oh, that’s all. For a minute you had me worried that I wasn’t going to hear what the point of your story is. Or is this just another one of your neverending stories with no point to it?”

The intervention worked. Babs resumed a faster pace of walking pace as she huffed, “Yes, smarty pants, there is a point, and if you’ll let me finish, you’ll hear it. Anyway, the boat we were riding in came real close to the crocodiles, and Mitchell started screaming his head off. But he loved seeing all them elephants bathing, especially the little baby elephants. We had to buy him a plastic elephant at the gift shop after we finished the ride. And the monkeys… he loved them too. Am I getting that ride confused with one of the rides we took at Six Flags? Does Disney World have monkeys in their jungle cruise ride or not? Anyway, them animals weren’t really animals. They was really just robots, but they looked so lifelike—”

“Lifelike? Sounds like Jeffrey,” Lilly said. Jeffrey was the name of the sexbot Babs purchased in September. Her incessant chatter after lovemaking caused poor Jeffrey to crash, never to power up again.

“You’re just being snippy, but that brings up a good point. What do they call animal robots? Jeffery was a sex robot, but they called him a sexbot. Do they call an animal robot an anibot? No, that don’t work. What about botimal? No, that don’t work either—"

“I think they call it animatronics,” said Lizzie.

“That’s a great name. Them animatronics looked so life like, you’d think you was in the jungle seeing a real animal—"

“Babs, walk a little slower, Sweetheart. It’s hard to keep you in focus talking while you’re moving that fast,” Tim said.

“You mean it’s hard to keep her in focus while her mouth is moving that fast,” said Lizzie.

“Ho, ho. Excuse me if I forget to laugh.” Babs stuck her tongue out as she slowed her pace. “Anyway, as I was gonna say, they got almost all the same kind of plants in that ride as they got in these here woods and even more. That reminds me, the funniest thing on that ride is when the guide on the boat says ‘There’s over 500 varieties of plants in this jungle, and I’d like to point some of them out to y’all.’ And then he points to a plant and says ‘There’s one.’ Then he points to a different plant and says ‘There’s that one.’ And then he points to another plant and says ‘There’s a different one over there.’ Avery and I laughed so hard that—”

“Okay, Babsie. We concede. You win. You are an expert on roughing it,” Lilly said. “Everyone be sure to stay up close. It’s like Cordell said. We don’t want to get separated.”

“Not casting aspersions on any one of us in particular,” Lizzie said, “but I don’t know that getting separated is such a bad idea.”

“We should have brought one of those ugly little things with the big tires that they use to ride in the woods. What do they call those things?”

“They call them Toyota Prius.”

“No silly. Besides, a Nissan Cube is much uglier than a Prius.”

“But a Kia Soul is uglier than a Nissan Cube.”

“They all look pretty ugly, but that’s not the vehicle I was thinking about,” said Lilly.

Sonny rescued Lilly and Lizzie from more boring conversation. He said, “Y’all mean ATVs, off-road vehicles. That is a great idea. It would be a lot easier to get to Area 53 in an ATV.”

“I was thinking more along the lines that we could hop in one right now and go back to the Escalade, not to Area 53.”

“We should have just had Cord lift the Escalade over the fence and rode in that,” Lizzie said as she struggled to move through a clump of fetterbushes.

Lilly said, “I don’t think even Babs’ Escalade could make it through this stuff.”

“We should have brought my little puppy. He can chew through anything. He ate a big chunk out of the carpet in one of my guest bedrooms the other day. This stuff would be like eating whipped cream to him.”

“That cute little thing. Eating carpet? I don’t believe it,” Lilly said.

“Believe it. His daddy was a John Deere bush hog.”

The chatter went on like this until Sonny raised his hand to call a halt. He turned and walked back past Allen, Lilly, and Lizzie then stopped. A worried look came over him. No one was behind Lilly and Lizzie. He said, “I wondered why I hadn’t heard Babs talking for a while. Babs! Tim! Y’all somewhere back there?!”

Chapter 27

Monday, November 10th, 1:45 AM CST

Tim concentrated on getting video of Babs. Cordell had drilled that priority into him prior to meeting up with the ladies. "Don't let her out of your sight. I want everything she says and does on tape," he said. "She's my goldmine." This meant maneuvering around thick bushes and bramble while keeping a moving target in focus. He also made sure he was close enough to pick up audio from her wireless microphone, recognizing her chatter would charm TV viewers. Babs continued her non-stop narration of the rest of the Jungle Cruise story as she maneuvered around fetter- and palmetto bushes. Nighttime darkness did not help. The end result was neither of them realized they had violated Cordell's strict instructions about not getting separated until it was too late.

Tim stopped moving and interrupted her story. "Babs… Babs. Where's the rest of the group?"

Attempting to untangle herself from a buttonsage shrub, Babs looked up. "Ain't they in front of us?"

"I don't see them."

"Oh shoot! They probably missed the best part of my story."

"Best part of your story?"

"Yeah. The part where the Avery got his foot caught in the robot alligator's mouth… I thought the guide would never stop laughing. Little Mitchell was so scared that robot alligator was eating his daddy's foot. He didn't know it wasn't a real alligator, that it was just a robot alligator. What would you call a robot alligator? Botgator or allibot? Rogator? I wish Gidget or Daffy was here. They are always good knowing about those kind of things—"

"Babs! Babs. It doesn't matter what you call it. We're lost."

"Silly, just call them on your phone."

Tim pulled out his iPhone. Several attempts to call Cordell and the other ladies failed. "No luck. Something's wrong with cell reception out here."

"Let me try." Babs also got 'Service Unavailable' messages when she tried calling. "What we gonna do?"

At that point, a clump of fetterbushes nearby began to tremble. Fetterbush is an evergreen bush native to the moist soil of northwest Florida. It grows anywhere from three to six feet tall and has very dense foliage. Animals generally travel around it, which is one reason it is sometimes used as a hedge. Suddenly, these fetterbushes seemed to separate, and a large part of the clump emerged from the rest. Creature-like, plant-like, terrifying—words fail to describe what it was. Too frightened to think to pull out their pistols, Babs and Tim froze. Fetterbushes do not move! Was it an alien?!

The thing's emergence from the clump of fetterbushes mimicked a cell dividing into multiple cells when it reproduces. One of the new 'cells' now stood apart from the others. Over six feet tall and almost three feet wide, a solid mass of green fetterbush, no arms, no legs. It did appear to have four large, bulging 'eyes' located where a potential 'head' might be. Each eye contained neither iris nor pupil such as might be seen in a human being. Instead, the eye was a solid black circle, one and a half inches in diameter. All four eyes moved in a synchronized manner—up, down, and sideways—as if intently inspecting its prey. The creature slowly moved to a point five yards in front of Babs and Tim. They stood immobilized, although Tim retained sufficient mental capacity to remember to capture what happened next on video.

Her eyes fixed on the thing, Babs whispered to Tim, "Do you think it's one of them aliens?"

"I'm just trying to figure out whether it's animal, vegetable, or mineral," said Tim.

"Maybe it's one of them tree people like on *The X-Files*." Babs referred to an episode set in northwest Florida where Mulder and Scully were attacked by a mysterious tree-like humanoid with an ability to merge into a tree. She hesitantly held up her right hand, imitating Mister Spock's split-fingered Vulcan salute. "We come in peace."

The fetterbush replied with a similar salute and said, "Live long and prosper."

"Damn! Why can't the rest of the girls be here? I knew I was right all along. It's a real live alien from outer space."

An 'arm' partially separated from the bush, although remaining attached at a point where its 'shoulder' might be. The tip of the arm grasped its four eyes and flipped them up. Two human eyes stared at Babs and Tim. It said, "No ma'am. We're not aliens, although we're close. We're Army Rangers."

"Rangers! Like the Boy Scouts?"

"Uh… no Ma'am. We're more like a cult." The fetterbush turned his head and said, "Okay guys. Come on out."

The rest of the fetterbush clump separated into three parts. Each part had two arms and two legs. All three parts flipped up their four eyes which were actually night vision goggles. These were the GPNVG-18 models that had four lens tubes instead of two in order to provide a more panoramic field of view.

"What are y'all doing here?" asked Babs.

"I might ask you the same thing, but I already know the answer," the Ranger said.

"You do?"

"Yes Ma'am. We watched your show Thursday night."

"You did?"

"Yes Ma'am. We love your show. The show Thursday night was better than the first show. That food fight at Preble Hill was great. It reminded me of RASP training."

"RASP? What's that?"

"Ranger Assessment and Selection Program—eight weeks of pure hell."

"What are y'all doing here?"

"We're on a training exercise, Ma'am."

"What kind of exercise?"

"If I told you, I'd have to kill you."

"Well, we're trying to get to Area 53. Can y'all help us?"

"Follow me."

Chapter 28

Monday, November 10th, 1:55 AM, CST

Cordell watched and listened to Tim and Babs' fetterbush encounter in silence. He had not spoken a word since his two visitors interrupted him forty-five minutes ago. Neither had the visitors spoken after the initial command "Don't do nothing stupid" was followed by "Keep yer trap shut." They also watched the monitors intently while keeping their weapons pointed at him. Cordell's eyes nervously migrated between the monitors and his visitors. Audio was also being transmitted to the van so they could hear every word picked up by Tim's and Allen's camcorders. Cordell's anxiety had steadily increased as things unfolded, but it doubled when Babs got lost. *Don't tell me I'm losing my top star!* He had to act.

"I don't care what you say, I'm gonna call Babs," he said. Surprisingly, the black-suited men did nothing as he dialed her cell number. His phone displayed a 'Service Unavailable' message, and repeated tries yielded the same result. A keen observer would have detected traces of smiles on both black-suited men.

Both men wore identical black suits, white shirts, and black ties. Just like their clothing, their manner said that they were all business. They belonged to an organization whose history can be discovered by googling 'men in black'. Wikipedia documents UFO sightings as early as 1947 where those reporting the UFOs were subsequently visited by men in dark suits. These men sometimes advised those reporting not to talk about their sightings. Other times they threatened more serious consequences. The movie *Men In Black* traces its conception to these intimidations.

Allen and the two ladies did not see Sonny approaching until he stood before them and said, "I didn't find them. Cordell ain't gonna be happy with me." Sonny's biggest worry was money. Cordell had promised him half the fee he intended to pay his ex-special operations guy. Repeated attempts to call Cordell, Babs, and Tim had all received 'Service Unavailable' messages on everyone's phones. Sonny had subsequently backtracked their steps in an effort to locate Babs and Tim. Now, he returned empty-handed.

"Well, just get back out there and keep looking," said Lilly, in a commanding voice seldom heard by others. Actually, a commanding voice never heard by others.

"Look, I've got three of y'all to worry about, and I did see some good signs."

"What kind of good signs?"

"I backtracked to a point where I could see Babs and Tim's tracks. They apparently wandered around for a while and then met up with somebody. I should say somebodies—"

"Somebodies?" asked Lizzie.

"Yeah. Looked like four people. My guess is they ran into some military guys here on some sort of training mission. Probably Rangers. From the tracks and disruption of the foliage, I'd say these guys were camouflaged as a fetterbush clump. It looks like Babs and Tim began following them. I figured I better get back here and make sure I don't lose you guys."

"What do we do now?" asked Lilly.

"We could go back to Cordell," said Lizzie.

Sonny shook his head. "I don't like the thought of leaving Babs out here following a bunch of fetterbushes—even if they might be Rangers—and us hotfootin' it back to the van. We're not that far from Area 53 according to the map, and it looked to me like that's the direction the Rangers were headed."

"Let's go that way," said Lilly.

Though it seemed as if all three of the ladies might be headed in the right direction, Cordell's anxiety continued. *If things don't go just right, we could have the makings of a ratings disaster.*

Chapter 29

Monday, November 10th, 2:20 AM CST

Sonny felt terrible. When he first realized Babs had gotten separated, he silently cursed himself. He had overpromised Cordell—a fault bestowed on others all too often in his past—and now it had come back to bite him in the butt. It appeared Babs and Tim were following some sort of military small unit which was presumably on a training exercise. He hoped the two tenderfeet were in good hands and safe. Hope was about all he had at this point. At least they appeared to be headed in same direction as he was. Best of all would be if somehow everyone rendezvoused at the Near Earth Object Detection and Holding Compound. He believed Babs would ultimately be safe but dreaded Cordell's wrath if his group returned without her. *Have to kiss that fee goodbye. I never should've tuned her out during that stupid Disneyland story.* Little Mitchell's woes on the Jungle Cruise were too much for Sonny to bear.

One problem continued to plague them. All attempts to call Babs, Tim, and Cordell had flopped. Similar results came from attempts to call Kanesha and Frigerator. They kept getting 'Service Unavailable' messages on all their phones. Why?

After her last attempt, Lilly said, "I wish these iPhones worked. When you most need technology, it lets you down. I'd feel a lot better if we could talk to Babs."

"It's the soldiers Babs is with that you need to worry about. Her rambling can be challenging after the first ten minutes. Her shaggy dog stories should be banned by the Geneva Convention." Lizzie's attempt at humor failed to mask the worried tone in her voice.

"Sonny," Lilly pointedly asked, "are you sure Babs is with Rangers?"

He lied. "Yep. I could tell by the footprints in the mud. Them was made by Army combat boots. I'd recognize them anywhere after three years humpin' around in them. And I saw signs of where the Rangers had camouflaged themselves. Don't worry. She's in good hands with those good ole boys. Those Rangers will take good care of her." *I hope.*

Another problem arose. Babs was not the only person getting old. Age began to catch up with Lilly, Lizzie, and Sonny. Periodic stops to catch their breath became more frequent. Seldom used leg muscles burned. Backs began to ache. Joints were not in great shape either. All complained of sore feet. The ladies' whining steadily increased, and it grated more and more on Sonny's nerves. He tried tuning them out, apparently having learned nothing from losing Babs.

Lizzie said, "How did I ever let myself get into this kind of a snafu?" By Sonny's count, this was the seventh time she had said this since they began their journey.

"My feet are killing me. Can we stop for a while?" asked Lilly.

"Yes. Any more of this whining, and I'm gonna snort roach poison when I get home." Sonny pointed. "Looks like a clearing. We'll take five over there."

Lizzie ceremoniously flopped down on the ground as soon as they entered the clearing. Lilly found a relatively smooth oval rock about a foot and a half in length and foot high. A sly smile spread over Sonny's face as he watched her carefully lower her posterior onto the stone. She said, "This feels like heaven to my calves." All pulled out their canteens and sipped slowly as Sonny had advised. Lizzie then passed a flask of bourbon around from which they gulped rapidly.

Five minutes later, everyone was refreshed. Lizzie asked, "How much further?"

"About twenty minutes," said Sonny, "depending on how fast we walk."

"What do you know about this Near Earth thing?"

"Not much. Cordell's special ops guy says this Near Earth thing has only been here a couple of years. It isn't exactly a secret on base, but security around the area itself is tight. You have to have an official reason to get into it. It's considered top secret so personnel know they can be jailed if they talk about it outside of the base."

"Why all the secrecy about aliens and UFOs anyway? If there's people here from another planet, let us know so we can show them some Georgian hospitality," said Lilly. "I got a great recipe for peach cobbler that nobody's never not loved."

"Aliens' digestive systems will probably be different than ours," said Lizzie.

"Well… then we'll just have to figure out something else to serve them… chicken salad? There ain't nobody that don't love chicken salad."

"I bet chickens don't love chicken salad, but that's just idle speculation."

Sonny said, "Answer me this. Why would three reasonably sane women want to break into a secure federal facility?"

"You've got a pretty loose definition of sane," said Lizzie.

"I'm beginning to think that. What you're doing is no misdemeanor. It's a felony. Why are you risking jail?"

Lilly said, "Because we support each other. Babs and us backed Daffy when she lost a bet that meant we all had to streak the Georgia-Florida game last month. Now, me and Lizzie have to support Babs after she accepted a challenge to her veracity."

"You mean that wasn't the Kardashians doing the streaking?"

"Nope. It was us."

"I watched it with several other guys, and we were split fifty-fifty on whether it was the Kardashians or somebody else. I thought it *was* the Kardashians," Sonny said.

"You were wrong," said Lizzie. "It was the five of us."

Sonny nodded. *That explains why it looked like two of the Kardashians had put on a lot of weight.* He said, "It's beginning to make sense why you would risk going to jail over UFOs and aliens. You folks *are* crazy. You don't really think you'll find aliens and UFOs on this base, do you?"

"Babs thinks so. She believes in a lot of strange things. Once she gets her mind set on something, it don't do no good to try and convince her otherwise."

"I admire that. The boxer Sugar Ray Robinson, said… If you want to be a champ, you have to believe in yourself when nobody else does. That's Babs. But *why* does she have to believe in something as nutty as Area 53 inside an Air Force base?"

Lilly said, "The local newspaper and TV stations slammed her on this Area 53 business. They called it a hoax that only an eccentric like Babs would fall for. Mitzi and the other Mammas harassed her. The City Council even passed a resolution denying the existence of Area 53 and aliens. Didn't matter. Babs stood by her guns. We even tried to talk her out of doing this. I told her I thought Area 53 was just another Internet hoax. But Babs believes there is an Area 53 with aliens and UFOs in it. So, here we are."

"Allen, how long have you worked with Cordell?" Lizzie asked.

Allen lowered his camcorder and said, "About five years… on three or four projects."

"Seems like he's got a hit with *Real Widows*."

"He was desperate for a hit. It does look like he's struck gold with your show. He's on wife number five, and alimony's killing him."

"Sounds like a candidate to be my number five," said Lizzie. "But anyone not regularly going to Dribblers Anonymous meetings is a candidate to be my number five—"

Before Lizzie could finish, Lilly screamed and jumped up. The other ladies followed suit. Allen kept filming.

"What is it?!" asked Lizzie.

"That rock! It moved!" Lilly said pointing to her improvised seat.

"Ain't no rock," Sonny said. "It's a gopher."

"That ain't no gopher. Gophers are soft and furry. That thing was hard as a rock."

"That's because this gopher is a tortoise. They're called gopher tortoises or just gophers. They're native to northwest Florida."

"You knew I was sitting on a turtle, didn't you? Ho, ho. Excuse me if I forget to laugh."

Sonny smiled again. He had been wondering when the creature was going to wake up. "Let's head 'em up and move 'em out."

The whining resumed almost immediately once they continued walking. Sonny gritted his teeth. Lilly spoke first. "I don't know why we spent all that money on new clothes. These leggings look like a worn-out net off a shrimp boat."

"Look at my shoes," Lizzie said. "I'd be embarrassed to drop them off at Goodwill."

"Look at my nails. Ngo spent thirty minutes Friday doing them."

"Our nails look good compared to our hairdos. Bedhead on steroids."

"I never realized we were going to have to walk this far."

"When are we going to stop again?" asked Lizzie. "My back is killing me."

"Mine too. I think I'm getting a charley horse." The ladies even grumbled about the Mammas. Lilly said, "If it weren't for Mitzi and those damn Mammas, we wouldn't have to be going through all this torture."

"Sonny, I don't know how much more walking like this I can take," said Lizzie.

Sonny said, "Buck up, ladies. Remember, when the going gets tough, the tough get going."

Lizzie said, "Not us. We've always followed the alternate version of that saying. When the going gets tough, the girls go shopping."

"I'm with Lizzie," said Lilly. "We may have to stage a sit-down strike right here and now."

"If you girls don't behave yourselves, I'm gonna have to bend you over my knee."

"Me first!" said Lizzie. "Although it doesn't matter what the order is so long as you spank firmly and slowly."

Allen videoed their griping for another twenty minutes before Sonny raised his hand for a halt. "I think we're getting close."

Chapter 30

Monday, November 10th, 2:50 AM CST

The Alien escorted Babs and Tim inside the Near Earth Object Detection and Holding Compound. Their destination—the compound's Holding Facility—loomed before them. He wondered what the two Earthlings would think, and more importantly what the female would say, if they were aware of the enormous consequences ahead. Informing the host planet of the purpose of his visit was something never done. To do so would virtually eliminate spontaneity in their discourse, a critical element of the decision-making process.

The male said little as his function seemed to be relegated to documenting the female's activities. The female's non-stop chatter over the last twenty minutes had motivated the Alien's invitation to visit with him and the other two members of his Decision Group. Since his group's arrival three weeks ago, interactions with stale officials on Earth had been unhelpful in making their decision.

Discussions with representatives of the Earth's military and government organizations had left him and his companions frustrated, a feeling similar to that experienced on some other planets. Things went much better on planets where his group interacted randomly with beings who were representative of the population as a whole. This was not the case on Earth. Here they had dealt only with government officials—beings with no imagination, no passion, no energy. This female was obviously not a government official. She possessed all three. She might very well be the solution to the frustration experienced by the Alien and his companions.

Earth's representatives indicated they dealt with extraterrestrial visitors all the time. Perhaps this explained why their presentations to his Decision Group seemed rote and insincere. The words obfuscation and narcissistic also came to mind. The Alien felt confident this would not be the case with this female Earthling. Further spontaneous interaction with her would aid in his group's assessment of the planet's level of sophistication. This would be critical in making the correct recommendation—something on which Earth's future depended.

Babs knew the Alien as Monroe. She learned his name right after they met during a tortuous verbal exchange. She had introduced herself and Tim, then asked his name.

> *"XGttbzqnfdtkttt," he said.*
>
> *"Can you spell that out for me?" Babs asked.*
>
> *"X-G-t-t-b-z-q-n-f-d-t-k-t-t-t."*
>
> *"Your name has got more letters than I can say grace over. It probably would help if your name had some vowels in it."*
>
> *"Our alphabet has no vowels."*
>
> *"No vowels!? Well, I never! A language with no vowels. Does Japanese writing count? Does it have vowels? They are pretty useful, you know. Especially when you have a name like yours. Your name seems pretty hard to spell, although now that I think about it, it would probably be harder to spell with vowels. Too bad you don't have a nickname—"*
>
> *"In your language, my name would be pronounced Monroe."*
>
> *"Oh, I love that name. Monroe. We used to have a chipmunk in our back yard, and one of my little grandsons nicknamed him Monroe. I posted a picture of him on my Facebook page. He just looked like a Monroe... the chipmunk, not my grandson." Babs scrunched her face as she stared intently at the Alien. Viewed from several angles, the Alien in many ways looked very human-like. "You don't look like a Monroe."*

Babs pointed to the Holding Facility looming before them. "That is the biggest pyramid I ever seen. Come to think of it, I never seen a real pyramid, like the ones they got in Egypt… up this close I mean. Except for that Bass Pro Shop they got in Memphis. It's shaped like a pyramid, but it's all glass. Right next to the Mississippi River. Avery and I took two of the grandkids there right after we visited Graceland……"

Listening intently, Monroe made a mental note to look up 'Bass Pro Shop' on the information system in his spaceship, which was parked inside the Holding Facility. He had already run across Graceland while surfing the Internet, into which they had connected for research purposes. He possessed an uncanny ability to hear things, having four ears evenly distributed around his head, atop his powder blue cylindrical body. This was also the case with his four eyes, four noses, and four mouths. His four evenly dispersed legs extended below his waist. Monroe also possessed four similarly distributed arms, each originating from a shoulder and terminating with a hand.

To Earthlings, this multiplicity of organs and appendages might have appeared odd, even grotesque. In fact, it was the product of millennia of evolution that allowed him to see and hear in 360 degrees. It also afforded enhanced capability to grasp things as well as move in any direction. This augmented redundancy provided ample backup in the event of loss of an appendage or organ. He wore a form-fitting charcoal grey jumpsuit with openings for four arms and four legs, as well as neck and head. The tightness of his attire suggested a toned body devoid of excessive flesh. His sizeable head implied a considerable brain.

But to Babs, Monroe was just a guy from another planet. Being who she was, Babs failed to comprehend the abundance of Monroe's organs and appendages. Maybe their somewhat human-like appearances caused this lapse in Babs' perception. Perhaps her failure to take note of something this conspicuous resulted from the angles at which she typically looked at him. They were evenly distributed around his body such that looking directly at him from any one of four angles, one only saw two eyes, one nose, two arms, and so forth. An alternative explanation to this oversight possibly lies within Babs' brain. Maybe her constant chatter occupied most of the cells in her brain, thereby crowding out electrochemical impulses received from her eyes. The most likely explanation lay in the fact that she had forgotten her eyeglasses.

"......except that Bass Pro Shop has a pointed top. This pyramid doesn't have a pointed top. Wonder why it's flat on top?" Babs asked, then paused awaiting a reply. Such pauses were rare.

"The Holding Facility's flat roof allowed Space Force to install a variety of detection devices such as radar and infrared telescopes." Monroe spoke into an iPhone-sized device in one of his hands. Space Force purchased commercially available language translators off the Internet for $249. This type of device could translate forty-eight different languages and had been used successfully during other alien visitations. It was able to add Monroe's language to its repertoire within several hours. When an Earthling spoke to him, Monroe heard a translation via an earbud in one of his ears. When he spoke into the device's microphone, the translator's speaker broadcast a translation.

"And you say your spaceship is inside that pyramid... that Holding Facility. You said it's like an airplane hangar, but it's really a spaceship hangar? I don't think I've ever seen a spaceship hangar as big as that one. Come to think of it, I don't think I've ever seen a spaceship hangar… unless you count the buildings them space rides at Disney are in… the Buzz Lightyear ride was the best of the bunch. Six Flags don't have no space rides. I wonder why? Wait. Am I thinking of the Buzz Lightyear Space Ranger ride in the Magic Kingdom or the Buzz Lightyear ride in Tomorrowland? It probably don't matter anyway. There I go again, rambling on and on like I tend to do so much nowadays. I tell you—I'm gettin' old, and the older I get, the more I ramble. I don't make a whole lot of sense when I ramble.……" Some of this was not accurate. Babs rambled no more now than when she was younger. Her parents nicknamed her Chatty Babby when she was but three years old.

Babs' chattiness amazed Monroe. His advanced brain calculated she had talked non-stop ninety-eight percent of the twenty minutes since they first met. He exercised daily by walking the perimeter of the compound, inside the fence line. Best time for him was early morning as his eyes were sensitive to bright sunlight. He remembered hearing the female long before he saw her. She and five other Earthling males approached from the other side of the compound's chain link fence. That no security guards patrolled the area surprised several of the males as well as Monroe. Babs said a group of female Earthlings called the Jailbirds were protesting at the Main Gate and associated that protest to the absence of security around the Holding Compound. Her narrative on that subject lasted four and a half minutes by Monroe's reckoning. At its conclusion, he realized he had absorbed a substantial amount of information concerning the Jailbirds' clothing and grooming habits. Based on the perceived benefit from further interaction with her, he decided to invite everyone in for a visit. Four of the males who from their clothing he deduced to be military, politely expressed their regrets before departing. Their leader said, "Sorry Sir, but we gotta finish our training exercise." Ten minutes later, Monroe convinced security guards at the Holding Compound's front entrance to admit his two guests.

"......We only have that one little rinky-dink airport in Thomasville. It don't even have its own website, just a Facebook page. And it's only got a couple of itty-bitty hangars. You could put all of them into this thing. This is the largest spaceship hangar I've ever seen. Oh wait! Didn't I say that before? Does your spaceship have a name like they name boats? I can't wait to see it. The only real spaceships I've ever seen are the ones I've seen in movies like *Star Wars......*"

The Holding Facility was inside the Compound, sand-colored, and windowless. It mimicked a pyramid that had its top third lopped off. It occupied an area the size of two football fields placed side-by-side. As they approached, two gigantic doors parted in the middle, and each door began sliding back into the wall. Babs fell silent, mouth wide open, as she stared at a large frisbee-shaped object. Its smooth metal surface gleamed as if made of silver. In a scene reminiscent of the 1951 movie *The Day the Earth Stood Still*, a section of the object's surface opened. A ramp automatically began sliding out from the bottom of the opening. Monroe extended an arm toward the ramp, inviting his guests to go aboard.

"I gotta pee real bad," said Babs.

"A bathroom is over there." Monroe pointed to a door inside the Holding Facility. "The bathrooms inside the spaceship do not work very well for Earthlings. One of the Space Force personnel unfortunately found that to be the case."

Five minutes later, Babs stepped onto the spaceship's ramp as Tim recorded her journey. Monroe followed, thinking as would have been translated into English, *Babs seems to waddle up the ramp*. He presumed her human anatomy's short legs and expansive posterior made it impossible for her to do otherwise. His mind drifted. The Group's recommendation to the Supreme Council would be final. Was he correct to place so much reliance on his Decision Group's upcoming interaction with the female waddling before him? He could envision no other alternative.

Monroe remembered the last Supreme Council meeting before his Decision Group embarked on its current mission. The

Chairperson of the Council gave one of her typical long-winded speeches, although its first paragraph remained verbatim in his brain.

"My Fellow Council Members. We are embarking on our most ambitious effort to date to expand membership in the Confederation of Planets of the Milky Way Galaxy. As you know, our galaxy contains over fifty billion planets. Approximately one percent of these are capable of supporting life forms. Using Drake's Equation, scientists estimate twenty thousand of these planets actually possess life forms sufficiently evolved to produce civilizations. The Confederation's membership now includes only 243 such planets. We cannot afford to have each of the rest of these twenty thousand planets independently undertaking its own actions, some of which may have adverse consequences for our galaxy... the Milky Way Galaxy. We must seek out planets that have achieved a sufficient degree of sophistication and admit them into our confederation, into our fellowship... For their betterment and for our own well-being."

Thus, Monroe's Decision Group was but one of many groups dispatched to find other civilizations. He had been chosen to lead his Group because of his stellar reputation on his home planet. Of the other two members of his group, one had performed in an excellent manner. The third member's performance reinforced his suspicion that she had been chosen because of her family's connections to a certain member of the Supreme Council.

His Group had already recommended the Supreme Council add three planets to the Confederation. Sixteen others had been rejected. As a planet within the Milky Way Galaxy, Earth might very well be his group's fourth affirmative recommendation—providing it had achieved a sufficient level of sophistication. Past experience demonstrated admitting an unsophisticated planet yielded disastrous results. It was best to let unsophisticated planets continue to evolve on their own without outside interference. Monroe's research of Earth history on the planet's Internet provided such examples. European colonization of the American and African continents had resulted in disaster for their native populations.

On the other hand, he did not want to recommend that Earth not be admitted into the Confederation without a thorough investigation, and Monroe was nothing if not thorough. It would benefit the galaxy to have one less potentially rogue planet outside of its sphere of influence. Moreover, it would provide Earth with access to advanced science, technology, philosophy, and culture. Monroe felt this last item to be the most important of all. From his observations of Earth civilization during his stay, it appeared the planet acutely needed access to a much more sophisticated culture. But he could not shake his belief that his group's interactions with Earthlings to date were insufficient. An 'Admit/Do Not Admit' recommendation was too important. Further Decision Group interaction with unofficial Earthings must occur, something this female could provide. These thoughts raced through Monroe's brain as he watched Babs waddling up the ramp in front of him. Suddenly a ruckus behind him at the Compound's front gate interrupted his thinking.

Chapter 31

Monday, November 10th, 3:04 AM CST

Sonny, Allen, Lilly, and Lizzie had finished their third circuit of the Holding Compound when they saw Babs step onto the spaceship ramp. Even more unbelievable, the strangest looking thing followed her as Tim videoed. Their hopes to meet up with Babs and Tim somewhere near the compound had not been realized until now. On the three unpatrolled sides of the Compound, they had walked close to the outside of the fence line, unmolested by security personnel. On the fourth side, they gave a wide berth to the guarded front entrance—until their third pass.

The Compound occupied five acres of land which meant its circumference was over a third of a mile. Three circuits equaled one mile of walking during the past two hours. This plus the four miles to get *to* the compound totaled five miles of walking since they entered the woods. A person typically burns up about a hundred calories walking a mile. Each of them had burned five hundred calories while walking that night but felt as if the number was much greater.

Calories were not on Lizzie's mind just before they saw Babs. Lizzie had said, "I've burned up both of my feet and any enthusiasm I might ever have had for UFO hunting. Which was zero to begin with, so I guess that means I now have negative enthusiasm. Is there a word for negative enthusiasm?"

Allen offered a word while videoing. "Aversion."

"No, that's what I felt about having sex with my second… or was it my third husband? This is worse than that."

Sonny said, "We should have made contact with Babs and Tim long before now… if they made it here with the Rangers. That leaves two possibilities. One is the Rangers dropped them off with Base Security. The other is she and Tim somehow made it back to the van."

"A third possibility is they're still lost somewhere in these woods," said Lilly.

"The fourth possibility is they're all asleep somewhere in these woods after listening to two hours of Babs' shaggy dog stories," said Lizzie.

Sonny said, "That would be my bet. What now?"

"Allen is getting video of Area 53 here, so we've got what Babs and Cordell were looking for. We can't keep looking in these woods for Babs and Tim. That might take too long if they're still here. We can't go to Base Security, or we'll be thrown in the stockade. The only thing we can do is go back to the van and see if Babs and Tim are back there."

"What if they aren't there?" asked Lilly.

"We contact base security by phone and let them know to start looking for a wandering chatterbox being videoed by a lost cameraman."

"How do we get back over the fence?"

"Cordell must know what's going on from the video and audio he's getting from Allen's camcorder," Sonny said. Then he looked directly into Allen's camcorder. "Cordell, if you're listening, notify the bucket lift guy to be at the fence line by the time we get back there."

"Bucket lift—always my favorite mode of transportation," said Lizzie, then looked at Sonny. "And so romantic—"

The sound of the Holding Facility's massive doors opening interrupted Lizzie's feeble attempt at humor. The group turned their attention in that direction.

"Is that who I think it is?" asked Lilly.

Babs and Tim walked beside a very strange being. All headed toward the doors opening into the massive pyramid-like building. After the doors of the Holding Facility had opened, a large shiny frisbee-like object inside the facility became visible.

"What the heck is that thing?" asked Sonny.

Lizzie said, "I think that is evidence that Miss Babsie was right all along. This place is some sort of Area 53 where the Feds keep UFOs. But it doesn't matter. I've still burned up my enthusiasm for UFOs."

After Babs stepped onto the spaceship ramp, Lilly and Lizzie immediately sprinted—a relative term—toward the Compound's front gate. Allen followed with Sonny straggling in the rear.

"Wait! Wait! You can't take them away!" Lizzie screamed.

Lilly yelled, "At least let us say goodbye!"

Chapter 32

Monday, November 10th, 3:10 AM CST

Until forty minutes ago, Cordell's attention constantly shifted among the four monitors displaying video feeds from each of the four camcorders. During that time, he periodically switched the sound among the four audio feeds. Audio from all four camcorders at the same time would have been incomprehensible.

Cordell thought most of the video of Babs following the Rangers would wind up on the cutting room floor along with her morose whining about getting old. A full spectrum night vision camcorder produces a murky monochromatic image which is okay visually on TV for brief sequences. Any longer and it gets boring unless there is sufficient action and/or good dialogue. Babs' non-stop shaggy dog stories and whining merely reinforced the monotony of watching her and the Rangers walk through the woods. Cordell marveled at how the four men were able to put up with her constant chatter for an hour and a half. Must have been their youth.

He loved Allen's video of Sonny and the two women stumbling and tripping and complaining and moaning. It provided great visuals and witty dialogue in spades. Lilly and the gopher were priceless. The bit about the spanking should be worth at least a 0.05 ratings bump in the 25-54 women demographic. Allen's footage would be the primary component of two, maybe three full segments of the next *Real Widows* episode. Along with the video of the City Council meeting, the problem would be deciding what to include and what to defer to future episodes.

Bits of Kim and Alexis' camcorder feeds of the protest would be interspersed among Allen's video. The Jailbirds were a hoot. They staged several mock sit-downs among the Jersey walls. Kanesha somehow managed to shout pre-written slogans at the young military policemen and women in a non-confrontational, humorous way. They all chanted mock protest songs in support of the alien, the lyrics of which turned out to be very funny. Several of them had excellent singing voices. Cordell figured he'd loop the best of the songs a couple of times for effect. Bab's and the producer's plan had been spot-on as additional base security personnel kept arriving at the Main Gate throughout the protest. Maybe he could use the Jailbirds in other episodes later on? Maybe in a show of their own?

Short bits of Tim's video of Babs following the Rangers would also be interspersed among Allen's video. Cordell would have his audio engineer modulate Babs' monotonous yakking to thirty decibels, making it barely audible and overdub it with narration at 60 decibels.

As boring as the first hour's feed of Babs' chatter from Tim's camcorder was, so was its last forty minutes fascinating. Cordell watched this part in rapt silence, mouth wide open. His two black-suited visitors showed no emotion, no surprise. What did they know? Nothing like what was displayed in Tim's, and subsequently Allen's monitors had ever been seen on Earth.

The circuits in Cordell's brain buzzed as he visualized how to incorporate the video of Babs interacting with a live alien. Most likely, some of it would be the entire last segment, with a tease 'More to Come' message right before closing credits. So many possibilities. At least one additional episode primarily devoted to the Babs-Alien interaction would be hyped by a week of pre-show advertising.

The idea that they might wind up showing something like this had never occurred to Cordell. He never believed Babs was correct about there being an Area 53 with UFOs in it. His gut instincts about a successful reality show had paid off. It was pure luck he had tuned into the Florida-Georgia game and recognized Babs as one of the streakers. But he never viewed her paranormal ravings as anything other than part of her eccentricity. She had been just as crazy at FSU. Now, her craziness would result in phenomenal ratings. What he currently viewed on the monitor was not eccentricity. It was reality… reality beyond imagination. This was nothing short of fantastic. The show's ratings would go through the roof but pale in comparison with what this would do for his career. This would make him a legend in Hollywood. An international legend. He imagined the awards. A Golden Globe. An Emmy, maybe more than one… for unparalleled achievement in filmmaking. Cordell visualized a row of shiny statues on his mantle…

…If I can get this footage on the air. The network's lawyers felt confident they could protect video of three women bumbling about in the woods of a military base from censorship. But this! How

would they get the Federal government to allow something this explosive to be broadcast on national TV? Surely, they would invoke some sort of national security directive, and everything Tim and Allen had filmed would be classified top secret. He doubted the network's lawyers would be able to use their planned 'freedom of the press' argument to get this aired. It was dynamite—

One of the black suits interrupted Cordell's reverie. "I know what you're thinking, and it ain't gonna happen."

"I never thought any of this would happen. My plan was pretty modest. I figured we'd video the girls hiking through the woods. Video the protests. I never thought there would be something like an Area 53 inside Elgin. But I never thought *existence* of an Area 53 was essential to the episode anyway. I figured we'd maybe get some video of them trying to climb over or into something… anything. That's all you need for a reality show anyway—just a bunch of women doing something controversial and hopefully, something confrontational. I knew they'd be confronted by some military personnel. Get some footage of them being taken into custody. Put the lawyers to work. I figured we could edit two episodes out of all the video. But this…" Cordell's voice trailed off as he shook his head, eyes transfixed on Tim's monitor.

Chapter 33

Monday, November 10th, 3:15 AM CST

Monroe left Babs midway on the ramp and returned to the front gate of the compound. Two guards argued with four Earthlings who appeared not to be government officials. As best he could determine, these Earthlings knew Babs and Tim and wanted to join them. *This could potentially increase variety in our spontaneous interaction with Earthlings. Two additional females and two additional males. Babs has been invaluable so far in my assessment of her planet's degree of sophistication. Interaction with four more can only facilitate making the correct decision.* Monroe did not need to remind himself that such interaction was critical to the Earth's future. After a brief discussion, the front gate guards again yielded to Monroe's wishes, and he escorted them to meet Babs and Tim.

"Oh, Babsie! We been so worried about you," said Lilly as she hugged her lost friend. "What happened? Tell us all about it."

Monroe thought, *Earthling, be careful what you ask for.*

"Oh, oh, oh… you will not believe what happened. We met these bushes right after you left us—"

"Babsie," said Lizzie, "As I remember it, you left us."

"That ain't important. What's important is that them bushes took us right here where we met Mister Monroe here… He is a real gentleman… uh, I guess he's a man. I ain't had time to ask him yet. He's got a man's name, so I just naturally assumed—"

Lizzie looked Monroe up and down and said, "Babsie, we ain't been introduced to this nice gentleman yet."

"This happens to me all the time. I forget my manners. Folks, this here's Mister Monroe. He's from some planet whose name I can't pronounce, probably because it don't have no vowels in it. Mister Monroe, this here's Lizzie, Lilly, Sonny, and Allen. You've already met Tim."

Lilly and Lizzie both politely smiled and nodded at Monroe, while Sonny attempted a fist bump. Monroe, somewhat surprised by the gesture, recoiled then realized it was a form of greeting. He extended all four hands which Sonny bumped in succession. Via his translation device, Monroe said, "I cannot tell you how pleased I am to make all of your acquaintances. I and my associates inside our ship have travelled far to meet with beings on your planet. We hope to gain a better understanding of your planet Earth and its inhabitants. We especially hope to talk with all of you at length. I would be pleased if you would agree to meet with us inside our spaceship which has been our home for quite a while now. I would be happy to give you a tour of the craft if you so wished."

That did it. Nothing could have enticed Babs, Lilly, and Lizzie any more than seeing the inside of someone else's home—and a spaceship to boot. HGTV would be *so* jealous. Any fears about abduction to another planet disappeared as they scampered up the ramp.

Lizzie whispered to Lilly as they ascended, "I bet this old boy Monroe has got a wad of dough. Spaceships ain't cheap. He's probably his planet's Elon Musk… and he does fill out that uniform very nicely."

Many humans claim to have seen UFOs. Many photos and videos have been taken from a distance of things that may have been UFOs. The National UFO Reporting Center recorded over 150,000 UFO sightings in forty-seven years of reporting. Despite all this, no photos or videos taken by a human being inside a UFO and authenticated by reputable authorities have ever been made public.

Nothing remotely connected to these facts occurred to Babs as she stepped through the doorway into the spaceship, followed by Lilly and Lizzie. Sonny paused to scrape mud off his boots on the ship's door sill, then followed Monroe into the craft. From different angles, the two cameramen filmed the entire event. As he stepped around the women, Monroe said, "You realize that you are the first female Earthlings to enter this spaceship.

Plagiarizing Neil Armstrong's immortal words, Babs said, "I guess we took one small step for a woman, but one giant leap for womankind."

"You mean no government people have been inside here?" asked Lizzie.

"Some government officials have been inside for tours or meetings, but most of our meetings have been inside conference rooms inside the Holding Compound's Command Center. Oddly enough, the only government officials that have been inside this spaceship have been males."

"So much for diversity."

"Let me give you a tour," Monroe said, leading them down a corridor. First stop: the spaceship's berthing spaces. Three tubes, each somewhat larger than Monroe, occupied the central part of the room. The tubes appeared to be made out of some sort of transparent material tinted dark grey.

"Them look like the old-style phone booths we used to have in Thomasville," said Sonny. "I thought the only place that had phone booths anymore was Waycross."

Monroe said, "These are our sleeping pods. You would call them beds."

Flirting, Lizzie asked, "What else do you do in them besides sleep?"

Lilly made a face. "But they're vertical, not horizontal."

"Yes, we sleep standing up, not lying down," Monroe said.

"Just like horses," said Babs.

Lilly said, "I thought horses slept laying down."

Monroe hesitated before speaking. How could he correct his Earthling guests without insulting their intelligence? His mission was a diplomatic mission after all. He said, "Actually, both of you are right. Your planet's horses experience two kinds of sleep—slow wave sleep and rapid eye movement sleep. They either stand or lie on their chest during slow wave sleep, and they lie on their side while in rapid eye movement sleep."

Lizzie leaned into Lilly and whispered, "I bet Monroe's best rapid movement doesn't occur in his eyes. Hmm… four arms, four legs… what else does he have four of?"

Lilly giggled, then scanned the room. In addition to the sleeping pods, it contained several pieces of some sort of metal and plastic furniture that would have fit in very well in a DMV office. The room's large area rug looked as if it was purchased at a yard sale at Pee-Wee's Playhouse. Lots of bright colors and geometric shapes. The walls displayed various plaques, certificates, and photographs—the typical stuff one would expect to see decorating the walls in any military facility. Lilly politely said, "Your interior decorating is unlike anything I've ever seen in Thomasville."

"One of my companions whom you will meet later decorated the ship," said Monroe. He hoped no one would notice two of the photographs, over which he and the female member of his Decision Group had gotten into an argument prior to mission launch. He felt they were tasteless, but she insisted on hanging them and won out. It helps to have friends in high places.

Lizzie moved close to the photographs to get a better look. She said, "Pretty good framing on these photographs. Looks expensive. I think I see Monroe in a couple of them."

"Yes. Each of us brought some photographs. It is a long trip, and it helps to have something by which to remember home. I am in a couple of those with my family."

Babs zeroed in on the two tasteless photographs. One showed the female member of his group walking nude with several friends at a clothes-optional beach on their planet. In the other, she appeared to be mooning whoever took the photograph while riding on some sort of amusement park ride, also on their planet. Babs pointed to the latter picture. "Looks like someone was having fun. Who is it?"

"One of the other members of my crew whom you will meet later. Please pay no attention to it."

Lizzie eyed Monroe. "Too bad. I was hoping it might have been you."

Monroe ignored her comment. "Let me show you our dining room."

He next led them to a room whose walls were populated with dozens of small one-by-one-foot doors at chest high level. Lilly said, "There ain't no table with chairs in here."

"We do not sit on chairs at a table as you Earthlings do when we eat," said Monroe. He pointed at the rows of small doors. "The diner stands before a door and eats whatever is behind it. The diner can partake of multiple doors if so desired. Our food service technology places a different interplanetary food dish randomly behind each door after the food behind it is eaten. We do not know what we will be eating until we open a door. During a long space voyage, it introduces an element of surprise into the daily routine."

"That sounds like them new kiosks at McDonalds," said Babs. "I don't care what I order from them things, I never get what I think I ordered."

After the cafeteria, Monroe showed them a conference room and 3-D theater. His guests were particularly impressed with the short video highlighting some of his planet's geographical features. He was most anxious to show them the spaceship's engine room. Monroe was especially proud of the craft's advanced propulsion system and hoped to impress his guests. He said, "Let me show you the spaceship's engine room. I think it is best part of the ship."

"I thought I was looking at the best thing on the ship," said Lizzie, focusing on Monroe.

Sonny flashed a smile, and said, "That's what I been waitin' for. I bet this thing's got a kickass motor."

Monroe led them to the rear of the ship, opened a door, and ushered them inside. Lizzie looked at Babs and quietly said, "Don't touch anything." At times, Babs could make Inspector Clouseau look competent.

Monroe pointed at a large cylinder encircled with a series of transverse fins. One end of the cylinder connected to a receptacle on a wall, while another connected to a large tank filled with a fluid. The entire device occupied most of the room. He said, "This ship uses the latest in nano electrokinetic thruster technology for propulsion. It reduces interstellar cruise time by a factor of four," said Monroe.

"What kind of gas mileage do you get?" Babs asked. "Silly me. I bet this thing don't even use gasoline. What does it use?"

"An ionized electrolyte."

"I hope your electrolyte don't cost half as much as what we have to pay for gas around here. My Escalade drinks gas worse than my grandchildren drink Capri Sun……."

Two minutes into Babs' narrative about children's drinks, Monroe realized the physics of interstellar propulsion was beyond her grasp. The other Earthlings also seemed overwhelmed as he explained how the spaceship's propulsion system was based on electro-osmosis. He tried to explain in the simplest terms of which he was capable but to no avail. Even the male who initially seemed so interested in their propulsion technology failed to engage in any discussion. Sonny stood there with his mouth wide open.

Monroe stood immobile as Babs complained about the high prices of gasoline and Capri Sun and how things kept getting more expensive the older she got. He listened, finding it difficult to comprehend her inability to grasp the physics underlying electrokinetic thruster technology and electro-osmotic flow. On his planet, these were subjects taught at an elementary grade level.

Sonny innocently revealed his ignorance when he asked, “Mind if I open this door? A picture’s worth a thousand words.” He pointed at the hatch to the nano thruster array.

“That would not be wise,” said Monroe thinking, *especially if you do not want to be vaporized by the array’s EMF.* Monroe sensed his own rising frustration with his unsuccessful efforts to enlighten the Earthlings. *Perhaps, it is best to bring my companions into the evaluation process sooner rather than later*. As he led them out of the engine room, he said, “Let me introduce you to the other members of my group. I’ll have them meet us in the lounge.”

Chapter 34

Monday, November 10th, 4:10 AM CST

When Monroe and his guests arrived in the spaceship's lounge, the other two members of his Decision Group awaited them. Both aliens appeared similar to Monroe in terms of a multiplicity of arms, legs, ears, mouths, and eyes. They differed in height; at six feet five inches, Monroe was the tallest of the aliens. The shortest was five feet six inches. None had hair on the top of their heads, but one sported what appeared to be some sort of beard that encircled its entire head. Like Monroe, they dressed in form-fitting charcoal grey jumpsuits with openings for four arms and four legs, as well as neck and head. Skin color differentiated one of the three aliens from the other two. While one possessed skin the same shade of pale blue as Monroe, the bearded alien had skin a shade of lavender pink.

Monroe spoke to them in their own language for several minutes then turned to Babs and the others. "I updated my companions on the purpose of your visit and informed them of each of your names in our language. Let me now introduce you to each of them. This is *QNFDxbrxgttbzkttt*."

The lavender pink bearded alien stood and bowed slightly. Babs nodded hello in return and said, "Can you repeat that?"

Using a translator, the alien said, "Yes. My name is *QNFDxbrxgttbzkttt*. In your language, it would be pronounced Ramone."

Ramone's short, direct answer surprised Monroe. Ramone could be a smart-ass at times, and Monroe had expected some sort of flippant answer.

"I've always liked the name Ramone for a man. I think that was the middle name of one of my husbands."

Ramone said, "I am not a male."

Babs said, "I guess that explains your skin color. It's a beautiful shade of pink. Ramone is usually a man's name here on Earth, but no reason why it couldn't be a woman's name on your planet. We have some women here that have men's names just like you do. Like… uh, like… that woman Sean Young that starred in that Kevin

Costner movie… uh… I forget the title of the movie… No something. Anyway, I think Ramone is a wonderful name for a woman—"

"On our planet, we self-identify monthly as male or female, depending on how we feel. I am a female this month."

"Goodbye periods. Lord, do I wish we could do that here on Earth." After saying this, Lizzie leered at Monroe and said, "Although there are times I do enjoy being a woman."

Babs looked at Monroe. "What are you?"

"This month I am a male," he said. Lizzie nodded approvingly.

"I can relate to that," said Lilly. "I had a date in September with this guy, Ashley. It was one of those dates where we met each other on the Internet. When we met in person, this guy was drop dead gorgeous. To top it off, he was a real Southern gentleman just like what I've been trying to meet ever since my husband Wendell died last year. Only he wasn't no gentleman… Ashley, not Wendell. Except he was the day we met each other in person. Ashley was normally a woman except he identified as a man that day, which he said was lucky for me. Now that I think about it, saying that was sort of... What's the word I'm looking for… kind of—"

Ramone offered a word. "Arrogant."

Monroe thought, *What is going on with Ramone? Forty-two words and not a single wisecrack from her? That is a record on this voyage.*

"Arrogant. That's the word. Arrogant… for Ashley to say that it was lucky for me that he was identifying as a man that day. Why wasn't it lucky for him or her that I *was* a woman that day? That sounds just like something a man would say, don't it? 'Ain't you lucky I feel like a man tonight?' He must think the sun comes up just to hear him crow. We met on one of them online Internet dating sites. Oh, I think I already said that, didn't I? Apparently, he lied as much on his online form as I lied on mine. When we almost had sex at his house, he told me that he started out as a girl, got married, had two kids, then decided he didn't wanna be a woman no more, so he started self-identifying as man. But he didn't do it all the time. Sometimes he felt like a woman, sometimes a man, so he just switched back and forth like he felt at the time. There's a lot of people that do that sort of thing nowadays—"

"If more women did more self-identifying as men," said Lizzie, "think what it would do to tampon sales. It'd put Tampax out of business."

"Yeah, but beer sales would go through the roof," said Babs.

"Our planet has been self-identifying for several millennia," Ramone said, then smiled mischievously. "It works very well, although it complicates things from a clothing standpoint."

Monroe had seen her smile that way at other creatures. He shook his head. *Ramone... Ramone... Ramone. These poor Earthlings probably do not realize you are attempting humor.*

"Lilly can relate to that," said Babs as she nodded at Lilly. "She'd have to double the size of her shoe closet if Earth started going whole hog like y'all do on self-identifying."

Both Monroe and Ramone's translation devices remained silent as if malfunctioning. Finally, Monroe's device said, "I cannot translate the word 'y'all'. Can you provide more context?"

Babs nodded. "Oh sure. Y'all. It's like a combination of you and all. Y'all. We say it all the time in the South when we're talking about more than one person."

Monroe said, "Now, I understand. A contraction of two words to form a colloquial plural form of the word 'you'. We ran into something similar seven days ago from another Earthling from Pennsylvania. He said the word 'youse' which our translation devices could not translate. It turned out to be another colloquial form for the plural of the word 'you' for which the English language has no distinct formal plural form. Our research on your Internet to date has failed to yield a logical explanation for this oversight in your language."

"English has all kinds of dumb things like that," said Babs. "The worst thing is there's too many words that don't spell right. Take the word vacuum. How many c's does it have? How many u's? Most people don't know how to spell it. I always like to spell it with two c's and one u, and the stupid spell checker in Word always disagrees with me."

"We believe English to be one of the more difficult languages in the Milky Way galaxy," said Ramone.

"It's definitely the most difficult language on *this* planet. By the way, Mister Monroe showed us that nice movie about y'all's planet, but I never caught the name of y'all's planet. Where are y'all from?"

Ramone's whimsical personality surfaced as she extended one of her arms above her head and pointed upward, eliciting polite laughter from the third alien. Ramone was widely known for her lame jokes and harmless pranks. This pitiful one exemplified why Monroe had been skeptical of the Supreme Council's decision to include her as a member of his Decision Group. His companion had pulled this particular joke several times before on other planets as well as Earth.

Monroe rolled his eyes despite his best efforts not to, fearing the gesture might bring attention to the crude joke. Unfortunately, four eyes evenly distributed around your body can sometimes be a hinderance. There was no direction in which he could turn to hide his expression of annoyance. *I appreciate a good joke as much as anyone, but this one is terrible, and Ramone has worn it out.* He said, "Please ignore Ramone. You are one of many on whom she has pulled that old joke, six of them here on Earth."

Babs ploughed on. "I didn't realize it was a joke. Anyway, as I always say 'ask a stupid question.' But I seem to do that all the time. At least that's what my daughters always tease me about. At least two of them do. I have three daughters. And two sons. Don't ask me how many grandchildren I have 'cause it's too many at my age to remember without writing them down on a piece of paper to make sure I don't leave one of 'em out. I got so many grandchildren I cain't sling a dead cat without hitting one of 'em. Thank God I only got two great grandchildren. They are a handful, but I've gotten off track again, haven't I? But old women like me do that a lot. What were we talking about before we got onto how screwed up English is?"

"In answer to your original question, the name of our planet is KOI 5715.01. In answer to your last question, we were talking about self-identification, and you said Missus Lilly would have to double the size of her shoe closet if Earth started self-identifying to the extent we do on our planet."

Ramone said, "It sounds like Earth is trying to catch up with KOI 5715.01 if I understand Missus Lilly's narrative about the Ashley Earthling."

Babs said, "It does sound that way sometimes. At least it seems that way. At the rate folks are self-identifying on Earth, we're probably gonna zoom past you folks. Sometimes I read where there's supposed to be twenty or thirty genders, and other times I see it's gone up to fifty or sixty. LGB… XYZ, you name it. It's way too many for me to remember. After all I'm sixty-three. I wish them people that make up all these sexes and genders would think about old people with memory loss like me for a change. When you're sixty-three, your memory ain't too good, as I've been reminded about more and more lately. You know...I just realized we been yapping our mouths non-stop. Y'all must think we're the rudest things you've ever seen. We been talking so much, we ain't given y'all a chance to introduce us to this other nice gentleman... He is a gentleman, ain't he?"

The other powder blue alien stepped forward and said, "Yes... I am a male, at least for twenty more days of your calendar. My name is *ZZxbrptxgkttt*. It would be pronounced Salome in your language."

"Like the woman in the Bible?"

Salome nodded. "I have scanned your Bible. It is a very great book."

"Don't you love the stories in it? It don't have no pictures though. I don't know why the people that wrote the Bible didn't put pictures in it... at least for the kids. Too bad they didn't have Facebook back in the Bible days. Salome is a wonderful name, but not many people name their kids Salome nowadays. It is spelled S-a-l-o-m-e, isn't it?"

"Almost. My name is spelled C-a-l-o-m-e."

"C instead of S?" asked Lizzie.

Salome nodded. "Yes. ZZ in our language is equivalent to the letter C in your language. Our language has no letter equivalent to your S."

"Why?"

"The letter S duplicates the sounds made by the letter C and is therefore not needed," Monroe said.

Lizzie looked at Sonny. "You'll have to get a new driver's license with your name spelled right."

Sonny sneered. "Suits me. The picture in my current one sucks."

Babs decided to go in a different direction with the conversation. She said, "Too bad Daffy and Gidget aren't here. They're more fun than a sack full of kittens. Gidget's the one you definitely gotta meet. She reminds me of you folks. She don't talk that much. She didn't come along with us not because she didn't want to, but because she's on a cruise with Daffy. I know she don't think y'all are even real, but there's a lot of people I know that don't think y'all are real... Mitzi Merchant for one. She was the most... most... what's the word I'm looking for..."

"Skeptical," said Ramone.

"Skeptical. Yep. That's the word I was looking for. She's the most skeptical person I know when it comes to UFOs and aliens and......"

Monroe thought *I wonder where she is going with this narrative, but that seems to be the case with all of her narratives.* He typified the mindset of most inhabitants of his planet—no nonsense, get to the point, think logically—Ramone being one of the exceptions to this rule. To Monroe, this Earthling's ramblings proved to be invaluable. They enlightened him as to how those outside of her planet's government processed information and communicated the results. He tuned Babs back in just after she had switched narratives again.

".......and, it was one of my older brothers. He had this parrot that he named Caesar. That thing talked more than anything I've ever seen......"

Missus Babs has not looked in a mirror lately, Monroe thought.

"........and my older brother, he was studying at that time to be a taxidermist... you know, one of those people that stuff dead animals for show, and Caesar he up and died on him from some sort of parrot disease, so my brother puts him in the freezer until he can figure out how to taxiderm him or whatever it is they do to them animals. So, every time someone would come over to our house, they'd ask, 'Is Caesar in the freezer?' My momma didn't think that was funny at all. But, it wasn't as bad as the time my sister left her monkey's head in the refrigerator... Well, it really wasn't a monkey's head at all, just a monkey's skull. She got it for one of her nursing classes and left it in the refrigerator in a brown paper bag, and my daddy mistook it for his lunch, which momma always put in the refrigerator in a brown paper bag......"

Surely, we have gained invaluable insights into how the human mind works. Insights not revealed during our many conversations with all those government officials. To a person, they all exhibited rigid, narrow-minded thinking.

"......Mitzi wasn't just skeptical. She was downright hateful about aliens and Area 53 on her Facebook page. Gidget's just skeptical, but she's skeptical about a lot of stuff. I think it's because she's a pharmacist. I bet pharmacists are trained to be skeptical because they probably get a lot of people coming in wanting drugs they're not supposed to have, so a pharmacist has to ask herself 'Now, is this guy wanting this tranquilizer because he really needs it or because he's addicted to it.' I take a Xanax myself every so often, and they can be pretty addictive if you don't watch out—"

Monroe realized all of a sudden that he had missed the last two minutes of Babs' narrative. That had never happened before!

".......and I told Avery... this was after that prostate procedure that he had. I told him 'Avery, wearing Depends ain't no different than wearing contact lenses. People don't know that you're wearing contact lenses because you need 'em to see... just like people don't know you're wearing Depends because you need 'em to pee'......."

Lilly wanted to talk with the aliens about a subject near and dear to her. She said, "Y'all have some of the most interesting interior decorating in your spaceship. I don't believe I've ever seen a lounge decorated quite like this. It really makes a statement. Mister Monroe told us that one of y'all did all the decorating."

What appeared to be wallpaper covered the room's walls, floor to ceiling. Its pattern resembled the images seen in a child's kaleidoscope. Dozens of different colors in geometrically symmetrical patterns resulted in a psychedelic effect right out of 1969 Haight-Ashbury. Monroe motioned for all to take seats on several sofa-like pieces of furniture that occupied the room. These made abundant use of pea green, pink and peach hues in their fabrics. Shag carpets lay scattered on the floor. The room's coffee and end tables resembled the Modern style furniture designed by Charles Eames in 1940s and 50s.

Lilly's comments caused Salome to beam with pride. Monroe noticed; he knew his colleague appreciated the recognition. Decorating was the one thing that got Salome out of his shell. He was the introvert of the Decision Group. Monroe recalled the conversation he had with Salome's father the day before their spaceship departed KOI 5715.01.

"Monroe, I depend on you to look after my boy for me. After all, he is only two hundred and eighty-five years old, and this is

really the first time he has ever been out on his own, away from the nest so to speak. I don't count the trip to CoRoT 7b after he graduated from school."

"You can count on me to look after Salome. I will look after him as if he was one of my own. I am proud to have him as a member of my Decision Group. Salome is one of the most competent flight engineers we have on the planet."

"I know he is, but he is so shy. Frankly, I am surprised the Supreme Council selected him for this mission. I mean from a diplomacy standpoint. Face it, he is a wallflower when it comes to interacting with other beings. Why did they select a wallflower for a diplomatic mission?"

"Who knows the rationale behind any of the Supreme Council's decisions?"

Salome's father had silently nodded his agreement.

Monroe looked at Lilly and thought, *Thank you, Missus Lilly.* He looked at Salome. *Time to shine, my boy.*

Salome acknowledged Lilly's interest in his decorating with a bow and said, "Yes, I did, and thank you. I was assigned the task of decorating it, so I appreciate your compliment."

"You use visually stimulating colors to say the least," said Lilly.

"These colors were very much in vogue on our planet when we were preparing for our voyage."

"You also used some psychedelic patterns in your furniture and wall coverings. It reminds me of decorating styles popular during the 1960s and 70s here on Earth."

"On our planet, it is called 'Neo-Andromeda' style."

"Neo-Andromeda?"

"Yes. It is a style first introduced in the Andromeda galaxy that has rapidly spread to other galaxies, including our own Milky Way galaxy. I ran across something on your Internet called 'Retro Modern' that was a decorating style popular on Earth in the 1950s and 1960s. It does closely resemble the 'Neo-Andromeda' style—"

"I love the shag carpet here in the lounge. It's been making a comeback in American bedrooms and dens lately."

Salome nodded. "Yes. You cannot walk into any hotel lobby on a planet in the Andromeda galaxy and not see psychedelic wallcoverings and shag carpeting."

"Enhances the effects of the LSD," said Lizzie.

Lilly frowned. "Please ignore her."

Tim lowered the camcorder again, having doubled over laughing. He composed himself and resumed filming as Salome continued to explain. "This shag carpet came from PA-99-N2."

"PA-99-N2?"

"A planet in the Andromeda galaxy famous for handwoven shag carpets. Very expensive, I might add. It sells for the equivalent of one hundred and twenty of your Bitcoins a square inch."

Sonny's eyes got wide. "I'm glad I cleaned my boots off before I came in y'all's spaceship."

Salome glanced at Sonny's feet wishing he had done a better job.

"Salome, how about I rip up the old shag carpet in my basement, and you sell it for me on Andromeda?" Lizzie asked. "We'll split the profit."

Chapter 35

Monday, November 10th, 4:32 AM CST

"I remember the shag carpet in my momma's house," said Babs. "I remember when she covered all the beautiful oak hardwood floors in her house with shag carpet in 1968. We ripped all of it up in 1989 and refinished the floors. They looked beautiful after that… There I go. Dating myself again."

"What do you mean by dating yourself?" asked Monroe. "I thought dating on Earth typically involved two different people, usually a male and a female but sometimes two of the same gender."

"That was in the old days," said Lizzie, then winked at Monroe, "although I still prefer the old way of dating myself."

"Shush," said Babs, looking at her friend, then turning to Monroe. "When someone says 'dating myself' it means that he or she is revealing how old they are. What I meant was that I'm saying that I'm old, which at I am."

He said, "Missus Babs, I have noticed that you seem to think you are getting very old. You seem unhappy about growing older."

"Just wait till you're my age, then you'll know why."

"Why do you think you are getting old?"

"You know you're getting old when you pick up your meds at your mailbox instead of a pharmacy."

Lizzie nodded. "You know you're getting old when no one calls you between one and three o'clock because they know it's time for your afternoon nap."

"You know you're getting old when you aren't embarrassed to be driving slow and not being drunk at the same time," said Babs.

Lilly nodded. "You know you're getting old when you look at your shopping list, and the first three things are underwear, a mop head, and ant poison." She spoke from experience.

"I remember my third or fourth husband—I forget which—said he looked forward to turning seventy," said Lizzie, "because the only time he'd ever have to wear a tie again was at his own funeral."

A forlorn look came over Babs' face. She said, "I'm so old I put my empty wine bottles in my own garbage can instead of my neighbor's."

"Why do you consider doing that as a sign of old age?" asked Monroe.

"Because I'm so old I no longer care if my neighbors know how much wine I drink." The quizzical look on Tim's face prompted further explanation. She said, "My neighbors are a bunch of snoops. They listen for wine bottles breaking when garbage cans are dumped into the garbage truck."

"There is one good thing about getting old," said Lizzie.

"What's that?" asked Lilly.

"Losing your hearing."

"Did I hear you right? asked Sonny. "Why do you say that?"

"When you nod off at the wheel waiting at a red light and cars honk at you after it turns green, the honking don't wake you up… at least if you forgot your hearing aid."

I do not know how much more of this I can take. Monroe decided to intervene and repeated his initial observation. "Missus Babs, I have noticed that you seem to think you are getting very old. You seem unhappy about growing older."

Babs nodded. "Yeah, I am."

"Why?"

"Getting old is no fun. We know we are going to die at some point."

Ramone said, "I was researching Earth culture and philosophy on your Internet and ran across something one of your philosophers, Martin Heidegger said that pertains to your last comment."

"I remembered reading about him at FSU. I majored in philosophy—"

"Heidegger and I used to go to different schools together," said Lizzie. The old lame joke went over everyone's head.

Babs frowned at the interruption. "What did he say, Ramone?"

"Heidegger said that humans are beings unto death—"

Lizzie shook her head. "That only applies to men. Women are actually shoppers unto death."

Ramone paused, analyzing Lizzie's second lame joke. He said, "I understand. It was an attempt at humor—"

"Not very good humor," said Babs. "Please continue, Ramone."

"What Heidegger meant was that humans are the only animals on your planet that are aware of their own mortality. Humans have to confront the fact that they are going to die."

Monroe thought, *Ramone is being serious for a change. I wonder what she is up to?*

Babs nodded. "I been doing that a lot lately."

"Yet you say you are only sixty-three Earth years old," said Monroe.

"Sixty-three is old. Believe me it's old. And I feel all sixty-three years of it every time I look in the mirror. How old are you, Mister Monroe?"

"In Earth years, six hundred and thirty years old."

Lilly said, "Oh my God! What have you been eating? That's wonderful. You don't look that old. I wish I had skin as smooth as all of you have. Are y'all using some sort of Aveeno-like lotion that puts Aveeno to shame."

"Do you have commissary on this boat? I'd like to take home a couple of cases of your skin lotion," Lizzie eyed Monroe. "And maybe something else to remember this visit by—you interested?"

Monroe ignored the obvious flirtation and said, "Yes, we do have a commissary. We can stop by there on the way out if you wish." Casserole Ladies pass up a chance to go shopping? Fat Chance! He continued, "Missus Babs, you should consider yourself young, at least by my planet's standards."

"But I don't live on your planet, and here, sixty-three is old. How do y'all manage to live so long and be in such good shape yet be so old? Y'all aren't all vegans, are you?" asked Babs.

Lizzie leered at Monroe and said, "Monroe looks like a meat eater to me."

"We eat whatever we want from a variety of animals, vegetables, and minerals," he said.

"Yet, you live so long and seem so healthy," said Lilly.

"How long one lives is relative, just as the concept of 'old' is relative. To you, sixty-three is old, but to me sixty-three is very young. Age has both physical and mental components. Lifespans on my planet used to be about the same as here on Earth until two millennia ago when one of the wisest of our philosophers discovered the secret to a happy, long life."

All three ladies eagerly asked, "And what was that?"

"Afternoon naps, coital activity, and monkey bars."

Dumbstruck, all three ladies' jaws dropped.

Sensing their astonishment, Monroe elaborated, "Afternoon naps afford the body a chance to recharge or rejuvenate itself after periods of stress and exertion. That is why little children need them so much, when their bodies are growing. Yet, this need does not diminish with age; if anything, it increases."

"And to think I used to tease Avery for napping weekend afternoons," said Babs.

"Tell us more about coital activity," said Lizzie.

"Is there nothing better than sex after a short nap?" Monroe rhetorically asked.

All three ladies' heads nodded vigorously. Silently debating between sex and bowel movements, Sonny scrunched his face. Reluctantly, he nodded as well.

Babs asked, "But what about monkey bars? Do you mean the steel arrangement of bars that children climb on?"

"Yes, although a set of monkey bars on our planet is more elaborate than the monkey bars here on Earth. This is necessary due to the additional arms and legs we possess."

"But how do they help y'all live long and happy lives?"

"We regularly climb on them in much the same way as Earthling children do."

"You mean grown people on your planet climb on monkey bars?"

"Yes. Of course. Climbing on monkey bars, especially with one's children is a great source of pleasure as well as a healthy form of exercise. Many different muscle groups are stimulated."

Lizzie arched her back in a conscious effort to thrust her breasts forward for Monroe's benefit. She regretted buying the Ferragamo shirt. Its long sleeves hid her saggy underarm skin, but a high neckline totally failed to reveal any of her deep cleavage. She had looked at a much cheaper Zella Camo Tank Top. Its low-cut neckline and body-hugging style would work perfectly for the reaction she now wanted to elicit from Monroe. Unfortunately, she had reckoned the shirt would be warmer than a tank top on a chilly November night. She said, "I was wondering how you got those four big arms and chest."

"The activity of climbing monkey bars triggers chemicals in the body that stimulate pleasure receptors in the brain which has healthy benefits in itself. Climbing monkey bars is also a wonderful source of bonding with one's family. We have a set of monkey bars in our spaceship's gym."

"Maybe we could go there later, and we could do some bonding on them."

Babs shook her head. "I hear what you're saying, but I'm too old for naps, sex, and monkey bars to do me any good."

"Excuse me for a minute." Monroe lowered his translator and spoke with Ramone and Salome in his native language. "The Earthling seems to be very depressed about growing older."

"Yes, I noticed that," said Ramone.

"Your explanation of our secret to a long and happy life appeared to have minimal effect on her attitude," said Salome.

"I perceive the human brain to be frail in several respects, including its ability to cope with old age. That explains why we observed so much on their television relating to the selling of products intended to slow effects of aging. Their civilization has not evolved sufficiently to perceive the benefits of aging such as increased wisdom, additional time to correct past mistakes—"

"Do not forget the senior discount at GVttpkttty'c." Ramone's wisecrack referred to a fast-food restaurant chain on her planet.

"Ho, ho. Excuse me if I forget to laugh. Please be serious. This Earthling is such a nice Earthling. I would like to help her overcome her depression about growing older. Any ideas?" asked Monroe. He was known on his planet for his caring attitude and kindness to others.

Ramone's prankster nature again surfaced as she said, "Perhaps we could let her experience a few minutes on the massage bed in the gym but tell her that it is anti-aging technology. This Earthling seems to be very naïve and may believe it to be effective in that regard." The aliens lay on the massage bed when they wanted to relax. It acted on their bodies in much the same way as a masseuse might but with much more effect. On long interstellar voyages, it also helped keep their muscles toned.

You would know Ramone would come up with something like that... but what could it hurt? "You have an excellent idea. We could tell her that it will reverse the effects of aging and extend her life span, not that it merely massages flesh." Monroe looked at Babs, lifted his translator, and said, "Missus Babs, my companions and I have been discussing the problem you have with growing older and want to offer you a possible solution. Our planet has developed technology which we use to extend our lifespans. It is a technology that reverses effects of aging. We would like to offer it to you, if you so desire."

"What is it?" Babs asked.

"It is called an x-g-x-b-r-c-c-x-b-r-d-f-k-t-t-t g-g-k-t-t-t-z," said Monroe, neglecting to explain that this translated into English as 'massage bed'. "I would be happy to let you experience this technology for yourself to see how it rejuvenates the body. And all of your Earthling companions are welcome to try it as well."

Monroe turned to the other Earthlings. Everyone remained silent and slowly shook their heads, declining his offer. After all, Lizzie had said that the alien looked like a meat eater.

Chapter 36

Monday, November 10th, 4:49 AM CST

Everyone waited in the spaceship's lounge while Monroe escorted Babs to its gym. He instructed her to disrobe, then lifted the lid of the massage bed or xgxbrccxbrdkttt ggktttz as she knew it. The machine stood just over three and a half feet high, four feet wide, and eight feet long. The aliens considered the shiny metal device to be an essential item as it helped prevent muscle atrophy during long space flights. The surface of the bed as well as underside of the lid consisted of thousands of small flat, eight-sided disks, each about an inch in diameter and abutting each other to form what appeared to be a smooth surface.

"Please lie on your back on the *ggktttz.* The machine is programmed to adjust its temperature to whatever the being's body temperature is plus two percent for maximum comfort," said Monroe. After she lay down, he closed the lid and turned the device on. The machine made a humming noise, and Babs felt thousands of disks extend or contract from the bed and lid surfaces. They conformed to the shape of her body and began vibrating as they massaged it.

"Ooh, this does feel good," she said while enclosed in the massage bed. "What exactly is it doing?"

Darn! I did not anticipate a relevant question. I need to tell her something. "It is removing negative ions from within your body and replacing them with positive ions." Just like there are sins of omission, Monroe committed a minor fib of omission. He purposefully neglected to tell Babs that the bed's ion exchange only served to enhance the tone of the aliens' muscles.

"I'm feeling younger already. How much younger will this make me? How many years will this increase my lifespan?"

"I cannot say," said Monroe truthfully. "That is determined by the individual's interaction with the machine."

Five minutes later, Monroe turned the bed off and lifted its lid. After Babs had dressed, they returned to the lounge.

Lilly and the others looked relieved. She asked, "How was it?"

Babs beamed with enthusiasm. "Wonderful. That machine Mister Monroe put me in was the best. It felt like I was getting a massage all over, but it was a massage like I ain't never felt on Earth. I feel thirty years younger already."

"That's wonderful. But it's hard to believe a few minutes in a machine can make you thirty years younger. How does it work?"

Monroe said, "An explanation of the principles underlying operation of the *xgxbrccxbrdkttt ggktttz* would require more time than available to us, if you were to truly understand it. We must leave Earth shortly. I would offer a simple explanation by saying that on our planet, we believe you are only as old as you want to be. This machine has the power to make you feel younger."

"Well, all I know is I feel like I was a teenager again in high school when I had so much fun. There was a group of us that ran around together all the time. Talk about fun. We were always doing crazy things together. Like the time we ran over that dog—" said Babs.

"A wonderful sport, running over dogs," Lizzie sarcastically said.

The Aliens' limited interactions with Earthlings had been insufficient for them to understand the nuances of sarcasm when engaged in conversation. Monroe thought *We need to research this sport, Running Over Dogs, on the planet's Internet if we have time.*

"You know I didn't mean it that way. But it was funny. We were going down a dirt road, and all of a sudden, this dog—it was a great big yellow lab—I remember all the details just like it was yesterday. That anti-aging machine of Monroe's has done wonders for my memory. Anyway, that dog ran right out in front of my girlfriend's VW bug before she could stop it, and it went right under the bug. I could hear him go 'thump, thump, thump' as he tumbled over and over under the VW bug from front to back. When we looked back, the dog had rolled all the way out from under my girlfriend's VW bug. I'd have thought he was a gonner. A VW bug ain't that big, and a dog, especially a big yellow lab can do a number on it if he hits doing twenty miles an hour… the bug that is… doing twenty miles an hour. Anyway, this lab rolled all the way under the VW. But them is big dogs, and a VW bug is no match for big dog on a dirt road. I saw him take off out from under the back of the bug down that dirt road, barking up a storm and grinning like a possum eatin' poop. That bug didn't get the better of that dog. Do y'all have dogs on your planet?"

"No," said Ramone.

"What do y'all have for pets?"

"*XBRqnfdxgxbrzkczpptc*. They are somewhat like your armadillos, only a little larger. We have one on board. She just had a litter of the cutest little pups. They have long pregnancies—thirty-six of your Earth months."

Monroe thought *Another argument I lost about what to bring with us.*

"And to think how we bitch about nine months," said Lilly.

Babs frowned. "Oooooh. I don't know if I could handle an armadillo for pet."

Sonny said, "Armadillos are all over Georgia. They've gotten so bad about digging up my garden that I've had to start shootin' em at night. Do y'all keep them armadillo-like pets of yours outside like yard dogs?"

"Absolutely. They are lovable but pretty nasty. You would not want one inside your house. It would ruin your furniture," said Salome.

Monroe rolled his eyes. *Mister Nitpicky. Always the fussy decorator.*

"It would probably be easier to handle than my new puppy. At least cheaper." Lizzie looked at Monroe. "I'm in the market for a fifth husband just to pay for new furniture to replace all the stuff he's ate up."

Monroe said, "Fifth husband? You have been married four times?"

"Yeah, but who's counting? Unlike a lot of the young people nowadays, I think marriage is a wonderful experience. The more the merrier as they say. What about you?" Lizzie batted her eyes.

Monroe grew more uncomfortable with Lizzie's continued flirting. He was on a diplomatic, not romantic, mission. Besides, he had four spouses and eighty-seven children back home. He lowered his translator and spoke in his native language directly to Ramone and Salome. "This Earthling reminds me of an older widow that used to live in my neighborhood. The one that would not stay away after one my spouses died. Always bringing me homemade dishes to eat. But that is neither here nor there. I believe it would be beneficial to discuss our interactions with these Earthlings among ourselves in private."

Ramone lowered her translator. "I do not know about you, but I feel I have gathered enough information from interacting with these

Earthlings to make an Admit/Do Not Admit decision regarding this planet."

"I also feel that way," Salome said, speaking in his native language. "You were correct to bring these three female Earthlings on board for us to interact with. Our conversations with them have given me great insights into the true nature of people on Earth, which we did not derive from our previous interactions with government officials of this planet."

Monroe raised his device to speak with his guests. "My goodness. Where has the time gone? My friends, I do hate to end our discussion, but my companions and I must prepare our ship for departure. We have another planet to visit and are long overdue."

"Oh, that's too bad," said Lizzie. "Just when we we're getting to know each other better."

"Yeah. It's been real great meeting y'all. I wish y'all would come visit us in Thomasville for a while. Y'all could stay with me if you want. I promise I'd make y'all some good Southern home cooking," said Babs.

Monroe said, "Missus Babs, we would love to spend more time with you as well as Lilly and Lizzie, but we have a very tight time schedule and more planets to visit."

"Shame y'all couldn't come to the next meeting of our City Council," said Lilly.

Babs vigorously nodded. "Yeah. I'd love to see the expressions on their faces when y'all walked in......."

Monroe led his guests out of the lounge as Babs continued to chatter. He led them into a large room which he identified as the spaceship's commissary.

Sonny's eyes got wide. "This room is better'n a Cracker Barrel."

"What is a Cracker Barrel?" asked Monroe.

"It's a restaurant and the best thing since sliced bread. They sell stuff in their gift shop you can't find at Walmart. They got the best chicken n' dumplins."

The three women could not have been more hyper than kids in a candy store. Monroe waited while they perused the merchandise, thinking *Why does it take Earthling women so long to shop?* Each woman held several bags containing their selections as they left the room.

Lizzie continued to flirt with Monroe even as the group walked down a corridor to the spaceship's entrance. Monroe diplomatically listened, all the while thinking what a great contestant Lizzie would make on one of his planet's most popular reality dating shows, *The Naked Divorcée*.

Standing in the doorway to the starship, Babs suddenly pounced on Monroe, put her arms around him, and hugged very tightly. He responded in kind by encircling her with two of his four arms.

She said, "Mister Monroe, I cain't thank you enough for what you've done for me. I been feeling so blue lately about getting older. My kids are all older and too busy with their kids to spend much time with me anymore. And I didn't seem to have the energy to keep up with my grandkids when I'd play with them. I mean I been really down lately about gettin' older. I don't know what it was… I guess when you got no husband to worry about anymore…"

"But anyway, I feel like I'm thirty-years old again. That anti-aging machine of yours worked wonders on me. It's like I said. I feel like a kid again. After laying in that machine… You know, you should market that thing. Right here on Earth. You'd make a mint. You could get that pillow guy to market it for you on TV. That machine did wonders for me. I feel like a kid again. Oh… I think I already said that. Anyway, what you said about growing old and how we're only as old as we want to be... I never thought about it that way, but you're right. I been making myself miserable when I don't really have to. Well, I'm having no more of that."

"I hoped the xg*xbrccxbrdefkttt ggktttz* would help you. You do seem to be rejuvenated," said Monroe. *At last, an Earthling who has benefited from our visit.*

Babs nodded enthusiastically. "And I'm gonna get myself a set of monkey bars installed in my backyard as soon as I get back to Thomasville."

Lizzie said, "I know what I'd like to do when I get back to Thomasville. Unfortunately, Mister Monroe is leaving us, so I guess I'll just have to take an afternoon nap instead."

"I think I speak for all of us when I say that we want y'all to know how much we appreciate your hospitality," said Lilly. "And please tell Mister Salome how much I loved talking with him about his decorating. He had some interesting ideas that I want to try out when I get back home. Especially pairing pink with orange which I always thought clashed with each other. If it works on y'all's planet, no reason why it won't work here on Earth. Next time y'all are in the area, I'd love to have him come to Thomasville and go to some of the interior decorating stores in Tallahassee with me."

Babs nodded. "Y'all have been the nicest three aliens I've ever met. I do hope y'all will come back soon and spend some time in Thomasville with us."

"Babsie, time to turn loose of Mister Monroe. I think those men down there are waiting for us," said Lizzie, pointing to the bottom of the ramp where several men stood. They all wore black suits, white shirts, and black ties.

"They will escort you to the Holding Compound Security Office," said Monroe. "Farewell, my friends."

Babs led the contingent down the ramp. All waived goodbye at Monroe, and he waived back with all four of his hands. He then closed the spaceship door and returned to meet with the other members of the Decision Group. All felt they had enough information to proceed with an 'Admit/Do Not Admit' decision. Their opinions would determine the fate of the Earth.

Chapter 37

Monday, November 10th, 5:36 AM CST

Monroe, Ramone, and Salome sat in their spaceship's conference room. They spoke in their native language which was recorded and translated here in English.

Monroe said, "This is the twentieth meeting of Decision Group 346. We were chartered by the Supreme Council of the Confederation of Planets of the Milky Way Galaxy. Our charter is to make recommendations to the Council regarding admissibility into the Confederation of select planets. The purpose of this meeting is to consider planet Earth for admission. The members of this Decision Group including myself are *XGttbzqnfdtkttt, QNFDxbrxgttbzkttt,* and *ZZxbrptxgkttt.* We will make either an Admit or a Do Not Admit recommendation to the Council."

"We have been on Earth twenty-six days and have met with eighty-seven officials from the following United States government entities: Department of State, NASA, Aerial Phenomena Research Organization, Department of the Air Force, Central Intelligence Agency, Federal Bureau of Investigation, Office of Scientific Investigation and Research, and the Space Force. I note the limited array of individuals with whom we met was necessitated by our confinement to the Near Earth Detection and Holding Compound located inside Elgin Air Force Base."

"These meetings were similar to our meetings with government officials on other planets. These meetings generally tended to be scripted by bureaucrats who presented information which was mostly propagandistic in nature. We believed these meetings did not provide us with a realistic picture of the planet on which to base a recommendation. For this reason, we solicited further interactions with three female and three male Earthlings named Babs Neauxgeaux, Lilly White, Lizzie Sherbert, Sonny Biskit, Tim, and Allen. We did not learn the surnames of the last two Earthlings. None of these individuals has any connection with any government entity. Our interactions with these Earthlings were helpful in our decision-making process. I now ask *QNFDxbrxgttbzkttt* for her thoughts."

"I concur with *XGttbzqnfdtkttt*'c comments regarding our meetings with officials from the various government entities," Ramone said. "Those individuals appeared to be unimaginative and duplicitous, but this is to be expected from government officials on any planet. It is not necessarily a reason why a planet should not be admitted into the Confederation. Accordingly, I did not find in any of those meetings a reason to recommend either admission or non-admission of Earth into the Confederation. Thank you."

"*ZZxbrptxgkttt*?"

Salome said, "I concur with *QNFDxbrxgttbzkttt*. For this reason, I was pleased that *XGttbzqnfdtkttt* was able to locate Earthlings not affiliated with an official government entity. I found all of them to be very nice Earthlings."

Monroe said, "I concur with *QNFDxbrxgttbzkttt*'c comments as well as those of *ZZxbrptxgkttt* about the Earthlings. That said, our interaction with them generated some concerns for me. First was the Earthling Babs verbosity. She talked non-stop, which was beneficial in providing information on which to make an Admit/Do Not Admit decision. On the other hand, the other Earthlings from the various government entities also talked extensively during our meetings. Might this be a worldwide human trait? Interplanetary studies have shown that excessive talking is correlated with a tendency to mask shortfalls in knowledge and/or cognitive ability."

Salome asked, "Is she a politician?"

"I do not believe so, but she certainly has the verbal proclivity to become one. I also found her criticisms of my name puzzling. She complained that my name was hard to spell, too long, and needed vowels such as those used in the English language. Her comment 'Your name's got more letters than I can say grace over' sounded sacrilegious."

"The other Earthlings with whom we met today seemed to have difficulty with our names."

"Odd that Earthlings have multiple names—first, middle, and last—but have difficulty dealing with one long name," said Ramone.

"Many creatures invoke negative stereotypes when confronted with unfamiliar sounding names. Could it be some sort of indication of prejudice against aliens?" Monroe asked. He paused in contemplation for a few seconds. "I was also disappointed in the Earthlings' inability to grasp the principles underlying nano electrokinetic thruster technology and electro-osmotic flow. None of them seemed to understand my simple explanation. And the Earthling Sonny seemed so interested in learning about our propulsion technology, at least initially. Very disappointing."

Salome said, "Perhaps you are being too harsh in your judgement of these six non-governmental Earthlings. Remember, we have talked with eighty-seven government officials since landing on Earth. Only one of them—the NASA physicist—was conversant with nano electrokinetic thruster technology and electro-osmotic flow."

Monroe nodded. "Yes, and thank you for reminding me. All of the Earthling government officials failed to impress me, and not only with their inability to grasp scientific principles. However, I think the three of us can agree on one thing. Intelligence levels among government officials was typically lower than that of the population in general on all of the planets we visited. This includes the three we recommended for admission into the Confederation. I had hoped the intellectual capacity of Earthlings not associated with government, specifically these last six, would be higher than that of officials that govern them. Unfortunately, my interactions with this last group did not bear this out."

Ramone nodded his concurrence, then addressed another issue. "I was particularly upset when the female Babs admitted she slings a dead cat at her grandchildren. From the information I see on the Internet, domesticated felines appear to be relatively benign animals."

"She apparently has a lot of grandchildren as she cannot sling a dead cat without hitting one of them. This sounds like a brutal activity. Something a primitive society would do," said Salome.

"Earth's culture must have some odd aversion to felines. Remember how Babs said her friends were more fun than a sack full of kittens? I fail to comprehend the humor derived from one kitten in a sack, much less a sack teeming with young felines.

Monroe nodded his concurrence. "Obviously a perverse sense of humor. Something else concerns me. The female named Lilly admitted that she as well as her Internet date lied on their online forms."

"Do Earthlings not recognize the inviolability of a global system of interconnected computer networks using standardized protocols to communicate?!"

"Lying on an online form on Globenet," Monroe said, referring to his planet's version of the Internet, "would be punishable with six lunachrons suspension from online gaming."

Ramone said, "Yet, the female Lilly acted as if lying occurs on the Earth's Internet all the time."

"Going back to the Earthlings' brutal activities toward felines, I found the Earthling Sonny's armadillo comments to be more appalling—shooting them in his backyard at night simply because the animals were performing instinctive tasks."

Salome nodded. "Apparently, the Earthling never considered some sort of catch and release solution to the problem." Ramone nodded her concurrence.

Monroe asked, "What did you make of the Earthling's use of the word 'y'all'? They used it quite frequently."

"I was dismayed. Any language that permits use of the contraction of two words is indicative of that civilization's decline," Salome said.

Ramone nodded. "Remember what the great philosopher *OBEktttqnfdtxgkttt* said, 'Use of contractions in language is a sign of a slothfulness and a lack of sophistication.' An advanced civilization's language does not use contractions of words."

"Speaking of lack of sophistication, the Earthling Sonny expressed his belief that the restaurant labeled Cracker Barrel is the best thing since sliced bread," said Salome. "Surely, his existence thus far has been extremely limited if he places such a high value on the slicing of bread. I wonder how many other Earthlings would deem slicing bread an outstanding accomplishment?"

"Another thing troubles me. Why does Earth need so many genders? The female Babs indicated that they have as many as fifty or sixty genders," said Monroe.

"I thought she had either misspoken or was exaggerating when she said this. I know we practice gender inversion as most advanced societies do, but I cannot fathom any civilization having more than two genders. Maybe we misunderstood her," said Salome.

"Or maybe the human species has somehow extended gender identification beyond that which we believe possible. Let us check their Internet to see if this is accurate," Monroe said.

As requested, Ramone queried the Internet and quickly came back with results. He said, "It appears to be worse than the female indicated. I found an article at HelpfulProfessor.com that indicates there are eighty-one different types of genders and gender identities on the Earth."

"Surely you misread it! Does the article site any examples of these different genders?" asked Monroe.

"Yes. Here are just a few." Ramone read at random as he scrolled down a list included in the article. "Assigned female at birth, cis male, demigirl, gender questioning, Guevedoche—"

"Guevedoche?"

"This gender belongs to a small ethnic group of Earthlings. Females sometimes give birth to children who are born looking like females but grow male genitalia at age 12."

"I don't recall ever running across that on any planet before. Interesting. Please continue."

"Non-binary, novigender—"

"Novigender?"

"Apparently, these are Earthlings that feel as if their gender is ever-changing or hard to pin down. Here are some more genders—polygender, transsexual, winkte—"

"Winkte?" asked Salome.

"It is a Native American gender describing someone born male but possessing a female spirit. Do you want me to continue?"

"No need to. Eighty-one! Are you sure this article is written by a reputable source?" asked Monroe.

"The article is written by a person who possesses a doctorate degree. It must be a scientific article."

"Clearly sexuality on Earth eclipses anything known within the Milky Way Galaxy." Monroe paused before continuing. "Was it just me, or did either of you notice that the female Lizzie kept making romantic overtures toward me?"

"It was obvious," said Ramone. "It seemed to me she was prospecting for a suitor of substantial means."

Occasionally, Ramone does have a valid insight. Monroe nodded his agreement and said, "I think some sort of intragalactic sex was a secondary motive on her part. Her overtures became quite aggressive at times."

"Could this planet be inhabited by many females of this sort?"

Puzzled, Monroe shrugged all four shoulders. "I doubt we will be able to answer that question. What else about the Earthlings did you observe?"

"Religion on this planet exhibits unusual tenets," said Salome.

"How so?"

"I refer to the female Babs' comment that their Bible should have been published with pictures in it. Why would Earthlings want pictures of that which is unseeable and unknowable? Might this kind of thinking be prevalent among other Earthlings?"

Monroe and Ramone, unable to respond, simply shook their heads in pity.

"I think one of the most telling indicators of the Earth's unsophistication is the fact that they still have letter S in their alphabet," said Salome.

"I know of no advanced civilization using the letter S," said Monroe shaking his head. "There is something else. I noticed the female Babs referred to something called Facebook several times. None of the Earthling officials made reference to a Facebook. Do either of you know what it is?"

Ramone nodded. "I was doing some research on the Internet while you were exercising this morning and ran across Facebook by accident. It appears to be primarily a means of social interaction among older females. They interact by means of 'posts' on their Facebook 'pages'. These posts can include text and images communicating life events, philosophical musings, and pointless trivia about themselves. Also, a substantial number of humans appear to use Facebook as a means of expressing anger toward other humans."

"They may find it to be a less physically traumatic method of confrontation than an in-person dispute."

"I had not thought of that. Let me display some Facebook posts on the large screen to see if we can substantiate your deduction."

All three aliens looked on as Ramone accessed Facebook postings at random. After a minute, Salome said, "What a crude means of virtual social interaction."

"Yes, but this is because Facebook operates on the Internet, which only allows humans to interact socially via two of the five human senses—visual and auditory. The Internet, and hence Facebook, does not involve olfactory, tactile, nor gustatory senses," Ramone said.

"And these Earthlings believe Facebook to be an adequate substitute for physical social interaction?" asked Monroe.

"Apparently."

"Let us move on. The female Babs said she used something called Xanax. Please look up what it is."

As requested, Ramone queried the Internet then said, "It is a psychotropic drug used to treat anxiety disorders and anxiety caused by depression."

"Why would a female Earthling be using psychotropic drugs? Because of insufficient physical social interaction?"

"There seems to a lot of information on the Internet regarding the planet's abundance of drugs and excessive drug use. Apparently, the female Earthling's drug use is typical."

Salome asked, "Could the female Earthling's use of Xanax be correlated with her depression about growing older? Indeed, might not the entire planet's obsession with growing old be correlated with its excessive drug use?"

"That is a distinct possibility. It would be interesting to research this topic as well as correlation between human beings' excessive drug use and high levels of Facebook postings and online gaming on the Internet," said Ramone. "But these topics are probably beyond the scope of our mission."

Monroe said, "I concur but think we can surmise that excessive drug use on Earth is probably an issue negatively weighing on its admission into the Confederation. Anything else?"

"The male Sonny tracked mud and animal feces throughout this vessel, including the shag carpet in our lounge. Perhaps an indication of a careless deportment widespread throughout the human species," said Salome.

Monroe said nothing and instead nodded agreement while thinking *I have been waiting for Salome to bitch about the mud on his carpet.*

Ramone said, "I found the female Babs' story of an encounter between something she called a friend's 'VW bug' and a dog to be very disturbing, to say the least. It sounded like some sort of a sport involving large insects and canines."

"Something akin to slinging a dead cat perhaps?" asked Monroe.

"Possibly. Remember the Earthling Lizzie's reference to the sport of 'Running Over Dogs?'"

"Yes. She referred to it as a wonderful sport. I had thought canines were beloved animals on Earth."

"The female also mentioned that the canine ran off 'grinning like a possum eating poop'." Ramone quickly queried the Internet. "A possum is a small marsupial animal, and poop is a slang word for feces. Why would marsupials be happy eating feces? The way the female said it, it sounded like a not uncommon practice among marsupials on Earth."

"I find the sport of a large insect running over a canine to be more troubling than marsupials eating feces. Perhaps they medicate the canine with some sort of psychotropic drug before the large insect runs over it."

Salome said, "I venture to say that the canine's behavior after being run over by the large insect might have been a learned reflex resulting from some sort of psychological conditioning. We could query the Internet for more information on marsupials eating feces as well as the sport of running over canines."

Monroe shook his head. The Supreme Council appointed him to lead this mission because of his decisiveness. Too many Decision Groups had been sent out in the past, succumbed to prolonged indecision, and failed to return. He said, "I see no need to pursue this any further. I think we have sufficiently discussed the Earthlings' behaviors to draw conclusions regarding Earth's admissibility into the Confederation. I know we had planned on staying on Earth up to six months, but I believe our interactions with these three female Earthlings, as well as government officials before them, have yielded sufficient information. I recommend we take a vote, then leave this planet forthwith. Do both of you agree?"

"Agreed."

"Agreed," Ramone said.

After voting, Monroe informed the Space Force staff on Elgin they would depart Earth as soon as they completed their pre-flight procedures. Disappointed at not finding Earth sophisticated enough to admit into the Confederation, he nevertheless felt satisfied.

I truly think we made the right decision. Earth needs more time to mature. And what can I say about my crew? Did they not perform superbly? That Ramone! She never ceases to surprise me. For once, she behaved herself. She thought of someone else for a change and came up with a great solution to help Missus Babs get over her depression about growing old. And what about shy Salome? I cannot get over how he interacted with those Earthlings just as if they were old drinking buddies. His father will be so proud when I tell him how Salome was 'Mister Charisma' on Earth.

As they lifted off, Monroe also took pleasure in knowing the spaceship's food storage compartment contained six cases of M&M's. He got hooked on them during the Holding Compound's Halloween Party.

Chapter 38

Monday, November 10th, 6:05 AM CST

21st Space Surveillance Squadron Command Center, a building inside the Near Earth Object Detection and Holding Compound, contained several Interrogation Rooms. Babs and her five companions sat in one of them. All the interrogation rooms had four things in common—walls painted bright white, glaring fluorescent overhead lighting, grey metal chairs, and an off-white laminated-top table. Some Holding Compound staff suspected poor taste accounted for the decorating scheme; some suspected malice.

The men interrogating Babs and the others were from the Alien Interrogation Unit. AIU was a component of the 21st Space Surveillance Squadron. The Squadron Commander reported to the newest branch of the Air Force Department, Space Force. AIU adopted its nickname, Men in Suits or MIS as commonly known, one New Year's Eve while celebrating at the Elgin Officers Club. The two MIS men identified themselves to Babs and the others simply as Number One and Number Two.

Number 1 held Tim's camcorder in his hands as he inspected it for the umpteenth time. He said, "We're going to keep all of you here as long as it takes. You've been helpful so far, but we need to know everything, and I mean everything, you and the aliens talked about."

"I already told y'all everything I know, but I don't mind telling y'all again," Babs said, talking being in her sweet spot. "My friends and I do this reality show, *Real Widows of Thomasville*, and we had to come here to prove there's UFOs and aliens in Area 53, which there is because all of us met three of 'em. By the way, they are the nicest people... well, they really ain't people, are they? Anyway, they were the nicest aliens I've ever met... Duh, they're the only aliens I've ever met.........."

Number 1 and Number Two began to tune Babs out as he had heard Babs tell this story seven times in less than twenty minutes. They knew all about Babs and the *Real Widows* reality show, having worked overnight on Thursday with Kirby Johnson on the article denying existence of Area 53.

"........Mitzi has been ragging me forever about Area 53 being a figment of my imagination. I can't count the number of Facebook posts where she's gone off on a tangent about me and UFOs. But when she and them other Mammas mouthed off on our show about me getting older and me lying, that did it. I wonder if Cordell purposefully had them do that to egg me on? Oh well........"

Number Two leaned over while Babs was talking and whispered in Number One's ear, "She's a fountain of information. Actually, more like a geyser. I've learned more about alien culture from her in the last thirty minutes than I did interrogating the aliens over the last three weeks. I just wish we could keep her on track. You think she does this on purpose?"

Number One shrugged and whispered back, "I've been wondering about that. Maybe she's some sort of a disinformation plant."

"You know, those three aliens never told us even a tenth as much about their culture as she has."

"I just hope we don't run out of tape," Number One whispered in jest. The room's digital system accommodated a virtually unlimited amount of recording.

"........so, they got into an argument over whose asparagus casserole was the best, and I thought to myself, 'Y'all wouldn't have had this mess if y'all would've coordinated this stuff to begin with.' Nobody wants to see two asparagus casseroles at the same social function, even if it's a convention of twins. I swear... I'll never volunteer to coordinate another Garden Club Food, Fun, and Flowers Luncheon if I..........."

Both MIS Men tuned out even though they had not heard this story before. Several minutes lapsed before they tuned back in.

"........Ramone, he's... I mean she's the alien that's a woman this month, told me about his... I mean her children... Did y'all know that she has one hundred and seventy-seven children? I wondered 'how does she ever keep track of their names?' Especially the kind of names they got with no vowels. I hate to think of what Christmas shopping for presents for his... I mean her children must be like. Can you imagine buying diapers for all them? But I know she's a great father... or mother, depending on what time of the month it is. Wait, maybe I should've said what month of the year it is... Anyway, I told him 'I bet coming up with all those names for all them children is quite a chore.' I wondered whenever his or her wife… You know, depending on the time of month, it might just be his husband… Anyway, I'm getting off the subject. I should say that I would have figured that whenever he or she and his or her spouse have a baby, they just throw pieces of paper with letters of the alphabet on 'em into a bowl, then pull 'em out randomly, and lay 'em on the table, and whatever order they're in is the name of the baby. I would've guessed that you can do that when your language don't have no vowels. But Ramone said that ain't the way they name their babies. He… I mean she said that they got a much better way of naming babies—"

Suddenly, the door opened. A man leaned in and pointed at Number One. "The Squadron Commander wants to see you."

Number One said, "Be there in a minute. She was just going to tell us how the aliens name their babies."

The man said, "Now."

Number One looked at Babs. "Talk about something else until I get back. I want to find out exactly how aliens name their babies."

After Number 1 left the room, Tim asked, "When can I have my camcorder back?"

"I doubt you'll ever get it back, my friend. This is evidence," Number Two said.

Lilly said, "But we're cooperating. Why do y'all need evidence?"

"He's saying they'll need evidence for a trial," said Tim.

Number Two smiled. "Who says you'll go to trial."

"But we have a right to a trial," said Lizzie.

"Not when it involves national security. You folks broke into a top-secret facility."

"We didn't break in. Mister Monroe invited us in," Babs said. "And he was very gracious about it too. He was one of the most polite aliens I've ever met. Wait. Is it most polite or politest? I think it's most polite. That sounds better. I wish I had one of them translation devices like Monroe had. That thing would know whether to say politest or most polite. There's some words that always trip me up when it comes to knowing whether it's more or most and er or est—"

At that point, the door opened and #1 came back in. He motioned for the interrogatees to follow him as he said, “Come with me.”

Cordell sat in an interrogation room on the other side of the Command Center. His two black-suiters took him directly there after transporting him to the Holding Compound. He said, “It’s like I’ve been telling you two for three hours now. We’re here doing a real-life documentary for TV. I was parked on the side of the road which is public land. There’s no law against parking on the side of the road. I demand to call my lawyer.”

Number Three said, “And it’s like we been telling you, we know what you were doing, Mister Isler, and why you were parked outside a secure military base. MIS has been monitoring you folks ever since your show Thursday night. We love your show by the way. It’s the best thing on TV since *Beverly Hills, 90210—*"

“You gotta be kidding. *Beverly Hills, 90210* stunk. But *Real Widows* is the best thing on TV since the *X-Files*. But enough of that.” Number Four looked at Cordell. “You can demand to call your lawyer until the cows come home. It ain’t happening until you sign this agreement not to show any footage your camera crews recorded.”

“I demand to know what you’re going to do with me.”

“You’re on a need-to-know basis, and all you need to know is that you need to sign that paper.” Number Four pointed to the pen and paper in front of Cordell.

Cordell picked up the pen and signed the paper. Despite being weary from the interrogation, he smiled. His lawyers had successfully broken agreements before.

Chapter 39

Monday, November 10th, 4:30 PM CST

Babs, Lilly, Lizzie, Sonny, Tim, and Allen showed up as the Jailbirds lounged poolside at a beachfront house in Santa Rosa, Florida. Cordell rented it for staging the Area 53 project. Mild weather and a lot of alcohol and food made for a festive afternoon. As previously agreed, they abandoned their protest outside the Main Gate at 5:00 AM. Base Security personnel breathed a sigh of relief as the thirteen women waived goodbye and boarded their RV. After a stop at Waffle House for a well-deserved breakfast, they arrived at the beach house. Their Duval County Jailhouse friends were not there; nevertheless, the *Real Widows* producer told them to party by themselves on Cordell's dime. He also praised them, something rarely done by customers in their lines of work—drugs and prostitution. "Your protest successfully diverted enough security personnel to the Main Gate that the Real Widows were able to reach Area 53 without being detained."

The late arrivals looked pretty beat up. Pink said, "Like, you guys look like something the cat drug up. What happened?"

"We been tied up all day with security people on base. What a mess. At least they drove us back to Babs' Escalade. I would have hated to ride in a bucket lift over that fence twice in one day. That damn fence was topped with razor wire," said Lizzie.

"I never rode over a fence topped with razor wire, but I've climbed over lots of barbed wire fences," said Ebony. "Had to spend three months in the joint after the cops caught me all tangled up the last time."

Isabella said, "Barbed wire ees no beeg deal. I climb through a bunch of that stuff crossing the border in Arizona when I was twelve years old."

"Like, my worst experience with barbed wire was a john that liked to have it, like wrapped around his nuts when we had sex," said Peggy. "Like, I had to be *reeel* careful."

"Like, was that your only experience!? Where you been? There's a lot of barbed wire BDSM out there," said Angie. "Like, I get requests to use it all the time. Check out 'barbed wire sex' on the Internet sometime."

Lizzie joined in the one-upsmanship. "My third… or maybe it was my fourth husband always wanted me to wrap him in barbed wire when we had sex, but I wasn't about to get blood all over a twelve hundred dollar set of bed sheets. No matter how enjoyable it would have been to see that two-timing bastard suffer."

"When yo man is cheatin' on you, they's lots better ways of gettin' back at 'em," said Frigerator. She spent the night in the Duval County Jail with the Casserole Ladies, having been arrested for assault and battery. Her boyfriend cheated on her on a night when business on the street was light, so she came home early.

"Such as? I'm always interested in new ways of getting back at my future husbands."

"Kick 'em in the nuts like I did my man."

"Where were you when I was fifty?" asked Lizzie.

"Prob'ly in the Duval County Jail."

Lilly said, "We were just lucky that base security detained us."

"How you figure that?" asked Kanesha.

"If we had to walk back to the fence where Babs' Escalade was parked, we wouldn't have been able to get over it. Our phones wouldn't work, so we wouldn't have been able to contact the bucket lift guy to get us back over the fence."

"None of yo phones work? Wonder why?"

Babs said, "They weren't supposed to work. I found out why from them Rangers—"

"You did. What do you mean?" asked Lilly. "The abbreviated version, please."

"After y'all lost us, those four nice Army Rangers I was telling y'all about. They were there on some sort of training exercise—"

"That's what I said probably happened… that you and Tim ran into some Rangers and were following them," said Sonny.

Babs nodded. "Correct. They were dressed up like bushes. Scared the heck outta me, but they were very nice. Just a bunch of kids. Looked like they was just out of high school. Cute as a button… at least I bet they were when they weren't disguised as bushes. Anyway, they were on a training exercise. We told 'em that we were there filming for our show, and the oldest one of them, he wasn't any older than a lot of my grandchildren, said they loved our shows. And I said, 'Y'all do?' And he said that they especially loved the food fight at Preble Hill. He said it reminded of RASP training—"

Lilly asked, "RASP? What's that?"

"That's Ranger Assessment and Selection Program. It's pretty rough. The Ranger said it was eight weeks of pure hell—"

"I bet RASP was no competition for the Preble Hill Food Fight," Lizzie said. "Maybe the Rangers should have part of their RASP training at Preble Hill during the Masquerade Ball."

The lightbulb came on in Babs' brain. Her face lit up as she asked, "Why didn't I suggest that to them? Anyway, they were on a training exercise… you know… hiding out as bushes, trying to walk in the woods without making noise, heading in the same direction as we wanted to go—"

Lilly rolled her eyes. "And I asked for the abbreviated version."

"If you're gonna interrupt me, maybe you should tell my story."

"Oh no. You're doing a great job. Please continue. But we would be interested in finding out why our cell phones didn't work."

"Oh yeah. I did kind've get sidetracked. Anyway, that cute Ranger said that the base blocks cell phone service in certain areas of the base on purpose. He said they started blocking cell service in training areas after they found out teams were cheating by using their cell phones during exercises."

Lilly said, "So that explains it."

"Them Rangers said they would like to have been able to use their phone's GPS, but they wouldn't work, so they had to use their brains instead, and I thought to myself, 'That's a good idea. Why didn't I think of that?' Anyway, they told me that they had to go on these kind of training exercises all the time. Sometimes they'd go thirty-six hours without sleep. I'm half dead right now, and I only been without sleep for a day or so. I hate what going without sleep does to my face. I ain't slept well ever since we watched our show on Thursday night—"

Delphine who was from Haiti said, "My deeer Babs, that reminds me. I loved the first show, but the voodoo ritual under the oak tree—your chant in the Haitian Creole language—"

"Yes?"

"Your translation into English waz eencorrect."

"What do you mean?"

"You thought you said, 'Let our boyfriends tell them mammas to kiss their asses and think only about the Casserole Ladies.' Did you not?"

Babs nodded. "Yep."

"What you actually said in Haitian Creole translates into English as 'Oh great spirit, let me find an alien nearby here, so I can make a new friend.'"

Babs looked around, beaming and smiling ear-to-ear. "And y'all think my voodoo stuff don't work."

Lizzie smiled and looked at the Jailbirds. "Even though this discussion is very entertaining, I have to ask… Have any of you seen Cordell?"

"They have not showed up heeer yet. We been enjoying ourselves weeth yuuur refreshments," Delphine said, her accent revealing her Haitian background.

They unsuccessfully tried calling Cordell, although no 'Service Unavailable' messages were received. Jada said, "The show's producer has called base security looking for your Cordell guy. He also called the network lawyers, and they've been calling the base as well."

"Nothing like a lawyer on retainer," said Lizzie. "Just ask any of my exes."

Cordell finally arrived just before 11:00 PM. He explained his detention by base security. "Everybody but the Pope interviewed me. I got threatened with everything from pulling out my toenails to chemical castration. I finally signed their stupid agreement to not show any of the film taken on base, but they still kept me for hours after that."

"So, nothing Tim and Allen filmed will be shown on our show?" asked Lilly.

Cordell smiled. "Everything they filmed was transmitted to the van and was uploaded from there to the Cloud. It's all preserved, and our lawyers are working on getting my agreement nullified. That's why I didn't call you on the way over here. I been on the phone non-stop with them. They're working on the Feds as we speak. We got a lot to do. I want Tim, Allen and our producer to do some interviews with our protestors here. Get some good background stuff on the protest. We want to get some of the protest included in the next episode, or should I say next three episodes. We're gonna make hay out of this." Cordell looked at Lilly, Lizzie, and Babs. “I want the three of you to go to bed and get some sleep. We have to be in tip top shape mentally tomorrow morning.”

“Why?” asked Babs.

“We gotta be in court tomorrow morning at 10 AM.”

Chapter 40

Tuesday, November 11th, 9:30 AM CST

Judge Hammond's courtroom was located on the Naval Air Station in Pensacola, Florida. Babs, Lilly, Lizzie, Sonny, Tim, Allen, and Cordell sat with Leonard Birdwell, one of the network's top lawyers, at the defense table. Other than the Prosecutor, Bailiff, and Clerk, the courtroom was empty.

Counsellor Birdwell explained the judicial proceedings to his clients. "This is going to be unlike any courtroom drama you've ever seen on TV. This is a Specialized Federal Court. I've heard of them but never tried a case in one. I didn't even know this type of specialized court existed until Cordell called me yesterday."

"Specialized Federal Court?" Babs asked.

"Yes. They're not like the regular system of Federal courts. These only handle special cases. I was aware of five types of them—one that reviews cases involving the Armed Forces, one for Federal Claims, one for International Trade cases, one that adjudicates Veterans' Claims, and the Tax Courts. It turns out there apparently is a sixth type that handles certain types of National Security cases."

"Which is what our case is?" Lizzie asked.

"Bingo. Your case represents a violation of the National Security Act. These cases involve classified information—but not your average classified info—and for that reason, there is no jury. There's only a judge who is appointed by the White House. It's kind of like a FISA court."

"FISA court?" asked Lilly.

"Foreign Intelligence Surveillance Act. Judge Hammond is one of the few qualified to try these cases. He's been on the bench for over three decades. This is serious stuff."

"Why didn't you tell me this before?" asked Cordell.

"I did. You weren't listening. I wish I could have found a lawyer with experience in this particular kind of court, but I couldn't. National security cases as serious as yours are rare. From what I understand, Judge Hammond's ruling can only be appealed directly to the President of the United States. If Hammond sentences you to thirty years, you will probably serve thirty years in prison unless the President overturns his ruling."

Birdwell paused to let that sink in. His audience remained silent. He continued. "Your case is especially sensitive. Federal Courts are usually closed on Veteran's Day on November 11th, so the fact that Judge Hammond is hearing the case today says somebody very high up is pulling some strings. Be on your toes. Don't try any stunts. Don't try to look cute or smart. Answer his questions honestly and completely... but not too completely. Don't give him more information than he needs. Short, complete answers. Get to the point quickly. Got it?" Lilly and Lizzie deliberately looked at Babs. The defendants solemnly nodded.

Inside his chambers, Judge Hammond finished reading the case materials a second time then shook his head. He had handled a number of these specialized national security cases but nothing like this one. He thought, *Is this for real? A bunch of old women, Real Widows stars, breaking into a top-secret, secure Federal facility. How the Hell do I convict three little old ladies? How the Hell do I not?* He had watched the first two episodes and loved the show. The more he thought about it, this was exactly the sort of stunt Babs Neauxgeaux would attempt. Another thing disturbed him. Knutz was prosecuting. Hammond unconsciously shook his head in disdain. *Talk about a lightweight prosecutor*. The thing that most concerned him was the timeframe. The break-in happened yesterday morning, yet it was going to trial today!? Something was up, something way above his pay grade, and he was at a pretty high pay grade. *Someone very high up wants this thing wrapped up quickly. Probably someone in the White House worried about the PR aspects associated with jailing three older women. Better watch yourself! This is a tricky case, to say the least.* The Judge stood. It was time to get it over with.

As the door to the Judge's Chambers opened, the Bailiff said, "All Rise. The Honorable Judge Roland Hammond presiding."

Judge Hammond took his seat behind the bench and said, "Please take your seats. Let me explain how this court works. This is a Specialized Federal Court for Extreme Violations of National Security as proscribed by the National Security Act and subsequent amendments. The government will present its case first, then the

Defense, after which I will render a verdict from which appeal may only be made to the President of the United States."

The Judge continued to explain court procedures and other legal technicalities for several minutes, then looked at the Counselor Birdwell. "Are you ready?"

"Yes, Your Honor."

He looked at Prosecutor Knutz. "Are you ready?"

"Yes. Your Honor."

"Prosecutor Knutz. State your case."

Prosecutor Knutz rose and said, "A reminder, Your Honor. My name is pronounced 'newts,' like the salamander, not 'nuts,' like the inmates in an asylum."

"Noted. Proceed."

"Your Honor, the defendants…" said Knutz, then read the names of the seven defendants. "…are charged with willfully entering a top-secret, secure Federal facility without either appropriate security clearances or permission. To wit, they willfully entered the Near Earth Detection and Holding Compound as well as the Holding Facility located inside the compound yesterday. While inside this facility, they had access to classified information including the nature of the facility itself as well as the contents of the facility. Such violations of the National Security Act require a minimum prison term of not less than ten years in the Federal Prison at Leavenworth, Kansas."

"Very good. Counselor Birdwell, do you wish to make an opening statement?"

Birdwell rose. "Not at this time, Your Honor. We do have a number of issues regarding this case but prefer to raise them during testimony."

"Noted. Prosecutor Knutz, you may proceed with your case."

"Thank you, Your Honor. For my first witness I call Mister Cordell Isler. The witness will take the Witness Stand."

The Bailiff swore in Cordell who sat in the Witness Stand. Prosecutor Knutz directed Cordell to give an account of the events of the night. During Cordell's testimony, he explained how his role in the event involved monitoring the action from inside the van located outside the perimeter fence surrounding Elgin Air Force Base. When he got to the part where two men in black suits surprised him, Judge Hammond interrupted, looked at Knutz, and said, "Prosecutor Knutz, I understand from the briefing materials that these two men were agents from the United States Space Force. Is that so?"

"Yes, Your Honor. They were part of Space Force's Alien Interrogation Unit."

"Tell us what happened next, Mister Isler."

Cordell said, "Your Honor, those two agents stayed with me in the van and watched the action in the woods and at the main gate for several hours on the TV monitors. Then, they took me into custody, handcuffed me, and transported me in their security vehicle onto Elgin Air Force Base to the Near Earth Holding Compound."

Judge Hammond looked flummoxed, then said, "Let me make sure I understand. These two AIU agents took you from your van, which was parked on County Road 23 and drove you onto the base and into the Holding Compound?"

"Yessir."

Hammond's flummoxed look remained unabated as he said, "That was not clear in the Prosecution's briefing materials. I'm calling a recess. I want to meet with the Prosecution in my chambers."

Inside the judge's chambers, a gloomy expression passed over Judge Hammond's face. He said, "This is not the first time I've run into a screw-up by these AIU goons. What I understand from Isler's testimony, the AIU idiots apprehended him while he was outside the base, parked on the side of a county road."

"Apparently."

"So, you're telling me those AIU goofballs transported Cordell Isler against his will, which is usually the case when a person is handcuffed… transported him onto the base and into the Holding Compound against his wishes. Is that correct?"

"Yes, technically so, but they did it because they believed Isler was abetting Ms. Neauxgeaux and the others who were trespassing inside a top-secret Federal facility."

"Why was Isler not charged with abetting a crime instead of an actual trespassing violation? He trespassed, but it was under duress against his free will."

"I guess the Space Force AIU personnel didn't think to include it in the charges. They're not lawyers after all."

Judge Hammond shook his head. "Why didn't *you* think of it before bringing Isler into my courtroom?"

Knutz looked at the floor.

"Alright. I've heard enough. That part of the case would be overturned on appeal to the President, and I'm not gonna let myself look like a fool by letting that happen. We're gonna dismiss with prejudice the charges against Isler and focus the rest of the trial on the other six defendants. The ones who *voluntarily* trespassed into a top-secret Federal facility. Let's get in there and get this trial wrapped up." Dismissal with prejudice meant the government could not re-try the case against Cordell later.

Back in the courtroom, Judge Hammond said, "Charges against Cordell Isler are hereby dismissed with prejudice. Mister Isler, you are free to go. The Prosecution will now proceed with its case against the remaining defendants."

The Prosecutor called on Babs to take the Witness Stand. After the Bailiff swore her in, Knutz began questioning her.

"Ms. Neauxgeaux, I want you to relate your participation in the break-in of the Near Earth Object Detection and Holding Compound and the Holding Facility inside that compound. Leave out no details."

Babs smiled at the Prosecutor's order to leave out no details. She was being ordered to talk, and Babs very much enjoyed talking. Talking was in her sweet spot. She said, "First off, we didn't break into the Holding Compound."

"You didn't?"

"No. We was invited in by Mister Monroe. He was such a nice man. Well, I guess he really wasn't no man……."

Babs' statement caught Judge Hammond's attention. *Wasn't really no man? What's she mean by that?* He turned to Babs to ask for clarification. *She doesn't look too bad for a sixty-three-year-old. I wonder if Knutz screwed up her age in his briefing materials?* Hammond began thumbing through the materials. *It does say she's sixty-three.* He said, "Missus Neauxgeaux, excuse me for interrupting. Counsellor Knutz, would you approach the side bench?"

After Knutz stood before the side bench, Hammond motioned for him to lean in close and whispered, "Have you screwed up? My briefing materials say Neauxgeaux is sixty-three."

"That is correct, Your Honor."

"She doesn't look a day over thirty-three. What gives?"

Knutz shrugged. "Must be the water in Thomasville. Honestly, Your Honor, she attests that she is sixty-three."

Hammond leaned back and said, "Okay. Counsellor, you may return to the defense table. Sorry for the interruption, Missus Neauxgeaux. I want to ask just who is this Mister Monroe?"

"He was one of the nice aliens that was staying inside the big pyramid building in the Holding Compound, Your Honorship."

"So, the reason you went into the Near Earth Holding Compound was because he invited you in?"

"Mostly, yessir. He invited me and Tim to join him in his spaceship… and Lilly, Lizzie, Sonny, and Allen when they got to the front gate later on."

"I'm calling for a short recess. I want the Prosecution to join me in my chambers," said Judge Hammond.

Inside his chambers, the Judge asked, "Did you know that one of the aliens invited Ms. Neauxgeaux and the others into the Compound?"

"No, Your Honor, but—"

"No buts. Why did you not know that?"

"No one took a statement to that effect from the aliens. The AIU charges merely state that the defendants entered the compound illegally without permission from Holding Compound personnel and without sufficient security clearances. The short timeframe of this case did not allow for me to adequately depose the defendants."

"Is it too late to get statements from any of the aliens to the effect that they did or did not invite any or all of the defendants into the Holding Compound?"

"Yes, Your Honor. The aliens have already departed this planet."

"Then, who is to challenge the veracity of Ms. Neauxgeaux's assertion that she did not break into the Holding Compound, but was instead invited in?"

"Uh, I guess no one."

"And why was she not charged with breaking into the base itself?"

“The AIU referral to us didn’t include breaking into the Air Force Base in the charges.”

“Okay.” Frustration in Hammond’s voice was audible. “It sounds like the government cannot base its case solely on her breaking into a secure Federal facility without permission. How do you intend to proceed?”

Knutz hung his head. “I planned to base part of my case on Neauxgeaux and the others being in a secure Federal facility without appropriate security clearances. I need to get them to testify as to what they saw and heard inside the Holding Compound. Since the facility, and hence everything inside it was classified, by simply being there they accessed classified information without appropriate security clearances.”

“Mister Knutz, I’m going to let this trial proceed, but if I don’t hear sufficient evidence to this effect, this case gets dismissed. Let’s get back in there.”

Chapter 41

Tuesday, November 11th, 10:45 AM CST

After the trial resumed, Knutz said, "Ms. Neauxgeaux, please tell us exactly what you saw and heard when you were inside the Holding Compound."

Babs said, "Yessir. I'd love to tell y'all exactly what I saw and heard. Even though I'm sixty-three, my memory is as sharp as a tack. My memory used to be so bad I could hardly remember what I had for breakfast most mornings, and I have the same thing every morning. But after Mister Monroe put me in that machine, my memory's been much better, so I should be able to do a better job of telling what I saw—"

Hammond asked, "Who is this Monroe, and what is this machine?"

"Oh, Mister Monroe, one of the aliens, was the nicest gentleman… although I don't guess he really was a gentleman because he wasn't really a man, although he is a male this month, unlike Miss Ramone, the alien who is a woman… oops, I meant a female because Ramone really isn't a woman, since she's an alien too. Wonder what you call a female alien? You can't call them a woman, can you? Anyway, Mister Monroe… Is Mister the right title for a male alien? I wish I'd have asked him what his title was……"

Judge Hammond suddenly realized his mind had drifted somewhere during Babs' male-female designation quandary. He hated it when he drifted off like that in a trial. *How long was I asleep? Did I close my eyes? Was it long enough for anyone to notice?* He had forgotten what his question to Babs was, so he simply pretended to look like he was busy, then looked over at Babs as if he had been paying attention all along.

"……..and it's like what Avery always told me, 'Treat you wife like a queen, and she'll treat you like a john.' I thought he was talking about a toilet, which didn't make no sense. I didn't learn what he meant by the word john until we'd been married eight years, and I found out a john was a prostitute's customer. Then what he said made sense! But that was Avery. He had the funniest sense of humor. He had four brothers, and not a one of them had a sense of humor. I always teased Avery that his family must've got their sense of humor from a mortician somewhere back in their family tree……"

As she rambled, Babs' earlier comments about her past poor memory suddenly resurfaced among Judge Hammond's thoughts. Had he had forgotten to take his pills that morning? *If I can get home by one o'clock today, I can take them. If not, I'll just have to skip them today. I've been forgetting to take them more and more lately. Maybe I need a turn in Monroe's machine myself. Maybe if I start putting my pills next to my car keys.* Then, he realized Babs had just said something funny. He asked, "Missus Neauxgeaux, would you mind repeating that? I think I might have misunderstood you."

"Yessir. I was just saying that when I got up this morning and got dressed, I put on a dress especially for this occasion. I hope you like it. Anyway, I looked at myself in the mirror and said to myself, 'How in the hell did a buffalo get into this dress.' It's all that stuff we ate at the beach house yesterday. It was carb city, which puts tons of pounds on." Babs smiled one of her best smiles at Judge Hammond. "But you don't have to worry about that, do you? You must go to the gym every morning……."

Hammond beamed at the complement, then wished she had not reminded him about the gym. In addition to forgetting his pills, he had forgotten to go to the gym. *Wait. What day of the week is it? I only go to the gym on Mondays, Wednesdays, and Fridays. Damn! I can't even remember what day of the week it is, but I am in my late sixties.* This thought prompted follow-on thoughts about a middle-aged redhead with a cute butt that always wore real skimpy Nike shorts to his gym.

"……..And all them apocalypse movies… you know *Mad Max*, *Terminator*, and so forth… the characters in 'em look like they got their clothes from one of them S&M shops in Hollywood. I mean look at what they wear—leather, chains, silver belt buckles….."

Judge Hammond unconsciously nodded. *A lot of what she's saying makes sense, but it's just that she says so much of it. I bet the wardrobe mistresses on those apocalypse movies only have to walk across the street in Los Angeles to buy the costumes.*

"…….and why do those people in them *Star Wars* movies dress like they're Medieval monks? I mean my God, they're flying in spaceships at Warp speed but wearing clothes made with sack cloth….."

The Judge unconsciously nodded again. *When you think about it, it makes sense. This woman has more insight than any of those numbskulls clerking for me.*

"…….and that's what she said, so I told her, 'You can bet your Gucci's that whenever Alabama and Auburn play, I hope they both lose.' I knew that would get her goat. She's from Birmingham, which is right in the middle between the two schools. Then she said that I had a face for radio and a voice for sign language. Well, I told her that she must have forgot to Febreeze her underwear that morning……"

Judge Hammond panicked. Had his wife remembered to Febreeze his underwear? *I don't remember seeing a nicotine stain on them when I put them on in the morning? How can I check without being too obvious? Maybe I should ask for a quick recess.*

"…….of course, it don't matter to me who wins in the Iron Bowl," Babs said referring to the annual football game between Alabama and Auburn, "since I went to FSU—"

"You're a Seminole?" asked Hammond. "Me too? What year did you graduate?"

"1978, Your Honorship."

"I'll be damned. I graduated in 1976. One of the guys in my fraternity was from Thomasville. What was that guy's name? E… E something Wren—"

"Edell Wren. Yeah, I know Dell very well. His wife died several years ago, so all the casserole ladies—that's a term we all use for single older women on the hunt for eligible bachelors—anyway, all the older women in Thomasville have made a run on Dell, except Gidget. She thinks he's pretty much worthless. She told me, 'Dell Wren is as useful as a pocket on a shirt.' Well, I just told her right back, 'That may be true, but there ain't that many shirts in Thomasville.' What I meant was there just ain't that many older bachelors in Thomasville, which means Dell don't stack up that bad 'cause he don't have that much competition. He's only good for one thing, and though it ain't that good, what are you gonna do when you live in Thomasville? It's like I often say to myself, 'There's so much of our sex lives that's better taken to the grave'……."

Judge Hammond remembered his fraternity initiation. Dell Wren had been one of the senior brothers who swung a heavy oak paddle against pledge's butts, including Hammond's. Babs' comments about sex lives prompted him to jot a quick note to himself while she talked. 'Look in boxes in attic for old girlfriend letters, pictures, etc. and destroy.'

"……and so, I told them that instead of happy hour starting at five PM, why not start it at four PM? And instead of it ending at seven PM, end it at eight or nine PM. And why not have it every day of the week instead of just five days a week? I said, 'What are we supposed to do on Saturday and Sunday anyways!?"

Judge Hammond noticed that everyone in the courtroom nodded their heads in agreement. *She's off track again. If that moron Knutz isn't gonna get her to focus on what she saw and heard in the compound, I'm gonna have to.* He asked, "Can you get into more detail as to exactly what you saw and heard inside the alien spaceship?"

Babs' subsequent spaceship travelogue lasted almost thirty minutes and contained excruciating detail. Judge Hammond continued to have trouble staying tuned in. *I bet Knutz is letting her ramble on purpose. He thinks the more she describes the aliens and the spaceship, the more it strengthens his case that she accessed classified information without appropriate security clearance. I'm gonna get this thing wrapped up so I can get home and take my pills.* The Judge said, "Ms. Neauxgeaux, you have given a lot of detail as to what you saw inside this alien spaceship as well as your conversations with these three aliens. As I understand it, you say your primary motivation behind your actions yesterday was to prove existence of an Area 53 as well as UFOs and aliens in Area 53?"

"Yessir, it was," she said.

"Why did you want to prove that?"

"It started with Mitzi and those other Mammas. They insulted me. They said I was just a senile old fart making up the Area 53 stuff for ratings, that I'm an old liar. She said that they wasn't no Area 53, that they wasn't no UFOs in Area 53 which didn't exist anyway, and that they wasn't no aliens come down here in UFOs in Area 53. I couldn't let all our viewers think I'd been lying to 'em just for ratings, could I? And it wasn't just Mitzi and the Mammas. Kirby Johnson, that Department of Defense spokesman denied existence of Area 53 in the *Washington Post* the morning after our last show."

"That is true. I remember reading their denial in the paper."

"So anyway, Mister Monroe invites me in to socialize with him and the other aliens, and then I get arrested for being someplace that don't exist. I keep asking myself, 'Why am I being arrested for breaking into something that don't exist?' Is that fair, Your Honorship?"

Judge Hammond reflected on her question. *She's got a good point. This might very well be the opportunity I've been looking for. Let the higher ups squirm with that one.* He said, "I'd like to call a brief recess and confer with the Prosecution in my chambers."

Inside his chambers, Judge Hammond asked, "Does she or does she not have a valid point? We've established that she didn't break into the compound. She was invited in. Those AIU numbskulls failed to charge her with illegally entering the Air Force Base itself. So, all you're left with is prosecuting her for accessing classified information without appropriate security clearance inside the Holding Compound which is called Area 53. But the Federal government denies existence of Area 53. How am I supposed to convict her of accessing classified information in a facility that DoD publicly says does not exist? I can just imagine what the President will say when her lawyer appeals it. Even the President can't argue with that."

"Your Honor, I'll have to consult with the US District Attorney before I can answer that."

Prosecutor Knutz left the room and came back fifteen minutes later. He said, "Your Honor, the DA agrees to a dismissal with prejudice of all charges against Neauxgeaux and the others."

Chapter 42

Thursday, November 13th, 8:00 PM EST

Babs, Lilly, and Lizzie crowded together on a leather sectional in Babs' basement to watch *The Real Widows of Thomasville* on her ginormous television. A large plate of loaded nachos sat on the coffee table in front of them. The air buzzed with excitement, but not because of the nachos. Cordell and his staff worked twenty-four hours a day, Tuesday night through Wednesday to produce the third episode along with a massive promotional campaign. The ladies knew all of Thomasville, as well as most of the country, would be watching. TV ads teased the audience, questioning whether the Real Widows would be able to meet Mitzi's challenge to prove Area 53 exists. The most enticing ad asked, "Do aliens really exist? Just ask XGttbzqnfdtkttt" as a transparent image of Monroe grows larger slowly moving toward the camera. Nachos and margaritas in hand, Babs tuned in the show.

INTERIOR SCENE: THOMASVILLE CITY HALL, FRIDAY

Real Widows theme begins with ladies' background chatter as images of individual Casserole Ladies' faces float across screen with her name superimposed. After the last image, screen goes totally black and silent as a disclaimer appears: "The United States Air Force denies existence of Area 53, Unidentified Flying Objects, and aliens from other planets as portrayed in following episode of *The Real Widows of Thomasville*." After ten seconds, the disclaimer fades into a wide shot of Thomasville City Council Chambers. Narrator's voiceover introduction occurs as Thomasville's Mayor and four City Council members walk to their seats at the dais and sit. Camera pans room which is filled with people.

NARRATOR: [Voiceover] Today is Friday, the day after Episode Two of *The Real Widows of Thomasville* aired on national TV. You may remember Mitzi and her three Mamma friends challenged Babs. Mitzi challenged her truthfulness, saying she lied when she said Area 53 exists. Mitzi also said Babs lied about Area 53 containing UFOs and aliens from outer space. She accused Babs' of lying to improve her show's ratings. Mitzi even questioned Babs'… and by inference the other Real Widows' mental acuity for advocating such a wild conspiracy theory. She inferred dementia had overtaken the three older women, especially Babs. Mitzi called Thomasville Mayor Joy Flamingo immediately after last night's episode and asked to be allowed to speak at the Thomasville City Council meeting. She told Mayor Flamingo it concerned Thomasville's reputation. The meeting is about to begin, and Mitzi is first on the agenda.

All the ladies were anxious to see exactly what transpired at the City Council meeting. Needless to say, they ranted and cursed throughout this segment of the show. Even polite and genteel Southern lady Lilly cursed more during the six-minute segment than she had in the last decade. At one point, Babs hit the pause button and said, "I don't know how much more of this I can take. Wait till those councilmembers are up for re-election."

Lilly said, "I'm just surprised the government is going to let Cordell show the Holding Compound stuff."

"Cordell or somebody at his network must have some powerful friends in the Federal government," said Lizzie.

Babs pushed play. At the point where Councilmember Maybry berated Babs' belief in twelve moons, Babs pushed pause and said, "It ain't twelve moons! Don't nobody on that Council know nothing right? Everybody knows it's only seven different moons."

"Dr. Maybry must have been one of the first children trained in new math," said Lizzie.

As they watched the Council's votes on both of Mitzi's resolutions, the cursing increased. After the vote was over, Babs paused the show and said, "Thank God that's over. I don't know how much more of that I could've taken." She pushed play.

NARRATOR: [Voiceover as scene transitions to a wide shot of the room as the Council takes up other business.] It looks like Mitzi achieved a victory today. The City Council voted unanimously to reject Babs' assertions that Area 53 exists and that it currently hides UFOs and aliens. They also censured her and the other Real Widows for these assertions. A review of Facebook posts shows that many residents of Thomasville agree with the Council's decisions. Unless the Real Widows can prove that Area 53 exists and that there are UFOs and aliens in it, they are going to have tough time remaining in the small town in which they grew up. Indeed, they have already begun the task of proving Babs is right, as we shall see in a few minutes. [Narrator pauses, second camera zooms in for close up shot of her, and she stares intently into camera as she speaks.] Many of you out there may agree with the City Council. That there is no Area 53 or Area 51. That no aliens have ever visited this planet. That there are no UFOs. I caution you. Remember the old saying, 'Truth is stranger than fiction.'

Scene fades to a commercial.

Babs made a phone call during the commercials. After she hung up, she said, "Tomorrow the City Council is gonna look like the fools they really are."

EXTERIOR SCENE: PARKING LOT IN JACKSONVILLE, SUNDAY

Long shot of thirteen women boarding a RV. As each woman steps up into the vehicle, her first name floats across the screen.

NARRATOR: [Voiceover] These colorful ladies have been friends of the Real Widows ever since the latter attended the Florida-Georgia college football game in Jacksonville last month. They are boarding an RV in the parking lot of a Walmart in that city in an effort to help their friends. Let's listen in.
KANESHA: I want y'all to be on y'all's best behavior on this here RV.
FRIGERATOR: Open up that refrigerator and hand me one of those malt liquors, or I'm gonna show you some bad behavior real quick.
ISABELLA: Bad behavior? That's my normal behavior. [Raucous laughter follows from all riders.]
PEGGY: So, like… can someone explain to me like, exactly what it is we're supposed to do?

KANESHA: How many times I gotta tell you? We gone go to that Elgin Air Base Main Gate and protest that they's keeping aliens inside that base.
JADA: But why we gone do that?
LATONYA: 'Cause that's gone draw all the base security to the Main Gate.
JUANITA: But why are weee going to do that?
KANESHA: Doan nobody listen to me when I's telling y'all yesterday? Babs and them other white women is gonna break into the air base to prove there's aliens an UFOs on base.
ANGIE: Like, ya know… Yaaaz, I was listening to ya.
PINK: Aliens? Like, ya mean the ones that come across the border? The Mexicans like Juanita and Isabella?
KANESHA: No. Not them kind of aliens. The aliens from outta space.
BRIANNA: Are we gonna get to stay at the beach?
BUTTERFLY: That's what the producer-man say yesterday. Stay as long as y'all want, he say.
EBONY: Awright! This sound like a good deal. Protest tonight, then relax at the beach a couple of days on Colt 45 and Moscato. [Everyone cheers.]
DELPHINE: [After cheering stops.] But we might get 'rested protestin' at that base.
KANESHA: No way. Daffy tole me 'drop everything and get back in this here RV if it looks like they gone 'rest us. [More cheers.]

Scene fades.

<u>EXTERIOR SCENE: FENCE LINE OUTSIDE ELGIN AFB: MIDNIGHT SUNDAY</u>

Medium shot taken from an smart phone in the second row inside of Babs' Escalade focusing on three signs in posted on chain link fence: "Restricted Area Warning, Off Limits Trespassers Will Be Prosecuted, Warning Electric Fence 7,000 Volts."

NARRATOR: [Voiceover] The Real Widows sit inside Babs' Cadillac Escalade at midnight staring at ominous looking signs posted on a fence intended to keep people from entering a classified, highly secure Air Force base. Armed military police actively patrol on the other side of the fence looking for intruders.
BABS: How we ever gonna get over a fence with that many volts in it?
LILLY: I knew this was a bad idea from the git-go.
BABS: Not according to Madame Cassandra. She gave me the green light on this… uh what did we decide to call what we're gonna do tonight?
LIZZIE: I think it starts with the word 'cluster' and ends with a dirty word. We're going to have to accept looking like fools and liars, tuck in our tails, and get this tank back on the road to Thomasville.
LILLY: Better that we look like fools and liars than go to jail. Besides, orange ain't in my color palette.
BABS: It's not too late. If y'all want to bail on me, I'd understand. Orange ain't my favorite color either. But after what that damn Thomasville City Council did to us Friday, ain't no way I'm not going over that damn fence.
LIZZIE: We could do some serious jail this time, Ladies. How did I ever let myself get into this kind of a… this kind of a snafu?

Scene fades to medium shot of Narrator walking in front of a tall fence, behind which is a forest.

NARRATOR: That is the sixty-four-thousand-dollar question. The Real Widows have gotten themselves into a pickle since they accepted Mitzi's challenge on last week's show. Now, they have to break into a secure facility and risk going to jail in order to prove that Mitzi, the Thomasville City Council, and based on emails and letters we've received, much of the rest of the country are wrong. More importantly, they have to prove that Babs is right about existence of Area 53 and that it contains UFOs and aliens from outer space. Can they do it?

Scene transitions to a commercial. Babs pauses the show and says, “I don’t know about y’all, but I gotta pee.”

“I’m outta margarita. What kind of a hostess are you anyway?” Lizzie asked.

“I’ll bring the rest of the pitcher out after I pee.”

After all glasses were refreshed and another plate of loaded nachos set on the coffee table, Babs pushed play.

Medium shot from outside rear of Escalade.

NARRATOR: [Voiceover] Some people say the Real Widows are eccentric. Some say they are kooky. Some say wacky. However, they are, if nothing else, icons of fashion. We are going to have a contest for the best-looking camouflage. The ladies went shopping at the Dillard’s in Pensacola yesterday for clothes that would be appropriate to wear as they hike in the woods inside the base. We ask all our viewers to let us know who they think is wearing the best-looking camouflage outfit. Please rate each of the girls on a scale of one through ten, with one being awful and ten being wonderful, according to how well you think she is dressed. You can text your votes to 833956. Just text each lady’s name and a number from one through ten. We’ll tally the results and announce the winner on next week’s episode.

As each door to the Escalade sequentially opens, a close shot of one of the Real Widow exiting the vehicle, beginning with Babs.

NARRATOR: [Voiceover] Each of these ladies appears to be a little over dressed for tonight’s mission. Dillard’s may not have been the wisest choice for woodland clothing. Don’t forget to text your votes to 833956. We’ll announce the winner next week on *The Real Widows of Thomasville*.

After last woman exits vehicle, scene transitions to Main Gate of base. Thirteen women are carrying protest signs while marching. They shout protest slogans and sing protest songs.

NARRATOR: [Voiceover] Looks like the Real Widows' friends made it safely to the base. They seem to be having a good time putting it to the man. What do those signs say? 'FREE THE ALIEN', 'ALIEN RIGHTS', 'NO ALIEN IS ILLEGAL', 'DON'T GITMO AREA 53', 'ALIEN AMNESTY'. Oh, my favorite is 'WE ♡ ALIENS'. It certainly looks like Kanesha, Latonya, Ebony, Isabella, Pink, Jada, Frigerator, Angie, Peggy, Delphine, Juanita, Brianna, and Butterfly know how to protest.

Scene transitions to fence line where the women and two men stand next to a bucket lift.

NARRATOR: [Voiceover] One of the men standing with the women is Sonny, a Thomasville native whom the producers hired to guide the Real Widows to Area 53 inside the base. The other man is the *Real Widows* executive producer, Cordell. He's explaining the logistics of their trip.
CORDELL: "There is a highly classified area inside Elgin officially designated as the Near Earth Object Detection and Holding Compound. The commander of the Compound reports to the new Space Command. Unofficially, personnel that work at Elgin call it Area 53. It's approximately five acres in size. Its perimeter is secured by a chain link fence topped with concertina. Area 53 is located here. Here's the way we'll be going to get there. You folks need to stay together and close to Sonny. We don't want any of you getting lost. Rangers and Green Berets conduct training exercises in these areas. They chose these areas precisely because of the dense jungle and wildlife. It's pretty nasty. Snakes, panthers, wild boar hogs, razor sharp palmetto bushes, you name it.
NARRATOR: [Voiceover as scene fast forwards to women being lifted over the fence, beginning with Babs.] Looks like the Real Widows may have gotten into more than they anticipated. This stuff is seriously dangerous. And now having to be lifted over an electrified fence topped with razor wire.

Sonny will ride in the bucket with each Widow to help calm them during the ride. Let's watch.
BABS: [Being helped by bucket operator into the bucket. Sonny stands beside them.] Can this thing can carry both me and Sonny at the same time?
BUCKET LIFT OPERATOR: It can lift up to 375 pounds. How much do you weigh?
BABS: [Standing inside the bucket] I ain't gonna tell you that. That's classified information. Only my doctor and I know that.
BUCKET LIFT OPERATOR: How much do you weigh, Sonny?
SLEDGE: Two thirty-five.
BABS: I guess I'll have to go by myself.

Scene fast forwards through Babs, then Tim being lifted over the fence to Lizzie and Allen standing in bucket lift as it starts to rise with Lilly inside.

LILLY: [Screams during entire ride over the fence.] AYYYYYYYYYYYYYY!!!!!!!!!!!!!!

Chapter 43

Thursday, November 13th, 8:44 PM EST

The Casserole Ladies watched scenes of Sonny leading the group through the woods and Babs getting separated. Despite being videoed by infrared technology, the photography was very good. Tim and Allen were among the best cameramen. While the scene of Babs meeting the Army Rangers camouflaged as fetterbushes was in progress, Lizzie said, "Those young men better watch themselves around male dogs. Their camouflage was incredible. None of the camo outfits we wore even came close."

"I thought your Nike Camo Leggings looked pretty good," said Babs.

"Nah, clashed too much with my shirt. Wish I'd bought that tank top instead," said Lizzie. She looked at Lilly. "You had the best outfit that night. Loved the mix of reds and pinks in your top and leggings. Perfect camo ensemble for hiding, if you're in a bordello."

"That reminds me. We don't want to forget to text in our votes," said Lilly.

They watched as the Rangers led Babs to the Holding Compound where they met Monroe. Babs said, "I never realized he had four of everything."

"How could you miss seeing that?" asked Lilly.

"Well, when I was looking at him, I only saw one half of him at a time. I didn't see the whole Monroe like I am now."

Lizzie asked, "Did anyone see if he had four penises?"

In unison, Lilly and Babs said, "Not me."

"Darn. Looks like he had pretty big feet, and you know what they say about men with big feet. I guess you could make the same analogy about having four feet."

They watched the scene of Babs and the Rangers meeting Monroe at the fence line. When Monroe spelled out his name *X-G-t-t-b-z-q-n-f-d-t-k-t-t-t*, Lizzie said, "Pause it. That name seems familiar."

"Yeah, it does. Where have I heard it before?" asked Lilly.

"Not heard. Seen. I've seen it somewhere before… at Madame Cassandra's. Remember Babsie? She wrote it on that piece of paper after she did her rock thing."

"That weren't no 'rock thing,'" Babs said indignantly. "Them was her crystals."

"Whatever. Cassandra wrote Monroe's alien name on that piece of paper."

"Lizzie's right, Babsie. Monroe's alien name looks a lot like what the old witch wrote during her scam," said Lilly.

"It weren't no scam if Madame Cassandra wrote Monroe's name before I ever met him, was it?" asked Babs.

Lizzie and Lilly shrugged, and Babs pushed play. The scenes of Babs, Lilly, and Lizzie going where no woman had gone before were classic. Tim and Allen videoed the scenes inside the spaceship using regular camcorders instead of their full spectrum night vision camcorders. Murky monochromatic images were replaced with much better video quality. The show's editor selected just the right scenes and dialogue to create a believable storyline. The *Real Widows* very much appeared to be inside a real UFO engaging in discussions with extraterrestrial aliens. One of the more lighthearted scenes inside the spaceship occurred when Babs discussed philosophy with the aliens.

<u>INTERIOR SCENE: ALIEN SPACESHIP LOUNGE, EARLY MONDAY MORNING</u>

Medium shot of Babs, Lilly, Lizzie, Sonny, Monroe, Ramone, and Salome sitting inside the lounge.

NARRATOR: [Voiceover] As fascinating as Babs' discussion with the aliens has been so far, it gets even more interesting after they begin discussing religion. Babs majored in philosophy as an undergraduate at FSU. We understand that Ramone is a bit of a prankster, and it comes out in this scene.
SALOME: Babs my dear, we've talked about Earth's history, culture, government, and society. Could you tell us about Earth's religion?
BABS: Oh, I'd be glad to. Anything special y'all want to know?
RAMONE: One of the things we want to learn about when we meet with beings on other planets is whether they believe in a god or gods and an afterlife. Do Earthlings believe in an

afterlife? Do they believe in life after death? Do you believe that there is a greater entity such as the one you might call God?
BABS: Some people believe in God, some people don't, and some people just don't give a damn. Socrates, Heraclitus, Thomas Aquinas, they all believed in God and an afterlife. Sartre, Marx, and Heidegger are examples of philosophers that were atheists. Bertrand Russell is an example of the 'don't give a damn' folks. So, it's something that has been debated for a long time, and there still ain't no agreement.
SALOME: Our civilization gave up long ago trying to figure whether a god exists and whether there is life after death.
RAMONE: [Nods] I hope there is no afterlife. No heaven or hell.
LIZZIE: You sound like John Lennon.
BABS: [With a look of shock on her face.] Why do you want no heaven or hell?
RAMONE: Because I am reasonably sure that I will wind up in hell if there is. [Laughter off camera.]
BABS: I hadn't thought that way. I always figured on going to heaven. I go to church most Sundays.
MONROE: Does your culture believe that going to church helps Earthlings go to heaven?
LILLY: If it don't, then I've wasted a lot of Sundays. [More laughter off camera.]
SALOME: I wonder if that was why our planet eliminated the church requirement long ago?
RAMONE: My dear Lilly, even if there is no afterlife, you should not feel that you wasted your Sundays in church. You existed while you were in church, and existing is good in and of itself. I believe it was your Socrates that said, "To be is to do." What he meant was existing is living.
SALOME: Ramone, I think you got that backwards. I think what Socrates actually said is "To do is to be."
BABS: No, it wasn't. It was actually Jean-Paul Sartre that said, "To do is to be."
SALOME: I thought Sartre said, "Do be do be do."
BABS: Sartre never said, "Do be do be do."
RAMONE: Babs is right, Salome. Frank Sinatra said, "Do be do be do." [More laughter off camera.]
BABS: Ramone, that's an old joke.

RAMONE: I know, but Tim says it's a good one. [Scene fades with off camera laughter.]

Shaking her head, Babs paused the show. "I can't believe they pulled that one on me."

"I thought Tim would bust a gut," said Lizzie. "He prompted Ramone and Salome to pull that one on you while Monroe was doing that anti-aging thing on you in the gym."

At this point, every Casserole Lady's iPhone rang simultaneously. Each phone had a different ringtone. Lilly's ringtone was the music from the first stanza of "I'm a Little Teapot." Babs' ringtone was the theme from *Star Wars*. Lizzie's ringtone was Tammy Wynette singing 'D-I-V-O-R-C-E.' Daffy had sent texts to all three of them at the same time, letting them know they streamed *Real Widows* via the ship's WiFi and loved it. She also texted that they expected to be back in Jacksonville on Tuesday, November 18th, spend a night there resting up from the cruise, then come back to Thomasville on Wednesday, the 19th.

The ladies subsequently received another set of texts, this time from Cordell. Ratings for the show went through the roof. It was the megahit of the season for all reality shows. He wanted to let them know that the network wanted to extend the show for another full season beyond the current season.

The ladies watched the rest of the *Real Widows* episode, consumed the rest of the nachos and margaritas, and went to bed early. They had an important meeting to attend in the morning.

Chapter 44

Friday, November 14th, 10:00 AM EST

Lilly and Lizzie sat beside Babs in the first row inside City Hall. Babs had called Mayor Flamingo during the first *Real Widows* commercial and demanded to be allowed to address the City Council at their regular Friday morning meeting. Flamingo okayed her request and immediately called her old buddy Mitzi. Both agreed it would be a great opportunity to slam the Real Widow once again.

Lizzie looked around and said, "Looks like Mitzi and the rest of the Mammas are here as well."

"I knew Joy Flamingo would call her after I called," said Babs. "Those two are like two peas in pod and have been ever since they were in the same sorority at FSU."

A large reusable grocery bag sat on the floor beside each of the ladies. Every so often, one of the bags moved slightly, prompting a nudge from Babs' foot. By 10:15 AM, all members had taken their seats, and Mayor Flamingo said, "I call this meeting of the City Council to order. Will the Recorder please note that the following are present: Councilmembers Toddie Wurlitzer, Dr. Ted Maybry, Troy Seconell, Chastity Knott, and myself Mayor Joy Flamingo. We will dispense with the usual format of the meeting as I received a demand from Babs Neauxgeaux to speak to us. As y'all know, the third episode of The Real Widows of Thomasville was on TV last night, and she wants to talk about that in relation to our two motions last week. Ms. Neauxgeaux, please approach the microphone and make your presentation. As Babs approached, Flamingo glanced at her, then did a double take. Babs looked different. Younger. The Mayor wondered if she'd had some cosmetic surgery recently.

Babs walked up to one of the two microphones in front of the Council's dais and said, "I… that is we, and by we, I mean me, Lilly and Lizzie, and on behalf of Daffy and Gidget want y'all to know that we don't appreciate what this City Council did last week. Censuring me and rejecting my claims about Area 53, UFOs, and aliens was the height of lowdown. I hope after last night's show, y'all all feel like a bunch of fools. I hope… no I demand that y'all take back both of y'all's motions."

Mayor Flamingo looked at Mitzi, who also sat in the front row and said, "Mitzi, would you like to respond to Babs' condemnation of your motions?"

Mitzi glared at Babs. She looked different. Her archrival looked younger than the last time she had seen Babs. Had she undergone some sort of cosmetic surgery? Was she using Lizzie's plastic surgeon? She put those thoughts out of her mind as she walked to the other microphone and said, "Your Honor. I stand by both my motions. I haven't changed my mind since watching the *Real Widows* show last night. That show was nothing but a bunch of Hollywood magic. All them aliens and that spaceship was all done on a computer just like they do in the movies like *Star Wars*. That Area 53 they showed on the show was probably nothing but a movie set in Hollywood. And they probably filmed Babs and the others somewhere in the woods around here. Like I said, it was all a make-believe lie, and I stand by what I said at y'all's last meeting. I think y'all would be crazy to take back the motions that y'all approved unanimously."

Babs was incensed. She felt the positive ions from Monroe's machine surging inside her body. She was a tigress. The old woman approaching the twilight of her life had fled her body along with all those negative ions. Despite never having spoken before any kind of government body like this before, she was determined not to let Mitzi or the City Council run over her.

She said, "It weren't no lie. It was all real. There was an Area 53. There was a spaceship—We all went inside it. And those were real aliens. And they were the nicest people… well they really weren't people, but if they had've been people, they would have been the nicest people. Mister Monroe was a real gentle… gentlealien. They were all gentlealiens, except for Ramone who is a woman-alien this month. And they were all a lot smarter than a lot of the people in this room, including this here City Council. They have figured out how to do things y'all would not dream of… like making me younger. Like how they got spaceship motors that put any motor we got to shame. Like…"

Babs could see Lizzie shaking her head and holding a finger to her lips in an effort to send a signal to drop her current argument. Babs did so as she said, "Anyway, you folks… them resolutions y'all voted on last week show just how dumb all of you folks—"

"Babs," Mayor Flamingo said, "I'm warning you. If you continue to insult this City Council, I promise I'll fine you."

"Madame Mayor, if I may… " Dr. Maybry turned to look at Babs and paused. She looked younger than the last time he saw her at the Masquerade Ball dressed as an alien. He would have loved to ask her if she was getting some sort of medical treatments. Instead, he asked, "How do we know what Mitzi said ain't so? Them Hollywood people can make imaginary and unreal things look real. They do it all the time in the movies. Just like Mitzi said. I love them *Iron Man* movies, but I know they ain't no real Iron Man. It's all done by what they call CGI, computer graphics something. Robert Downey ain't flying around in no flying suit even though it looks like he is. Why ain't it the same thing with y'all's show?"

"Yeah Mzz Babsie. That Mister Monroe looked like he was modeling your next Halloween costume," said Mitzi.

"It'd be a better costume for me than the one you wore two years ago to the Masquerade Ball," Babs looked at the audience and asked, "The one where your belly spilled out over the bottom piece of that costume like water spilling over Niagara Falls."

Mitzi got really mean. "Aliens with four arms, four legs, and four eyes! Someone in Hollywood must've been smoking dope when he dreamed up that Monroe costume. I wonder if he had four dingdongs? Only Babs knows for sure—"

Mayor Flamingo said, "Please, please ladies. Let's elevate the tone of this meeting, please. Remember, these proceedings are videotaped. That said, Babs I'm inclined to recommend to this City Council that we not rescind our two motions—"

"Before you do that Mayor, just let me show y'all something," Babs said. She marched to her chair and reached into her grocery bag. She extracted a small frisbee-shaped object about six inches wide and three inches high. Its smooth metal surface gleamed as if made of silver. Triumphantly holding it in both her hands, she walked over and stood before the dais. Instead of placing it on the dais, she lowered her arms with a flourish. The disc did not fall to the floor as one would have expected and instead hovered in the air unsupported. The room remained silent as Babs beamed.

Mitzi finally found her voice and said, "That thing ain't nothing but one of them small drones like they sell everywhere. So, what's the big deal?"

"If it's just a drone, what's keeping it afloat? Does anyone see propellors?" asked Babs.

"It's got some sort of jet propulsion underneath it."

"It ain't no drone, and it don't have no propellors or jets on it. It's a model flying saucer. I purchased it in the commissary on Monroe's spaceship. I invite everyone to come up here and inspect it to see if they can find any jet exhaust anywhere on it. It's flying on its own, powered by some sort of anti-gravity stuff inside it."

Babs walked back to her seat, leaving the disc hovering by itself at the front of the room. Everyone in the audience was reluctant to approach the disc until one brave person finally walked up to it. She looked it over, top to bottom, and all over. She put her hands beneath the object trying to feel for jets of air shooting out. Finally, she said, "I can't feel nothing. There's no wires holding it up."

That set off a rush to inspect the disc. Virtually everyone in the room, including all Council members performed similar inspections. After everyone finished, the Mayor said, "I think we have all satisfied ourselves that this is technology none of us have ever seen before."

Councilmember Knott said, "Mayor, I'm not inclined to say that this technology is from another world."

"What does the rest of the Council think?"

"It looks like something from another, more advanced civilization than any here on Earth," said Councilmember Wurlitzer, "but I just don't know."

"It's some sort of Hollywood trick," Councilmember Seconell said. Left unsaid was his suspicion that this flying disc was of the same sort of Hollywood magic as they had pulled with Babs' makeup. She looked thirty years younger now. Those Hollywood makeup artists were magicians.

"I'm on the fence," said Councilmember Maybry.

From her seat, Babs said, "If that don't convince y'all, maybe this will." She put on a bulky rubber glove, reached into her grocery bag again, and extracted a small armadillo-like animal. In addition to its armadillo-like features, the creature appeared to be a mix of brown and green colors. It had a small set of wing-like appendages on its upper back. Call it an armadillo on Mescaline. She walked over to the hovering silver frisbee and held the small animal up for all to see.

“What is that?” asked Mayor Flamingo.

“It’s a baby Tankaby. The mother Tankaby had a litter of babies on the spaceship, and Monroe gave me one.”

“A Tankaby?”

“Yeah. They’re like pets on Monroe’s planet, but they don’t normally keep them in the house. This one’s only two months old.”

“Tankaby. How do you spell it?” asked Councilmember Maybry.

“Its alien name is spelled G-V-x-b-r-t-b-z-x-b-r-d-d-d-d-y, but it has a y in it. Monroe’s alphabet don’t have no vowels, except for the letter y, which in this case is used as a consonant. I wish they hadn’t had to leave so soon ‘cause I never got a chance to ask him about using a y as a consonant, but not being able to use it as a vowel ‘cause they don’t have no vowels in their alphabet. I think that may be one of the ways that Earth is more advanced than Monroe’s planet. Y’all might be asking ‘Why?’ Well, I think y is like a transgender letter in our alphabet. You know… sometimes it’s used like a vowel, like in the word funny, and sometimes it’s used like a consonant, like in the word y’all. So, y is like a transgender letter of the alphabet. Sometimes it’s vowel, sometimes it's consonant—”

Mayor Flamingo said, “That’s a very interesting theory Babs, but that animal thing is from another planet. You can’t just keep an animal from another planet. How did they let you leave Area 53 with that thing?”

“Those Men In Suits wanted to take it from me, but Monroe insisted they let me keep it, and they wasn’t gonna go against him at all. So, they said okay, but then they took it away from me after Monroe’s spaceship flew off. By that time, I had already grown so attached to the little thing. I cried my eyes out, but then, a man shows up on my doorstep yesterday with this cute little Tankaby in a little soft-sided pet carrier—”

“I can’t believe the Federal government would give something that an alien brought to Earth from a planet far away in space and let Babs keep it,” said Councilmember Seconell. “Let’s face it. This is just Babs Neauxgeaux from Thomasville, not the Queen of England.”

“Well, I have to really give the credit to the Judge Hammond.” Babs smiled coyly. “He graduated from FSU like me and gave me his phone number. Told me to stay in touch. He loves our show. So, I texted him about Tankaby, and he texted that he would try to pull some favors in from some folks he knows at the FDA and the

Department of Agriculture. There was some sort of overlapping responsibility, which was why it took so long to get them government bureaucrats to give it back to me. It was a gift to me from Monroe after all."

"You mean you're gonna keep it?" asked Councilmember Wurlitzer. She also wanted to ask Babs what facial moisturizer she was now using. Whatever it was, it was doing a great job.

"Salome says they make real good yard dogs, although he didn't call it a yard dog. He just said you wouldn't want to keep in your house. I figure it'd be great for keeping snakes and possums out of the yard"

Mitzi loudly said, "I'd rather have a snake or a possum in my yard than that ugly thing!"

"You're one to talk. That pug of yours looks like she ran into a brick wall with her face."

Councilmember Knott said, "I don't think the Tankaby is *that* ugly."

"What are you gonna name it?" asked Councilmember Maybry.

"I thought and thought about that, and I think the best name would be Daisy."

Councilmember Seconell nodded. "That's a great name for a Tankaby."

Councilmember Wurlitzer nodded. "Daisy the Tankaby. I like it."

"Me too," said Mayor Flamingo. "So, you're going to keep Daisy in your yard?"

Babs shook her head. "No, Your Honorship. Tankaby ought to belong to the City of Thomasville. This is something everyone should enjoy. So, I'm gonna donate it to the Thomasville History Museum. I was thinking they could set it up in some sort of petting zoo for kids. But they'd have to wear thick gloves."

"I think that is a lovely idea. I know my grandchildren would love to pet and feed it. What about the spaceship?"

"I'm gonna give it to my grandson Sammy. He loves this kind of space stuff."

"Your Honor, I also have something that I bought in the spaceship commissary that I would like to donate to the museum," said Lizzie. She reached into the bag beside her and pulled out a metal container about the size of a can of beans.

"What is it?" asked Mayor Flamingo.

"It's a can of some sort of vegetable that the aliens eat. It has something like a sourdough starter in it that continually regenerates more of whatever it is as the vegetable inside it is removed. It can never be depleted. Folks that visit the museum can sample it, and it will never run out of the food. I tried some, and it tastes like chicken, but what doesn't?"

"I have something to donate too," said Lilly as she reached into her bag and extracted a large gem-like stone. Oval-shaped—four inches in diameter widthwise and six inches lengthwise—its many facets sparkled with a beautiful aquamarine color.

"What is it?" asked the Mayor.

"It's a mineral from Monroe's planet. They give them like hostess gifts on planets they visit. Monroe says there's no mineral on Earth like it. It's kind of neat. It recharges your iPhone if you set it next to it. I think it makes a great doorstop."

Mitzi fumed as Babs and her buddies seemed to be winning the City Council over to their side. All her hard work vaporized by a bunch of junk and filthy animal. She shouted, "That doorstop is about as useful as reusable toilet paper."

Troy Seconell glared at Mitzi, then turned to Mayor Flamingo and said, "Your Honor, I propose we rescind both of last week's resolutions. I also propose we fund an additional wing for the museum and name that wing 'The Real Widows of Thomasville Hall' and that these ladies' donations be featured prominently therein, although the Tankaby petting zoo should be set up on the outside."

Mayor Flamingo said, "I have before the Council motions to rescind last week's two motions censuring the Real Widow, to fund an additional wing for the Thomasville History Museum and name it 'The Real Widows of Thomasville Hall,' and to feature these ladies' donations prominently therein. Each member of the council will now vote by saying either Yea or Nay. Councilmember Toddie Wurlitzer."

"Yea."

"Councilmember Chastity Knott."

"Yea."

"Councilmember Troy Seconell."

"Yea."

"Councilmember Ted Maybry."

"Yea."

Mayor Flamingo said, "I also vote 'Yea,' and that makes the vote unanimous."

With the vote, loud and raucous cheering broke out throughout the room. While the Casserole Ladies jumped up and down and hugged each other, Mitzi glumly sat in her seat. Her scheming with Cordell had backfired on both of them—to her detriment and to his benefit. Even more disheartening, her archrival had somehow benefited from her scheme. Babs looked younger than ever. After ten minutes of celebration, Mayor Flamingo brought the meeting back to order and asked, "By the way, who won the best camouflaged contest?"

Babs said, "You'll have to watch next Thursday to find out."

After the meeting broke up, Councilmember Maybry approached the Casserole Ladies with a question. "Babsie, you look thirty years younger. What happened to you inside that spaceship?"

"I had a treatment in the aliens' anti-aging machine," said Babs.

"Anti-aging machine. How did it work?"

"Mister Monroe told me it removed all my body's negative ions and replaced them with positive ions."

Dr. Maybry, a physician, had practiced in Thomasville but was now retired. Babs' answer puzzled him as it ran counter to existing medical thinking about positive and negative ions' effects on the human body. He said, "Really. So, the aliens think replacing negative ions with positive ions reverses the effects of aging?"

Babs nodded.

Dr. Maybry shook his head in astonishment. "That diametrically goes against current medical thinking. Negative ions are supposed to be good for the human body while positive ions are bad."

"How so?" asked Lilly.

"Medical science believes positive ions help cause things like asthma and depression. Negative ions do several good things for the human body such as enhance the immune system, act as antidepressants, and help lower blood pressure."

“That don’t sound right—negative being good and positive being bad.”

“Negative and positive only refer to whether an atom has more or less electrons than protons...” Dr. Maybry realized his explanation soared over the Casserole Ladies’ heads and further explanation would be useless. He moved on. “I wonder if current thinking in the medical community about ions’ effects on the human body needs to be revisited.”

Lizzie said, “That’s a comforting thought—medical science doing a one-eighty. Well Doc, it’s been nice talking to you, but we gotta go. I have a bloodletting appointment this afternoon.”

As they walked away, Lilly looked at Babs and joked, “Babsie, I hope our encounter with those aliens has taught you a lesson about keeping your positive ions up.”

Babs vigorously nodded. “I have. But I learned something even more important.”

“What’s that?”

“I am gonna start going to Madame Cassandra twice a month.”

Epilogue

Wednesday, November 19th, 2:33 PM EST

Babs anxiously knocked on Daffy's door. She had been calling and texting Daffy and Gidget repeatedly since breakfast to no avail. No responses. Nada. They should have come back by now. Even obeying the speed limit, which Daffy never did, it should have only taken her two and a half hours to drive from Jacksonville to Thomasville. No one answered her knocking, and Daffy's Lincoln was not in her driveway. Were they stranded, or worse on the side of the road somewhere on I-10? None of the Casserole Ladies had received a phone call or text from Daffy or Gidget since Daffy's text congratulating them the previous Thursday. Thinking their friends were too occupied with the Marx Brothers and sightseeing on Caribbean islands, they had not worried. This morning was a different matter.

Babs could not take it any longer. She had jumped in her Escalade and driven to Daffy's house to see if possibly her friend was inside and had fallen. Her friend was close to seventy after all. That now seemed improbable as Daffy's Lincoln was not parked in her driveway, and no one answered the door. Babs stood on the porch and wondered what to do. Daffy and Gidget left for their extended Caribbean cruise with the Marx Brothers on Tuesday, Oct 14th. They were supposed to have docked in Jacksonville yesterday and headed back to Thomasville this morning. Something was wrong. Babs texted Lilly and Lizzie.

Babs: Y'all heard anything yet?
Lilly: Nothing.
Lizzie: Same here.
Babs: I'm getting worried. What if something happened to them on the road from Jax?
Lizzie: That may be, but there's nothing we can do about it. We just have to wait and see.

Babs: I'm going to call the cruise line in Jacksonville and check on their boat.

Lilly: Good idea.

Babs called the cruise line and panicked when she heard the news. There had been a series of mysterious deaths onboard the ship beginning last Friday. Authorities in Port-au-Prince had detained the boat while an investigation was being conducted. The ship's communications network, which provided international cell phone connectivity, had been disabled to prevent malicious interference with the investigation. The cruise line was keeping a lid on news about the situation at the behest of authorities in Port-au-Prince.

Could another Casserole Ladies misadventure be in the making?

Acknowledgement

Our thanks to Dr. Tammy Winner, Professor of English in the MA Writing Program at the University of North Alabama in Florence, Alabama. She volunteered to have her Technical Editing class edit the manuscript for us. Once again, we thank one of our longtime dear friends, Donna Porter, for several priceless contributions to this book, especially the 'Is Caesar in the freezer?' bit. We also thank our beta readers Tina Schmidt, Pam Honeycutt, Katherine Harris, and Maura Wroblewski.

About the Authors

Billy Johnson lives in Florence, Alabama with his wife, Linda. They enjoy traveling and visiting their daughter who lives in Virginia with her family. Billy and Linda's previous Casserole Ladies zany misadventure is THE CASSEROLE LADIES, ISBN: 978-1-7374282-0-6. Billy has also published a collection of eight short stories in ATTACK OF THE iFONES and Other Vertically Challenged Stories, ISBN: 978-1-7374282-1-3. Billy wrote and illustrated a children's picture book titled LION IN MY BACKYARD, ISBN: 978-1-7374282-2-0. All Billy's books are available on Amazon. You can visit Billy's Facebook page at: https://www.facebook.com/Billy4GoodBooks.

www.ingramcontent.com/pod-product-compliance
Lightning Source LLC
Chambersburg PA
CBHW030926210726
48290CB00007B/2081

* 9 7 8 1 7 3 7 4 2 8 2 3 7 *